Praise for Elizabeth Brundage's
The Vanishing Point

"This mesmerizing and unpredictable saga unspools in crisp sequences that shift back and forth in time, with love and jealousy bubbling throughout...Brundage, author of the superb *All Things Cease to Appear,* has written another remarkable literary thriller...In this emotionally powerful work she leads us to an unforgettable truth, through scenes of searing intensity and luminous prose."

—Tom Nolan, *Wall Street Journal*

"A dark and moody literary mystery, centered on three photographers caught in a love triangle, Brundage's stylish novel probes the relentless demands of real-world problems on artists and their work."

—*New York Times Book Review*

"Elizabeth Brundage's *Vanishing Point* proves that she's one of the very best novelists writing today. It touches on crises that are politically immediate, of the moment, from climate change to income inequality to drug addiction. It gifts the reader with wisdom and insight. The novel brings into the sharpest focus how precious this thing is called life."

—Adam Ross, author of *Mr. Peanut*

"In this dark-toned mystery, Brundage develops an engrossing story about a love triangle involving three photographers...The first half of the novel brilliantly dissects the competitive and erotic entanglements that mark the characters, and Brundage is particularly good at using photographic theory to describe how each sees the world."

—*Publishers Weekly*

"A novel about what is seen but also what remains unseen in our lives. The interplay between the two is what makes great photography and a great story—and what makes *The Vanishing Point* a beautiful work of art."

—Elliot Ackerman, author of *Red Dress in Black and White*

"The interwoven lives of artists, failed and successful...Brundage's characters are convincing...Well written and affecting."

—*Kirkus Reviews*

"Complex and layered...*The Vanishing Point* is as lyrical as it is moving."

—Susan Miura, *Bookreporter*

"Brundage carefully outlines the tangled relationships of love and ambition among three students in stylized prose; her central concept of photography is evocative both literally and metaphorically...Recommended for readers of Anne Tyler or William Boyd."

—Melanie Kindrachuk, *Library Journal*

"An ambitious, literary novel, *The Vanishing Point* is distinguished by its characterizations, its pervasive air of melancholy, and its beautiful style. Not surprisingly, there is a great deal of thought-provoking attention given to the meaning and aesthetics of photography, and, like great photography, the novel is ultimately a work of memorable art."

—Michael Cart, *Booklist* (starred review)

The
Vanishing
Point

Also by Elizabeth Brundage

All Things Cease to Appear
A Stranger Like You
Somebody Else's Daughter
The Doctor's Wife

The Vanishing Point

A Novel

Elizabeth Brundage

BACK BAY BOOKS
Little, Brown and Company
New York Boston London

Back Bays Books / Little, Brown and Company
Hachette Book Group
1290 Avenue of the Americas, New York, NY 10104
littlebrown.com

Originally published in hardcover by Little, Brown and Company, May 2021
First Back Bay trade paperback edition, October 2022

Back Bay Books is an imprint of Little, Brown and Company, a division of Hachette Book Group, Inc. The Back Bay Books name and logo are trademarks of Hachette Book Group, Inc.

The publisher is not responsible for websites (or their content) that are not owned by the publisher.

The Hachette Speakers Bureau provides a wide range of authors for speaking events. To find out more, go to hachettespeakersbureau.com or call (866) 376-6591.

ISBN 9780316430371 (hc) / 9780316430388 (pb)
LCCN 2020945987

Printing 1, 2022

LSC-C

Printed in the United States of America

For my children

All photographs are time exposures of shorter or longer duration, and each describes a discrete parcel of time...Uniquely in the history of pictures, a photograph describes only that period of time in which it was made. Photography alludes to the past and the future only in so far as they exist in the present, the past through its surviving relics, the future through prophecy visible in the present.

—John Szarkowski, *The Photographer's Eye*

Part One

Portraits of Adults

A portrait is not a likeness. The moment an emotion or fact is transformed into a photograph it is no longer a fact but an opinion. There is no such thing as inaccuracy in a photograph. All photographs are accurate. None of them is the truth.

—Richard Avedon, *In the American West*

Julian

It was on the subway that night, heading home from work, when he discovered the news about Rye Adler. Peering over the shoulder of a fellow commuter, he saw his long-lost friend looking back at him. Under his gloomy, unsmiling portrait read the headline: Rye Adler, Photographer of the Rich and Infamous, Is Presumed Dead at 52. Shaken, he stepped off the train at 86th Street and climbed up from the din of the underground into the late March dusk, taking the damp air into his lungs. For a moment he stood on the sidewalk, bearing the wake of irritable strangers, then started west as a cold rain began to fall. He remembered a bar he'd gone to a few times over on Amsterdam, and he walked the few blocks without an umbrella, ducking under ledges and awnings. The place wasn't crowded, and once he'd crossed its dark threshold, entering a sanctuary of bloodred booths and muffled chatter, he doubted his ability to ever leave. He sat at the bar in his coat and ordered cheap bourbon because that was what he'd drunk with Adler back in the day, when they were grad students in Philadelphia and in love with the same woman.

Unlike his old friend, Julian hadn't made it. Not like he'd hoped.

His mother always consoled him that it took longer than anyone predicted, but now that he was almost fifty, the prospect of any true recognition seemed doubtful. His friends all had the impression that he was doing well, better than they were, even, but this perception was entirely superficial, based on his skillfully curated social media pages and the sound bites he used at cocktail parties and gallery openings. Early on, he had, like Rye, achieved a certain distinction for attending the famed Brodsky Workshop, known among photography insiders as a breeding ground for the best talent, but for reasons that remained mysterious to him, things hadn't turned out like he'd planned. Out of pride, he'd convinced himself that he wasn't a failure; he was simply more suited to commercial work, and by anyone else's standards he'd had a fine career. He'd made plenty of money. But advertising was a whole different animal, or maybe *mindset* was the better word. You had to narrow your focus and put the needs of others before your own. Others: that vast, proverbial melting pot of humanity. Whenever he lost track of what that was, he took a field trip to Walmart and roamed the aisles. He and Rye were on opposite ends of the anthropological spectrum: where Rye exploited his subjects in the name of high art, Julian promoted the products that kept them alive.

He finished his second drink and thought of calling his wife, a habit he had yet to break. He had to assume she'd seen Adler's obituary. He pictured her wandering around in a morbid daze, crashing into things. He would never forget their last night together out in Westchester, how she'd sat on the back steps in her mother's old coat, smoking like a teenager. And later, after he'd held her for the last time, how she'd cried in his arms. He knew it was mostly his fault. As his therapist liked to say, he had trouble committing to things. While he'd succeeded in staying married to the same woman for exactly twenty-one years, he'd never actually felt committed—just the word made him feel wrapped in a straitjacket—and he could admit to being a shitty father even though he still couldn't talk about it, couldn't even say his son's name out loud without breaking a sweat, that was the truth of it. How he would ultimately resolve this in his mind, he didn't have a clue; maybe he never would. He felt really bad about that, but, to be fair, it wasn't Julian who'd asked for the divorce. Ever since the thing with his assistant, she'd stopped talking to him. Shortly thereafter, he'd been served with divorce papers at his office, and Vera, his assistant, had gone into the bathroom to cry. It was kind of a scene. Embarrassing him like that in front of the people he worked with hadn't been nice. But his wife could be ruthless when she set her mind to it. Under the circumstances, he was glad he'd insisted on keeping the apartment. This was where he belonged. Here in the city, alone.

He sat in the bar till closing, then walked home in the cold, pulling up his collar. The lobby of his building, with its deco floors and granite walls, seemed morbidly serene, and the lonesome elevator, as it rose to the fourteenth floor, was like a rattling cage. He shuffled down the corridor to his door and retrieved the paper from his mat. As he stepped inside, he encountered the screaming emptiness of his apartment. There was no longer any evidence of their life together. Even their wedding photograph, which had long reigned on the surface of the credenza, was absent. After that last night, when he knew it was over with her, he could no longer bear to look at it and threw it into the incinerator.

He poured himself a drink and stood for a moment in the silent living room, staring out at the night, the city's cold geometry. The vacant streets seemed to ache with a prescient gloom. He spread out the paper on the coffee table and reread the article about Adler, which listed his numerous awards and accolades, his long-standing Magnum membership, and his gift for capturing the inner lives of celebrities, quoting some of the editors he'd worked with, none of them able to comprehend how he'd met with such a fateful end. It was a tragic little story, really. As previous articles had alleged, he'd possibly taken his own life, hurling himself off a bridge somewhere upstate, but his body had not been found, and nobody was really sure if it was suicide. To anyone who knew Adler as well as Julian did, suicide was certainly not an option. They were having a memorial service on Sunday up in Hudson. He knew he had to go.

He wasn't especially tired. He lay on the couch, its fabric like cold asphalt and its architecture equally unyielding, remembering that September of '98 when they first met, back when they were still equals and nearly feral with ambition. The Brodsky Workshop was competitive; it took only twelve students a year. Unlike the others', Julian's CV was pretty unremarkable. He'd gone to Rutgers, then worked a couple years at the *Star-Ledger,* Newark's stalwart chronicle of the times, covering mostly sports and local elections, the occasional crime. He was still living at home, working out of a darkroom he'd built in his mother's basement, when he'd decided to apply. He could vaguely recall the work he'd submitted to get in: stark black-and-white shots of his neighborhood out in Jersey, the unbearable stillness of the houses on the cul-de-sac, the overgrown lot behind the Pathmark, where, at thirteen, he'd gotten caught shoplifting, the window of the pizza parlor in the village, piled to the ceiling with slim white boxes.

As proud as he'd been of those images, it soon became obvious that Rye's were better. When they tacked up their assignments on the wall, Adler's stood out. They were street scenes, mostly. People you might see every day but captured with a certain unapologetic tenderness. The woman in the pink kerchief, for example, standing on the corner, smoking a cigarette, accusing you of not noticing her just like all the other people in her life, the husband she couldn't trust, the mother who drank, indifferent teachers blind to her potential, all evident in the premature lines on her forehead, the shabby, slightly dirty white handbag clutched under her arm, the fraying collar of her coat. Adler didn't just look at someone; he looked into them, without judgment, with the sort of empathy they couldn't find anywhere else.

By the end of the first week, everybody knew Rye Adler had

something special. Everybody wanted to be around him. To know what he knew. To see how he saw. Even then, when he was still in his twenties, people who mattered were calling him a visionary.

Almost by chance, they shared an apartment that year. Julian had been living out of his suitcase in a cramped, seedy motel room when he saw a ROOMMATE WANTED notice in the workshop lounge. You might say that everything that followed was set into motion the second he pulled off that tab with Rye's number on it. It was one of those older walk-up buildings around the corner from the university. The apartment was on the second floor over a hardware store that featured, in its large storefront window, a cat named Nicholas who dozed all day in the sunlight and patrolled the aisles by night; occasionally they'd wake to a murderous disruption. Of the two small bedrooms, Rye's was slightly larger and had built-in shelves stacked with books of all kinds. Thumbtacked to the wall were assorted black-and-white pictures he'd taken of his parents in their Marrakech home, his mother's glance of expectation as she fondled her beads, his father peering up over a French newspaper, and a poster from his favorite film, *Blow-Up,* which Julian hadn't seen. Julian's room was narrow and spare, with a twin bed and a dresser and a window that looked out on an alley. It suited him just fine. In the living room were a couple of mismatched chairs Rye had pulled off the street and a plant with leaves like elephant ears that clung to the dirty bay window. From the moment he moved in, Julian concluded that as roommates they were incompatible. Where Julian preferred a quiet, nearly monastic existence, Adler had a sort of impromptu celebrity that attracted a nightly brigade; it wasn't unusual to find strangers sleeping on the floor the next morning. Even though it sometimes annoyed Julian, he never complained; he knew that living with someone like Rye was, for him, an accident of destiny. As a result, he didn't mind being the one to clean up the mess, the countless beer bottles, ashtrays, dirty plates, and when Rye would emerge hours later still in his boxers, his hair mussed, surprised to find the apartment clean, he'd tease him for being such a neat freak. Julian didn't let it bother him. Rye often treated him with measured tolerance, like he was a slightly annoying little brother. And in turn he put up with Rye's idiosyncrasies, the ever-present containers of takeout in the refrigerator or Rye's dirty laundry getting mixed with his own. Once, at the Laundromat, he'd discovered one of Rye's Hawaiian shirts at the bottom of his pile and, as a symbol of his devotion, washed and even ironed it and, with great satisfaction, presented it to Rye like a gift, but his roommate only shrugged and said thanks, as if he'd just handed him the newspaper or something, and it occurred to Julian that Rye was used to people doing things for him. Unlike Julian's Levi's and JCPenney sweaters, Rye bought his clothes at flea markets and second-hand shops, preferring, he said, the life-worn threads of dead men. He rolled his own cigarettes with cheap pipe tobacco and smoked like a drifter, pinching the butt between his two stained fingers, but as much as he personified a man on the skids, he had an arrogance only bought with money. One night, a little drunk, he admitted that his father had made a fortune as a civil engineer, an architect of bridges. They'd moved around a lot. No matter where they lived, he told Julian, his mother always insisted on fresh flowers. In contrast, Julian's father was a mid-level executive for a women's clothing company. He'd worked in the city on Seventh Avenue until he dropped dead of a heart attack when Julian was fifteen. Julian grew up an only child in a split-level house in Millburn. They had a Ping-Pong table in the basement and a white poodle named Lulu. His widowed mother had taken a job at Lord & Taylor, at the perfume counter, to make ends meet. She'd come home reeking of hyacinths.

Rye had a girlfriend from college, Simone, his soul mate, he'd bragged to Julian, who occasionally made the trip from Manhattan, where she was getting a PhD in English at Columbia, and would arrive beleaguered, with a bulging sack of books that would end up scattered around the apartment, defaced by coffee rings, Post-it Notes, and crumbs that would sprinkle from the bindings, and, for the duration of her visit, there was evidence of her presence on every possible surface, her knitting projects, rarely finished, bunched on the couch, her sloppy, malodorous vegetarian concoctions lining the refrigerator shelves, and strands of her hair in the sink and on the bathroom floor, not to mention the occasional pubic hair—Julian was always relieved when she left.

Unbeknownst to Simone, Adler had come down with a fever for one of the girls in the workshop, Magda. He wasn't the only one; everyone was a little in love with her, even Brodsky. She was like a girl you happened to glimpse in a moving car, detained by some awful consequence, the type you wanted to save. She was local, from Port Richmond, the Polish neighborhood. Her parents had come over in the seventies, when she was a toddler, and along with an accent, she'd retained a certain reticence, unwittingly engineered by her Eastern Bloc roots. In stature, she was not delicate, and had a face that might have been drawn with thick crayon, the round bones in her cheeks, the wide mouth, the hungry, dark eyes. She dressed like a gypsy in baggy men's trousers and outsize sweaters that concealed her sizable breasts and wore clunky shoes with straps, trawled out of Salvation Army bins. Her only vanity, it seemed, was the waxy ruby lipstick she drew on her lips. She seldom spoke up in class; perhaps she was intimidated—the women, three in all, had it rough. During the weekly critiques she'd stand in the back, lurking thoughtfully, her arms crossed over her chest. When her own work was critiqued, her back went rigid with defiance, like a Resistance fighter in front of a firing squad. She was good, and some of the men were jealous. Things were said to stir a reaction; they didn't. She was stoic, unhindered. She worked as a figure model at the art school to make extra cash. One time he accidentally pushed through the doors of the studio where she was modeling naked on a platform. He remembered the cold look on her face as their eyes met across the enormous room. He backed out gently, before anyone else saw him, but something was established in that moment, something dark and indelible, seared into his memory like a brand.

When he finally mustered the courage to ask Magda out, he came home one afternoon to find her and his roommate coiled in the sheets.

It was another reminder that Adler was always a step ahead of him.

One weekend toward the end of the year, Rye invited Julian out to his mother's summerhouse on Long Island, an old saltbox on the tip of Montauk. There were a few other Brodsky people there: Marty Fine and his boyfriend, Lars, Magda, of course, and Rye's sister, Ava, who'd driven down from Boston. Ava was still in college, a junior at Harvard, studying metaphysics. She was a smaller version of Rye, but shy, pale as sour milk, the sort of girl who preferred the company of books to people and rarely left her dorm room. The house had been closed up for a while, some of the furniture covered with sheets, but it was an extraordinary old place, wood-paneled, musty, overlooking the ocean. Rye and Ava shared the pretense of being average—his scruffy, second-hand clothes, her worn-out green-suede loafers (they were Gucci)—but they had an undeniable exclusivity that set them apart. It was what money did to you, he guessed, allowed you to believe you didn't need anyone, gave you permission to be aloof. They wandered around the house with its narrow hallways and large, drafty rooms, the smattering of priceless antiques, sun-faded couches, oil paintings of sailboats and the sea. He could only imagine what it must have been like growing up here in the summer. Julian's own summers had been limited to the local Y camp, where, at fourteen, he'd started as a CIT, with a whistle around his neck and a jumble of lanyard in his pocket. Nobody in his neighborhood had a pool; they'd relied on sprinklers to cool off during the hottest months. But this place, you had the ocean calling to you from every single room.

It rained most of that Saturday and they dug out some old board games, Clue and Scrabble and even Twister, and listened to a stack of Sinatra albums. Finally, when the sun appeared, they piled into the wood-sided station wagon and drove into town to buy oysters; Rye had a shucking knife with his initials on it. He paid for everything, tossing his money onto the counter like a gambler buying chips. Back at the house, as the windows grew dark, they drank iced Stoli and smoked his mother's stale Pall Malls in the small, outdated kitchen, the cabinets warped from the sea air. Opening the oysters, Rye cut himself, and some of the blood ran into one of the shells. Nobody noticed, but Julian chose that one. He swallowed the oyster whole, like a wad of phlegm, relishing its metallic taste.

After they ate, they climbed down the rickety stairs to the beach. The wind was cool off the water, and they were all a little drunk and shivering. They dug a pit and built a bonfire and circled around it like some kind of a cult, silently watching the flames. Magda was standing across from him, the firelight coating her bare arms, her neck. She had the hard, irreverent beauty of a goddess, he thought, and found he could look at nothing else. She met his eyes over the flames in what seemed to Julian a signal of collusion, for they were interlopers here, kindred by their middle-class roots. But the moment didn't last. She took Rye's arm and draped it around her shoulders, securing their underhanded alliance at least for the weekend.

They stayed up late, watching a monster movie on the old TV set, drinking whatever was left in the liquor cabinet. At some point, like thieves, Rye and Magda crept upstairs. He could still remember watching her slim, pale calves as they disappeared into the darkness. A little later, Marty and Lars drifted off to their room. He knew he wouldn't sleep and stayed up with Ava, smoking too many cigarettes. They were both pretty drunk and he could tell that, like him, she was suspicious of the prospect of true contentment. They lay on the musty couch together with her feet near his head and his feet near hers, and she told him how their mother had died recently and the place wasn't the same without her, and she kept thinking any minute her mother would be coming downstairs to tell her to go to bed, and how without any parents she felt all alone in the world, aside from her brother, who was usually too busy for her, and he said that even though his mother was still alive, he, too, felt alone, and they both fell asleep listening to the roar of the ocean, and when he woke up the next morning she was gone and she'd covered him with a blanket. He knew he'd never forget that kindness.

A photograph is a kind of death, Sartre said, a moment, taken like a prisoner, never to *be* again. Was the photographer, in essence, a coroner of time? They were reading the best minds on the subject, Szarkowski and Sontag and Berger and Barthes, and would gather nightly at The F-Stop to drink and argue the medium's purpose and their role as photographers: Were they merely documenting the mundane evidence of life, or was a photograph the result of some inferred context? Were they looking out a window or looking into a mirror, as Szarkowski suggested?

In those days, they were still shooting film, mostly black-and-white, which was easier to process than color and cheaper and stood apart with its built-in austerity from ordinary snapshot photos. Julian was using the same SLR he'd had for years, a Canon AE-1, but Adler had acquired an arsenal of used equipment, including an old R. H. Phillips 4 x 5 view camera that he'd lug around the neighborhood on its tripod, persuading people to let him take their picture. While everybody else was home sleeping, he'd be up all night in the darkroom, producing luminous Cibachrome prints—a janitor, a busboy, a street preacher, various panhandlers, including a blind woman (an homage to Paul Strand), grifters, hookers, working people of all variety—packing all the pathos of a Dickens novel into one startling shot. He had a painterly hankering for saturated colors—the egg-yolk yellow of a waitress's polyester uniform or the weedy brown of a mechanic's coveralls—and bestowed his subjects with a dignity they seldom experienced in real life. When Rye put up his photos, a solemn reverence would descend on the room.

Julian didn't make portraits. He didn't like people in his shots. Instead, he was drawn to empty lots, condemned buildings. To him, there was a silent poetry in the sky over a vacant city park or the rubble of a razed building. Or a parking lot at dusk, the chorus of streetlamps, the empty carts inert as cows in a field. His images, he felt, were pure, almost religious—not that he was or ever had been at all religious; in fact, for all intents and purposes, he was agnostic—but, uncannily, he believed there was an aspect of God in his work. He didn't know why this was. It certainly wasn't deserved. For one thing, he was the product of a mixed marriage. As a result, his parents had forsaken religion and, unlike his friends growing up, he had not been forced to endure Sunday school. When people asked about his faith, he'd developed his own excuses for not taking part. Mostly, he didn't feel he belonged. Whenever he found himself inside a church or a temple, he felt like an outsider. He couldn't get beyond the rhetoric. He didn't *feel* the presence of God. At the very minimum, God as a concept seemed pretty far-fetched. But when he took a photograph of some barren place, some sad and lonesome aftermath that reflected the indignities of man, the routine apathy displayed in the lurid destruction of a city playground, for instance, the resulting image seemed to shimmer with some unseen light, the promise of another dimension beyond what Julian could perceive with his own eyes, as if God were playing a trick on him. It wasn't anything he talked about, but it caused a certain amount of private confusion, and sometimes when he was very drunk and behaving badly, courting the very edge of civility, he would feel a yearning to repent.

At his final critique, it was Rye Adler who spoke up, as if they'd all decided beforehand. In his vague, roundabout analysis he seemed to suggest that Julian's photographs were vacuous. *Your work has no soul* was how he put it, delivered with such earnest gravity that no other student dared refute it. Not even Brodsky, who only gazed at Julian with brutal indifference, as if condemning him to a life in exile.

In his final collection of prints, Julian had tried to emulate Atget's Paris—the mystery of a lonesome staircase, an unpopulated alleyway, an abandoned dinner table—but no one detected the comparison.

You're an impartial observer, Rye concluded. There's nothing at stake for you. I don't know how to feel when I look at one of your pictures.

Why do you need to feel anything? Julian asked.

Rye looked at him cautiously but did not reply.

As they filed out of the room, Julian stood there with his hands in his pockets, staring at the floor. He felt like a failure. That's when Magda came up to him and put her hand on his shoulder. Don't listen to them, she said. It's not what's there that matters. It's about everything that's not.

He clung to those words, even though nobody really cared what the women thought.

Over the years, he reflected on that single afternoon, the flat gray light of the studio, the rain streaming down the windows, the faces of the other students watching as Adler's comments took effect like a dangerous drug, disabling some essential organ, a death sentence conferred in a single, impulsive moment.

When the program ended, Julian moved to New York and rented a gloomy one-bedroom apartment in a rent-controlled, prewar building on Riverside Drive. Intent on working for the magazines, he made the rounds with his portfolio. Editors would stare at his pictures, glumly, and say nothing. None of them seemed to understand what he was trying to do. Eventually, when he ran out of money, he took a job as a junior account executive at a small advertising firm known for pharmaceutical marketing. As the new hire, he got stuck with all the boring accounts nobody wanted. He didn't mind. He liked the routine, working alongside the pros, the long hours, the sense of importance he felt when he'd finally leave the office late at night and sit alone at his kitchen table, drinking a cold beer. And he liked the money. He appreciated the fact that he didn't have to be a creative genius. It was good work, and he was good at it. For the first time in his life, he actually felt useful, like he had a purpose. Every now and then he'd run into someone from the workshop and they'd grab lunch and commiserate over their struggles, agreeing that things hadn't exactly turned out as they'd planned. It was on one such occasion, sharing a table with Marty Fine at a deli near his office, that he learned Adler was on assignment for *National Geographic,* thus knighted by industry royalty. As Marty droned on, Julian sat there, gritting his teeth. A few weeks later, idly turning the pages of the yellow-bordered magazine in his therapist's waiting room, he came upon an article about a cholera outbreak in Somalia, the result of tainted water, with two startling photographs credited to Adler of children orphaned during the crisis, with eyes that confronted you and demanded your attention. Eyes that had seen too much. They stared out at Julian with inalienable longing. He found he couldn't stay for his appointment. He had to leave. He had to get out. He walked along the park, reproaching himself for wasting his life. Adler was putting himself out there. He was doing important work. And what was Julian doing? Selling stool softeners! He didn't have the connections, was the problem. Adler knew people. And Julian didn't know anyone, at least no one who mattered.

In a morass of self-loathing, he walked thirty, maybe forty, blocks before he realized there were tears streaming down his face.

Soon after, there was no escaping the evidence of Rye's success. It seemed like every distinguished magazine in the country had a shot or two of his, and he was described at certain parties as the eye of a generation.

Adler wasn't just getting paid. He had made it.

On the day of the memorial, he woke at dawn, the sky pale as newsprint. He glanced out at the neighboring buildings. Most of the windows were still dark. The trucks were just rolling in to make their deliveries and the streets were relatively empty. His head ached. He had drunk too much the night before. He filled a glass with tap water and swallowed a couple aspirin. He took his time getting ready, putting on a good suit, buffing the tips of his shoes with a shoe brush. You never knew in life, he thought vaguely, when it would all end.

He looked around the apartment, the sullen arithmetic of the furnishings. It resembled a suite in an airport hotel, impersonal and forlorn, and it occurred to him that his marriage was the exhausting trip he was recovering from, stuck in this in-between, this ascetic cubicle of regret. You couldn't go back, he understood that now. You had to press on. You had to forge ahead.

He pulled on his overcoat and walked down to Penn Station in the wind. The station was crowded with commuters, and his train was delayed. He bought a cup of coffee and an egg sandwich and stood at the counter, trying to ignore his increasing ambivalence about making the trip upstate. He knew he had to do it, to show his face. It would be awkward, yes, but it was necessary. It could not be avoided.

When he finally boarded the train, he sat by the window in the nearly empty car, aware of his obscure reflection in the dark glass. The train moved slowly out of the tunnel into the suddenly sharp light of the city. They passed the old yellow-brick tenements with their small windows lined up like the holes on a punch card. Finally the river appeared, the brown marshes, the occasional hawk. The river was black, the sky dull and white. As the train moved upstate, the distant Catskills took on a shuddering majesty. Old, once elegant homes stood along the shore. The melancholic view pleased him and, as the train gained in speed, conveyed the convoluted abstraction of a dream.

He dozed off for a few minutes, and when he woke, the train was pulling into Hudson, an old-fashioned depot stuck in time. He stepped off the train and watched it pull away. He stood there, looking in both directions, up and down the track. A few men were waiting by their cabs, smoking. Julian nodded at one, and the driver opened the back door. He was an Indian, with dark, kind eyes that seemed to glitter in the early light. They drove up the main street, passing brightly lit storefronts. The wind came in gusts, ruffling the awnings, swirling scraps of litter. People on the sidewalks had to shield their eyes. One woman put her hands to her face as the wind disrupted her hair.

Rain is coming, the driver said in a delicate accent.

It sure looks like it, Julian said.

The driver let him off at an old grange on the outskirts of town. You could see the fields stretching behind it. A small plaque identified the building as a Reconstructionist synagogue. Inside it was dim and dank, the wood floor scuffed, the old pews from a church. A lectern served as the *bimah,* and the eternal light was a flickering candle suspended by macramé ropes. He surveyed the small crowd, surprised there weren't more people. Other than him, not a single person from the workshop. Well, that didn't necessarily surprise him. He assumed Adler had left those people behind. He had risen to another stratosphere, Julian thought. One reserved for a privileged few.

A damp draft circulated, and like the others, Julian kept on his coat. He took a yarmulke from a wooden box and fondled it into place on his head, then sat in a pew by the door. As the rabbi approached the *bimah,* the room filled with a sudden darkness. In the clerestory windows he could see the wild treetops and the slowly moving black clouds. He looked over at the empty space beside him and imagined Rye sitting right there, winking at him. The thought made him shudder.

He scanned the rows of heads and saw Simone up front, sitting with her daughter, the Somalian child they'd adopted as a toddler who was now in her twenties. Julian had always found it puzzling that, with all the gorgeous women at Rye's disposal, he'd chosen a rather unassuming wife, the sort who disdains the usual feminine trappings for political reasons. He supposed Simone had an earthy attractiveness; her hair was starting to gray and she wore very little makeup. He imagined she was the kind of woman who could assemble a great meal with only a few ingredients. Or the person you'd think to call in an emergency. Unlike Julian's impulsive wife, she had stayed the course. She was an academic, he knew, a poet. A few years back, he'd seen a piece on the two of them in the magazine section with pictures taken on their farm—the old country house, the big green field, the dogs—a lifestyle, it seemed to him, of reckless indulgence. He'd burned the article after he read it.

The rabbi read in Hebrew, then translated the 23rd Psalm. Just now it seemed to be very apropos—the one line in particular: *Thou preparest a table before me in the presence of mine enemies...*

Wasn't that the truth. Even back then, there were people who wanted to knock you down. The world really hadn't changed all that much. They were all still wandering the desert, taking what they could, trying to survive.

Simone's daughter rose and approached the *bimah*. She had a small, heart-shaped face. Unhurriedly, she unfolded a piece of paper, then traced her thin fingertips along the page.

Rye was a great and unusual man, she said. He was my father, and my best friend.

She told the story of how Adler had found her alone in a makeshift tent with her dead parents. She had memories of indescribable hunger. You went into another place, she said. It was abstract and consuming. Even now she could summon that terror.

Rye saved my life, she said. He nurtured my existence. And I will never forget him.

She began to cry and stepped into her mother's waiting arms. They parted, and Simone took her place at the *bimah*. In a low, halting voice she spoke about Rye's work, his dedication to excellence, his high ethical standards, et cetera, et cetera. Julian was getting bored.

She paused a moment, staring out at them, tears rolling down her cheeks. He was an adventurer, she said. That's how he saw life. And he never stopped looking for his people. He never stopped telling their stories.

Overcome, she stumbled, and the rabbi took her by the arm and ushered her back to her seat. The group watched as he comforted her, reassuring her in whispers that scratched the silence. A few rows ahead of him, a cell phone vibrated, and a young woman with short auburn hair and a shiny black raincoat rose and liberated herself from the pew, stepping over knees and feet, mumbling apologies. She started down the aisle, moving with the purposeful devotion of an employee. As she pushed through the door, a draft rippled across his back and a momentary brightness filled the room. He could smell the perfume that lingered in her wake. Tea rose.

Please rise for the *Kaddish,* the rabbi said.

When the service ended, everyone stood around for several minutes, blinking like people who'd come out of the dark after a tedious movie. Some began to file out, while others hovered around Simone, offering their condolences. He didn't feel ready to see her.

He stepped outside into the drizzling cold. The girl with the auburn hair was standing under an overhang, smoking. Below her raincoat he could see the wrinkled hem of her skirt, thick gray tights and clunky black boots she'd likely found in a consignment shop. Something about her sad eyes and knobby knees gave him hope. She resembled the St. Pius girls he often saw on his lunch hour who clustered at the chain-link fence in their uniforms and rumpled knee socks, sneaking cigarettes.

Is this the smoking section?

It is now, she said.

Can I bum one?

She retrieved a pack of unfiltered Camels from her pocket and gave it to him. Help yourself.

You don't mess around.

She smiled. That's true. I don't.

He cupped the flame as she lit it for him.

I'm Julian Ladd. He waited to see if his name registered; it didn't. Rye and I were in the Brodsky Workshop together.

Of course, she said. I'm Constance. I'm—was—his assistant. She reached out her pale little hand, and he shook it.

Is it true what they're saying?

Sorry?

About Rye. That he—

She looked at him with annoyance. That's the conclusion.

I never knew him to be depressed.

She shook her head. It's horrible. They found his shoe—

It's always just the one, isn't it?

She nodded as if the thought had never occurred to her.

One shoe in the road, never two, or in this case, one shoe in the river. It's almost Lacanian.

Her phone chimed. She looked relieved and glanced at the text. I have to go. She took a final drag on her cigarette and dropped it to the ground. You're coming to the house, aren't you?

He hadn't planned to, but he told her he was and needed a ride.

You can ride with Louis.

Who?

Over there.

She pointed at a bear-size man with a thick beard who was getting into a vintage red Mustang. Julian walked over and introduced himself.

Nice wheels.

My tribute to Eggleston. Need a lift?

Thanks. Julian got in. Very nice. What year is it?

'Sixty-five. Bought her at a police auction. She runs pretty good considering her age. It was an interest we shared, me and Rye. There's a nice old Porsche in his garage. What do you drive?

I live in the city. I bought my wife a Range Rover to drive to the supermarket.

Louis glanced over at him and smiled. That's pretty funny. That kind of says it all, doesn't it?

Yes, it certainly does.

They both chuckled.

We're getting divorced, Julian said.

Welcome to the club, my friend.

There wasn't much traffic on the Taconic, and you could feel the wind gusting against the car. In the short time since they'd left the grange, the sky had grown dark. The clouds looked yellow.

Louis peered up over the wheel. That can't be good.

Hail was always a surprise. A million little white balls pummeled the hood of the car. Jesus, Louis said, slowing down. Holy shit.

Some of the other cars pulled over to the shoulder, but Louis kept going. The land looked battered. When the hail finally stopped, the white sky seemed to throb in the aftermath.

Well, that was fucking weird, Louis said.

They drove in silence, like soldiers after a battle, their tank riddled with bullets. After a while, they turned off the highway onto a two-lane road flanked with open fields.

I used to print for him, Louis offered soberly. Back in the day. When he was still shooting film. At one point, we even went back to doing dye-transfer prints. Very time-consuming. But nothing really compares. Are you a photographer?

We met in the Brodsky Workshop.

Ah, the infamous Czech visionary.

I'm in advertising, actually. I gave up photography a long time ago.

Smart move. Tough to make a buck these days. I'm lucky if I get hired for one of the catalogues. It's not the same anymore.

No, it's not the same.

I blame the downfall of western civilization on Steve Jobs.

You can't stop progress, Julian offered ironically.

When they shut down Polaroid, I went into a dark place. Back in 2010, I actually made the trek out to Kansas to Dwayne's Photo with fifty rolls of unprocessed Kodachrome a couple days before they stopped developing it.

Really? How was that?

Sad. About a hundred times more morbid than this—and our friend Rye would agree. Kodachrome made the world a lot easier on the eye.

Julian nodded. I didn't shoot much color.

Ah, a purist. I hear some people are going back to film. That's what the editors tell me. But the business has changed; there's no money in it anymore. Not for dweebs like me, anyway. You can barely get by on what they're paying these days. Freelance—it's free all right. And I get it, you know. The technology's outsmarting us. I suppose there's no going back.

It doesn't matter, really, Julian said darkly. The world's ending.

Yeah, Louis snorted. That's what I hear.

Julian looked out at the wet, barren landscape. It appealed to him. He wondered if the weather was so bad in the city. He thought of his apartment, the sound of rain filling the empty rooms. And then he thought of his wife and was momentarily paralyzed by the realization that, even now, after everything she'd done to him, he still loved her.

They turned into a narrow lane so thick with pine trees it was like going through a car wash. They crossed a bridge over a wide stream, then followed a circular gravel driveway up to the house. It was an old stone Colonial, one of the earliest homes in the area, Louis told him, circa 1670. There was a large red hay barn, and a three-bay carriage house with a light over a doorway, a blur in the hard rain.

This is some place, Julian said.

Yeah, this is real money.

I didn't know they were so well off.

It's all hers, Louis said. Her father owned Hogan Foods.

Ah, Julian said, as if he knew. That explains it.

I guess we should park over here. Louis pulled off the driveway onto the grass alongside a few other cars. The rain was thrashing down. As they got out, two drenched dogs lumbered over to greet them, their tails wagging.

Hey, boys, Louis said, Hey, Pal, Rudy. That's a good boy. You, too, Rudy. Come on, now, let us get inside.

They tramped through the muddy grass to a small side porch. The air smelled of woodsmoke. Julian could feel the rainwater seeping into his socks. They entered a mudroom and hung their wet coats on pegs and wiped their shoes on the mat. He slid his hands through his wet hair and followed Louis into the living room. They'd become fast friends, and Julian was reminded of high school, when, through some anomalous act of cordiality, he was invited to a party. Some of the other mourners were standing around, eating off paper plates. They were an esoteric little group, Julian thought, obviously New Yorkers, and he assumed they were people Rye had worked with. You could always spot the editors. They looked underfed. They were wearing dark, expensive clothes, the women in shawls and high heels, the men in designer suits that looked a bit snug, the jackets short and boxy. The room smelled of perfume and leather, wet wool. Simone and her daughter were ensconced on the sofa in front of the fireplace. It was a rather austere room, he thought, sparsely furnished with antiques, the wide-plank floors scratched and worn. It occurred to him that he was famished. He found Louis in the dining room, navigating a trestle table laden with deli platters.

Some spread, he said, helping himself to a bagel and smoked salmon.

Jews, Louis whispered. They do good funerals.

They stepped up to the bar, where Adler's assistant, Constance, was making the drinks. What's your pleasure?

Well, there's a loaded question. Some of that scotch, I guess.

As she poured the drink, he noticed a tiny tear tattooed on her wrist. Cheers, she said, and handed it to him. Here's to dead friends.

Yes. Dead friends.

They seemed to be kindred spirits, he thought. She had a slight overbite and a little mouth crammed with teeth. He guessed she was in her twenties.

To happier days, he said.

She looked off into the room for a moment, her eyes watery and dull. They're her friends mostly, she said, motioning around the room. He didn't have many.

That doesn't sound like Rye.

How well did you know him?

I'm not sure, actually.

You're not alone, she said darkly. Nobody knew Rye. Not really. When was the last time you saw him?

It's been quite a while, he said, and left it at that.

He stepped away from the bar and took in the view of the brown fields, the twisted black trees. It was still pretty raw up here. The rain had let up for now, and he could see the white sky, the distant Catskills. He swallowed the last of his drink and shook the ice around in his glass. One more, and then he'd go.

He went back to the bar, but Constance wasn't there. He spotted her across the room, talking to a gray-haired man in an expensive suit. It was Henry Cline, the famous curator. They seemed engrossed in conversation, he thought, already drunk enough to feel a little possessive of her. She was a thin girl with the emphatic stature of a fashion model. Like the Degas ballerina, she stood with her hands clasped behind her back, a look of utter fascination on her face. Here was a girl who lived on ramen noodles and Smirnoff, just pretty enough to garner a few strategic favors from an old pervert like Cline.

He found the scotch and refilled his glass. There was a muffled energy in the room, as if they were all inside a giant balloon. It was a grand old place, drafty and damp. Books everywhere. Big painted chests and cupboards crammed with pottery. Abstract paintings on the walls—not his taste. Arranged over an antique bench was a group of family photographs: their daughter at various ages, Rye's parents when they were young expats, and one of Ava, the moody academic in a black turtleneck, staring into the lens with an unsettling intelligence, as if she were looking right at him. There was a black-and-white shot of Rye at Deerfield, his hair long enough to curl around his ears, his hands pushed into the pockets of his khakis, a button pinned to his corduroy blazer that said DIVEST NOW and a smile on his face of pure, unadulterated privilege.

Even now Julian envied it.

As he stepped into the large foyer and encountered his own reflection in the hall mirror, he was embarrassed to see that he'd broken a sweat. He wiped it off with the sleeve of his jacket. He had no business being here. He needed to make his exit, and soon.

But he stood there a moment longer, in no particular hurry, his gaze drawn to the top of the staircase, where a greasy light poured in through the Palladian window. Somehow, he couldn't stop looking at it, his eyes tearing from the glare.

After his third drink he approached Simone. She looked almost startled to see him. Julian, is that you? She rose from the couch, extending her arms.

Hello, Simone.

How good of you to come. They hugged, and he could feel the bones in her back under his fingers. How long has it been?

Many years, he said. I'm so sorry, Simone.

She held on to him tightly. When they broke, she analyzed his face. You look exactly the same.

Do I? So do you.

They were just words, he thought. Because in truth they had both changed. They weren't the same people now.

Have you met Yana? She turned to her daughter, who rose from the couch and ambled over. Yana, this is a friend of your father's.

Yana crossed her arms over her chest and stared at him with unambiguous distrust.

Good to meet you, Julian said.

I'm suddenly very thirsty, she told her mother, and left them alone.

Simone smiled apologetically. This is very hard for her. I'm sure you understand.

Of course it is. It's a terrible thing.

She was squinting at him as if he'd been obscured by some strange light, some disfiguring aura. Tentatively, like she didn't really want the answer, she asked, How are things going for you, Julian?

Well enough. I'm in advertising.

Is that so?

Pays the bills.

More than that, I'm sure.

We do ads for some of the big pharmaceuticals. One of our accounts is Motus.

She shook her head, unaware of it.

It's an OTC laxative.

OTC?

Sorry. Over the—

Oh, right. Of course.

The preferred remedy of opioid addicts. Needless to say, we've had a banner year.

How sad. She shook her head. This world is—

He nodded in agreement. Yes, he said. It is.

They looked at each other a moment. He coughed. I was hoping to see Rye's sister. We met once—

Ava. She's stranded at O'Hare. Electrical storms, apparently.

Pity, he said. It would have been nice to see her.

Simone asked if he was married, and he told her he was getting divorced.

I'm sorry to hear that. Any kids?

We have a son.

She studied his face, perhaps understanding that he wasn't going to talk about the boy, at least not here, not now.

Tell me, she said, shifting gears. What ever happened to that awful girl in your class?

He stood there, frowning with confusion. He could feel the pounding of his heart. Which awful girl?

Rye photographed her that year. It nearly ruined us. He sold it to the Met. It's still hanging there somewhere, I'm told.

I'm not sure who you mean, Julian managed to respond.

The Polish girl—

Just then, her cell phone rang, a welcome intrusion. Excuse me, she said, and turned, cupping her ear, allowing Julian to politely recede and head back to the bar. He needed another drink. Of course he knew the photograph she was referring to.

It was a few years after the workshop when the news of Adler's show started circulating around the city. As hard as it was to deal with his friend's success in relation to his own failure, he'd been happy for Rye at the time—an exhibition at the Met was a big deal—and he made himself go. He'd left work early, claiming to have a dentist appointment. Like a thief, he roamed the galleries, skirting the peripheries, his head down, hoping he wouldn't see anyone he knew. It was unsettling to be surrounded by so many of Adler's portraits all at once, a whole chorus of humanity, but there was no photograph that affected him more than the one of Magda. She was sitting unclothed on a wooden chair near a window. The room was dark, save for the window light on her skin. Her body was sculptural, exquisite, and the expression on her face was one of longing, a smoldering discontent, as if in that moment it had become clear to her that she could never possess Rye, that whatever they had together would be over the moment he took her picture.

Julian stood there a long time, stirred by the image—her eyes, her breasts, the open window, the sheer, almost ghostly curtain—conscious of the people lurking behind him, trying to get a look. In a matter of seconds, he'd turned into what Berger called the sexual protagonist, eyeing her nakedness as though the photograph had been made just for him. Of course he knew all too well that was not the case.

Bereft, he drifted out into the street.

Compared with Adler, he was nothing more than a well-meaning amateur. He deserved the solemn purgatory of the advertising world. He left the museum that afternoon with a clear understanding of his own inadequacies and went home and packed up his cameras and drove them out to a storage place in Queens. It was like a burial, he remembered. He'd gone out afterward and gotten drunk, and he hadn't taken a picture since.

Constance refilled his glass. You look like you need it.

Thanks, I do.

She's good at that.

What?

Undoing people. Finding your weakness, whatever it is. She drills straight for the heart. Boring into it until you bleed. You can't hide anything from Simone.

Julian shook his head as if he didn't know what she was talking about.

At least you get to go home, she said.

Some of the guests were pulling on their coats. The thought of his empty apartment made him anxious. It was so terribly quiet.

Constance took out her cigarettes and motioned for him to follow her outside. They grabbed their coats from the mudroom and stepped onto the small side porch, then crossed the grass to a large slate patio with an awning and rain-soaked Adirondack chairs. The rain had slowed to a misty drizzle, but it was colder now, and raw. They stood under the awning, and he watched as her delicate fingers worked a couple cigarettes out of the pack as if they were preparing to draw straws.

You're a very bad influence, he said, taking one.

You're not the first person to tell me that. She smiled.

It was nearly dark. The sky looked bruised.

I'm finding this whole thing very depressing, he said finally. But in truth he wasn't unhappy to be here. The situation, unfortunate as it was, allowed him the coveted agency of an insider. Ironically, he felt closer to Rye than ever before.

Poor Rye, Constance said, and he noticed a single tear running down her cheek. I hate to think of him floating around in all that cold water.

He put his hand on her shoulder. I'm all right, she said, and gently shrugged him off. I suppose I was a little in love with him. But everybody was a little in love with Rye. He was such a genius.

He nodded, but the comment annoyed him. He dragged hard on his cigarette and blew the smoke down to his feet.

They were having problems. He was basically sleeping up there. She jerked her chin toward the carriage house.

What kind of problems?

The usual stuff. She thought he was cheating.

Was he?

She shrugged. Not with me.

Julian watched her smoke. She had very pale skin and freckles, and he could see how young she was, and how sad.

I can't say I'd blame him, she said. She's kind of cold.

He smiled, a little surprised by her candor.

Sorry, she said. I'm just honest.

They stood there smoking together like kids cutting school. A strange glow fluttered behind the clouds.

It sure is quiet out here, he said.

The winters are very long. I'm thinking of moving to L.A.

My wife lives in the country. Not the real country, Westchester.

I didn't know you were married.

We're getting divorced. She doesn't love me anymore. I'm coming to terms with it.

I'm sorry, she said.

When you're in it, you can't see. Then suddenly it's over and you see everything.

Thunder rumbled. He could feel the ground shaking under his feet. Then the sky filled with light so bright it might've been noon. He vaguely entertained the notion that this was The End. What if it was? he thought almost hopefully. He imagined the reports on TV, people running through the streets. This weather's crazy, he said.

Get used to it. It's only going to get worse.

Another blast shuddered through the clouds, and the house suddenly went dark.

Great, Constance said. Just what I need.

Inside, they were lighting candles, and you could see the tiny flickering flames reflected in the old panes. It was almost like being back in the seventeenth century, when the Dutch were still here, and the world wasn't ruined yet.

It began to rain, a celestial tumult.

I have to go in, she said. She took a final drag of her cigarette and tossed it to the ground. I have a feeling it's going to be a very long night.

Wait, he said. Look at that—

They stood there together behind a curtain of shimmering glass. He'd never seen such a hard rain. He wondered how he'd ever make it home.

* * *

It was after midnight when the lights finally came back on. They'd been sitting around the fireplace, resigned to the darkness, maybe even grateful for it. There were only a few of them left, and they were all grabbing their coats, getting ready to go. He knew he had stayed too long.

I'm sorry, Simone, he said uneasily. I should have left hours ago. I'm afraid I've missed my train.

No, I'm glad you're here, she insisted, really I am—this she added as if to convince herself. She looked at him, and he could see the day on her, the weariness in her eyes. You can stay in the studio. There's a futon up there.

I don't want to impose.

She shook her head. Please, she said. I want you to.

Constance took him out to the carriage house, carrying a folded blanket and shuffling along in a pair of untied Bean boots. They stepped inside the three-bay garage, where Rye's old black Porsche was parked. They both stared at it. There was something eerie about the dull shine on the steering wheel, the tongue-red of the leather seats.

Up here, Constance said.

Julian followed her up the narrow stairway. Constance was his Virgil, leading him through the dark woods. He didn't know what they would find.

On the landing, she took a key on a string from around her neck and unlocked the door. They went in, and she kicked off her boots and dropped her coat to the floor. He took off his loafers and set them neatly by the door. It was cold and drafty and there were many windows covered with old yellow shades. She turned on a small lamp. Here, she said. There's a—

Let me, Julian said.

He pushed some old newspapers into the woodstove, then a couple pieces of wood, and struck a match. Almost immediately the flames sprang to life. He closed the stove's door and looked up at her in the golden light.

Not bad for a city boy, she said.

I have many unexpected talents.

She dug around in a cabinet and pulled out a bottle of Jameson's. She handed him a glass and took one for herself, and they sat on the old couch, its oxblood leather scratched to shreds by the dogs.

He asked how long she'd been working there, and she told him two years. She'd gotten the job through a professor at Vassar.

That's the only way you can get these jobs, she said. Rye had me printing, keeping track of his files, corresponding with editors. We'd sit together in front of the computer. It was a tedious process. He was never satisfied. I don't think he ever fully adapted to digital. He was pretty old-school. But mostly I work for her.

Doing what?

Taking care of the dogs. Going to the market, cleaners. She's fussy.

Really?

Prone to tantrums.

He nodded like he understood.

People with money, she said bitterly. They're just different.

He asked her where she stayed.

Just down the lane, she said in a mock-British accent. There's a farm down the road with a little guesthouse.

Will you stay on? Now that he's gone.

I don't know.

They sat for a moment, drinking their whiskey.

So, this is where he worked?

Yes. She looked around as if the past two years had been nothing more than a dream. Do you want a tour?

It was like the scene of a crime, the futon in the corner, its filthy sheets strewn on the floor. A few old glasses out on the tables, dust. The smell of the dogs. As he looked around at the disarray, he felt an oddly appealing sense of déjà vu, for the space was not all that dissimilar to the apartment they had once shared.

She showed him the office, the towering flat file, a large mid-century Bauhaus-style desk, a pair of Barcelona chairs. She dropped into a desk chair on wheels that squealed like a barn animal whenever she moved.

He wasn't here all that much. He was always going somewhere. Her voice trailed off. I think that was the trouble between them. He'd go away, then come back. They'd fight. He'd come up here. He'd be in here all night, working. And then he'd leave again.

She opened the door to the darkroom and switched on the light. Newly printed photographs hung from a line.

That was Tokyo, she said. Right before. He was there for *Vanity Fair*.

He glanced at the pictures coolly. Nothing special, he thought.

I should go, she muttered. It's very late.

He found her coat and held it up for her, and she turned around and pushed her arms into the sleeves, and for just a moment, he laid his hands upon her shoulders, admiring the downy little hairs on the back of her neck. Slowly she turned and looked up at him. I'm sorry I stayed so long, she said.

You have nothing to be sorry about.

They were speaking in code. He felt sure there was something between them, some obscure and essential connection. They were like operatives bound by information that was at once incriminating and revelatory.

At the door she stepped into her untied boots and gazed up at him with wet eyes. He wasn't satisfied. In his work, I mean. He said he'd lost his edge.

Haven't we all, Julian thought.

He was searching for something…

What do you mean? Like what?

She shook her head, trying to find the right word. Transformation, she said finally. He said he was tired of all the bullshit. He couldn't trust anyone. He was tired of not believing in anything.

What, like God?

She nodded. It was only then that he noticed the cross at her throat. For some reason he thought of his wife's pale neck, her own disassembled devotion.

What if there isn't one? What then?

She considered the question and countered, darkly, What if there is?

He offered, but she wouldn't let him walk her home. He watched her crossing the yard, her hair blowing around her face, hugging herself in the cold, until the darkness absorbed her and she completely disappeared.

Part Two

The Decisive Moment

Photographers deal in things which are continually vanishing and when they have vanished there
is no contrivance on earth which can make them
come back again.

—Henri Cartier-Bresson,
The Decisive Moment

Rye

The sun is setting in Tokyo. He sits at a table near the window, where the golden light finds his hands. The bar is crowded with wealthy tourists, a parade of affluence—the clothes, the handbags, the shoes, the casual apathy of the very privileged.

He is feeling estranged from his own life.

Such random exclusivity, he thinks.

He suddenly cannot bear it.

Why is he here?

Maybe he doesn't care anymore. Maybe he's lost his empathy.

He remembers the refugees, hordes of them, crossing the broken earth from Sudan, how they'd faded and faded as the sky grew brighter, hotter, erasing their features as they blackened in silhouette.

Simone, before the trip. She'd let him photograph her.

When he was searching for her in the forest of birch trees.

And she became a stranger to him.

Maybe his soul is involved. Maybe his soul is yearning for something—someone—else. Is it her age? No, in fact she is more beautiful to him now, more beautiful in her vulnerability. Her culpability. But this is something ethereal—her scent, perhaps—he can no longer smell her. He can no longer find her in the dark. Her scent is indeterminate. And now he is walking in circles. Or maybe he doesn't actually desire her. If he is really honest. Loves her, yes, but desire is something else. He knows desire because he is a manufacturer of it. And desire is about loss. It's about disruption, chaos.

He finishes his beer, watching the woman across the room at a small table drinking a Kir, waiting, he imagines, for her husband, who is unforgivably late.

He rides the elevator up alone, up, up, sharing the space with his reflection in the mirrored walls. What does he see? Nothing. A man he does not recognize—

In the room, he packs his small suitcase, gathers his toiletries, and secures his cameras in the camera bag, lovingly as kittens. His flight isn't until morning, but he's had enough of the crowded Tokyo streets. He stares out at the dark night, the twinkling lights, befuddled by some vague premonition, the lavish comforts of the room somehow compromised by an encroaching danger. Like water, he thinks, seeping under the door, gradually spreading to the corners and rising ever so silently over the bed as he sleeps.

He's having breakfast in the hotel café when her name flashes across his iPhone screen.

Magda P. likes your photo. Magda P. started following you.

(And in this decisive moment, everything changes.)

He hasn't spoken to her in over twenty years. They'd known each other once, briefly, long enough to know she was the kind of woman who could bring the darkness out of you.

He clicks on her name, and a single photograph appears on her Instagram page. The picture is blurry, shot from a moving car, but there are two discernible figures, a boy and girl in their early twenties, standing on a highway exit ramp, holding up cardboard signs. The boy is in better focus, while the girl stands a distance behind him, smoking, a small pink backpack at her feet. The boy's sign simply says HUNGRY. The picture has no likes, and Magda P. has no followers.

Instinct tells him to block her from his account, but the concierge's voice startles him. Mr. Adler, your car is here.

Ah, yes, thank you.

It's a black Mercedes. The doorman holds an umbrella as he gets into the back seat. The air is cold, and it begins to rain. Even in the watery light the colors find him, the red paper lanterns, the yellow windows of shaded glass. He'd spent the week photographing the artist Masato Nakamura in an industrial warehouse near the university, where he teaches and where his work is on display. It's Rye's third time in Tokyo, an invigorating, inspiring city, but now, after Magda's abrupt interference, his melancholy deepens and he is eager to get home. The rain is a blue shimmer at his window, and the shadows of raindrops dapple his hands like a rash.

A few miles from the airport, he pulls out his phone and again looks at Magda's photograph. Obviously she started following him so that he would check out her page and see it, and now that he has, he wonders what she wants with him.

Using his thumbs, he enlarges the picture and studies the scene on the exit ramp. It's impossible to tell where it is; it could be anywhere. Both the boy and girl are wearing hoodies. Their thin bodies share the same hunched posture, as if they have been standing there for days and have grown weary, their hoods like shrouds. The boy is tall and gaunt, his eyes projecting a vague sense of indifference—or is it arrogance? Rye can recall holding up a cardboard sign of his own back when he was around that age, but it was one of protest—anti-apartheid, anti-nuke—and that seems to him a telling difference. And yet, perhaps this is a protest of another kind, subversive and complex.

Again he studies the boy's gaze, the cool detachment, something nagging at him like the memory of a dream he cannot fully recall. But it isn't until much later, on his layover in Chicago, while washing his hands in the men's room and glancing at his own ragged reflection, that he understands why the boy's face is familiar.

It looks exactly like his.

Simone is waiting for him in Albany outside the baggage claim. He sees her through the glass doors, leaning against her dirty white Saab in her farm coat and muddy boots, the green wool hat she knitted herself pulled low across her forehead. A countrywoman, he thinks. A country wife.

He heads outside and tosses his bag into the trunk. *Konnichiwa.*

She hugs him hard, and he can smell the cold fresh air on her neck.

They break apart, and he tries to avoid her infrared gaze. Suspicious by nature, she evaluates his appearance, intent to uncover some deception. He knows she has never fully trusted him. It is the nature of his work, he reasons. The continual distraction of strangers.

They get in the car, and she pulls out, and they wind around toward the airport exit. The car smells like gasoline and old leather. As much as he's tried to persuade her to get a new one, she refuses. It's a standard, and he watches her thin, capable hand as it manipulates the stick shift. There is something that happens to his wife when she drives. Contained in her seat, she handles the wheel like a race-car driver. He doesn't tell her, but her driving makes him nervous, and he finds himself clutching the strap. It's a side of her personality that continues to intrigue him. Unlike the other areas of her life, where she is cautious and deliberate, in the car, on the open road, she defies the rules. She dares to be free.

How was the flight?

Long. Screaming babies.

Oh, dear.

How's Yana?

She got that new job. She's very excited.

Does it pay anything?

Not enough. But—it's something.

Yeah, it's something. Good for her.

Are you hungry?

The word on the boy's sign comes back to him. HUNGRY.

Do you want to stop somewhere? We could stop at Jackson's.

They drive into the country on narrow back roads. A gentle rain falls on the windshield, and the wipers maintain a monotonous rhythm, keeping time in the deepening night. They stop in Old Chatham at the pub and order lamb chops and a bottle of cabernet. He studies his wife across the table, her hair pulled back hastily in a leather clip. She has always denied her own beauty, and yet tonight, even in yoga pants and a moth-eaten cashmere sweater, she draws glances from strangers. He is glad to be here, back in his town, a place where the space is open and free and he is accepted for who he is and also ignored for it. His wife looks at him carefully, like one of those early paintings of the Madonna, eyelids half closed, compassionate, full of grace.

You look a little ragged, she says. Like you've been cut out with scissors.

This helps. He holds up his glass, drinks.

He wants to tell her about Magda, this intrusion from his past, but knows he cannot, and he finds himself wishing they were closer, more open to each other, no matter the trouble. But this notion, of course, isn't realistic. Because Magda is the last person on earth Simone wants to hear about.

They drive home in silence on unnamed dirt roads.

You're awfully pale all of a sudden, she says. You okay?

I just need to sleep.

It's like the onset of a virus, he thinks, the only relief from which is stoic endurance while the illness runs its course.

* * *

In the morning there's a new picture of the boy and girl, standing under the awning of a Chinese takeout, waiting out the rain in the piss-colored light, their eyes distant, absent, passive. The photo had been shot with a long lens, perhaps from across the street. Rye enlarges the image, noting the vague details of light and dark, the hoods shadowing their faces, their entwined hands, the girl's fingers bright with rings.

Morning, sleepyhead, Simone says, climbing into bed with him. You were snoring!

Was I?

Are you better?

Yes, I'm better.

I made you pancakes, she says, and rolls onto her back, stretching her arms over her head. The sunlight has found them in the bed, the white sheets, the old Shaker quilt. He pulls her close, breathes her in. They look at each other; they don't look. And he fills his hands with her.

They spend the morning together, a rare occurrence. They walk through the orchard, the ground littered with apples. He pockets a few good ones. They wander down to the creek, the air cold enough for snow. The creek is gray under the early mist. They watch a lone heron lift from the shore. The house is warm when they return, and she makes him a cup of espresso, adding a tablespoon of sugar and warm milk just the way he likes it. They sit at the table, husband and wife, old friends. Her long silver earrings catch the sunlight as she lifts the cup to her lips. When they are finished, they drive into town to the Co-op to buy ingredients. She wants to make her famous beef bourguignon, she tells him, because it makes the house smell cozy.

At heart, she is a city girl, particular and demanding, but here in this kitchen, with its stone floors, the white clay sink, the old black range big as a piano, she is as resourceful as a farmer's wife. Yellow apples, wormy, deformed as crones, some with brown leaves, spilled out onto the table. No matter, Simone will take her knife to them and put them in a pie. He watches her at the cutting board, her narrow shoulders, an apron tied around her waist, her long arms and rather large hands. With such long, elegant fingers she might have been a pianist. But now this meal she arranges is her music, her symphony. She is very smart, his wife. Fluent in four languages. A translator by profession. But her favorite language is silence.

He takes the dogs and walks out across the pasture. Pal, the black Lab, stays close, while Rudy, his yellow cousin, canters up ahead, scavenging the long, rippling field. The sky is white. It gives nothing.

In the afternoon, he works in his studio, readying his work for submission. The trip is a blur to him now, the streets of Tokyo, the delicate, prescribed behavior of its citizens, unlike Americans, tramping through the continent like drunks at a party, oblivious, uncouth.

Here on the farm, he can forget the world out there. But the newspaper revives his conscience like too many smelling salts: the warming oceans, the diminishing planet. The government with its partisan schemes.

The world has changed; it continues to change.

He can feel something coming. A knowing anguish has settled in his bones.

He makes a fire in the living room, a cold room full of windows, the floors bare. Just this old couch, two faded wing chairs. The shelves crammed with books. It's always a little cold this time of year, the fragile windowpanes thrumming in the wind. He has grown used to the sound after all these years. The walls are white, the room bright with winter sunlight. And there are framed photographs—not his, the ones he has collected over time—Abbott and Kertész, three small Atgets, Adams's *Moonrise*. They're all of them dead now. Just as one day he will be dead, his pictures hanging on some stranger's wall.

He checks his phone again, but there's nothing more from Magda. Simone appears in the doorway in her Muck boots and wool coat. He looks up, stranded in the moment, and puts down his phone. Work, he says.

She nods. She knows when he's lying to her. We're going out to walk. Do you want to come?

I've got all these emails to answer.

She nods again, says nothing.

He watches her through the window as she sets out. The dogs bark happily, circling her legs, and she laughs and runs, and they follow her. She stalks the icy grass, limber as a pony, her unbrushed hair a nutty gray like the old split-rail fence. The atmosphere in the house changes when she's not inside it. The quiet lies over everything like dust. A quiet that becomes increasingly louder. He doesn't think he can live without her. And yet he knows, come morning, he'll be ready to go, their separateness a habit.

He opens his laptop and googles Magda Pasternak. There are a few by that name, but none that seem to fit. He remembers an old file of early work on his desktop and looks there. Sure enough. It's the picture he took of her in her mother's kitchen. That first time they'd been alone together.

She's been right here ever since, only a click away.

He rarely shoots in black-and-white anymore but he recalls his earnest attempt to emulate Kertész's picture of his wife, Elizabeth, the shallow depth of field, the soft gray tones, the intimacy between the photographer and his subject. He studies the photograph critically, her face, her dark eyes, the light, and sees only its flaws. But not her. No. She is astonishing.

It was a row house on Salmon Street in the old Polish neighborhood. Her mother was still at work. She'd led him up the narrow staircase. The walls were painted a cornmeal yellow, the hallways stacked floor to ceiling with books—anatomy, philosophy, poetry. Her mother worked for a textbook company. They sat in the small kitchen and shared a bottle of beer, drinking out of juice glasses, talking about their favorite photographers, his Robert Frank, hers Koudelka—she liked his gypsies best, running her hands down each page as if caressing the faces.

She had the trace of a Polish accent. As she was showing him around, he could only think of touching her, holding her. Let me take your picture, he said. The light is nice now.

All right.

Maybe sit by the window.

She moved the old wooden chair by the window. Here?

He nodded.

This chair is a little broken, she said. Most of our furniture came from the church. When we first came to the U.S.

How old were you?

Three. I've been here my whole life, basically. But really, I don't feel American.

No? Why not?

It's hard to explain. You have to feel it in here. Inside. He watched her light a cigarette and blow out the smoke. Like you belong, you know? Like you're really free.

You don't?

She shook her head. What is freedom?

He shrugged. You can do anything.

No—there is no such thing. Where are you from?

Here mostly. But my father's work took us to Morocco; he was an engineer.

So you are rich?

I'm not my father. Anyway, he's dead.

Mine, too.

What did he do?

He worked for an amusement company, fixing the machines. Pinball, Skee-Ball. Do you know those games?

Sure.

He would drive around in his truck. In Poland he was a doctor.

She put out her cigarette. What do you think about your picture?

I have a beautiful subject.

Beautiful pictures are boring.

They don't have to be, he said.

Here, let me try something—

She pulled off her sweater, then very slowly unbuttoned her blouse.

Magda—

For you, she said. A little gift.

You don't have to—

But then she unhooked her bra and it was too late. Better? We will be like Stieglitz and O'Keeffe.

It was safer behind the viewfinder. He brought the camera up to his eye and peered at her. The flat gray light fell across her neck and chest and the curve of her shoulder, and there was the slightest shine on her lips. He could see the clouds behind her and the rooftops of the neighboring row houses and the green spires of the church, and he took a few shots and set down his camera, and she rose, and they stood facing each other like wrestlers about to compete. He staggered toward her, and she clutched him, and they shuffled through the narrow hallway, backward and forward and backward, circling, kissing, into her bedroom and onto her hard little bed. He could still remember how they clung to each other, as if during their lovemaking they'd been transported into another realm, free of gravity, with no beginning and no end.

A few years later, when the Met had miraculously decided to do an exhibition of his portraits, the young curator Henry Cline chose her photograph as the starting point, declaring it a pivotal marker in his career, one that had ultimately secured his fate.

He wonders if she'd even gone to see it. He tries to imagine her standing there, looking at herself. They had stumbled into a brief affair—it had surprised them both—and he'd left without so much as a goodbye.

Again he studies the photograph. Her dark eyes seem to taunt him, as if she has caught him in the act of wanting her again.

He hears the dogs barking.

A chime sounds on his phone: I need to see you, she writes. Can we meet?

Simone raps on the window, alarming him, and cries, Look what Rudy did!

Rye looks up and sees Rudy at the window, wagging proudly, a dead rabbit in his mouth. Simone shakes her head and smiles, and he feels a sudden pressure in his chest, the love he has for her, and the guilt he endures for denying it. Guilty for all the things he has done to compromise their love, and for the thing he is about to do now.

Of course, he types back. Where and when?

Much later, he wakes on the couch. The room is dark now. He can hear the howling wind, and he can feel the cold air seeping through the windowpanes. His eyes are closed. He listens to the old house with its creaking floors as Simone comes and goes across the boards, picking up, putting down. She tiptoes in to check on him. He wants to be left alone. But she dotes on him. Covering him with an old quilt. Stoking the fire. Even the glorious smell of her cooking doesn't cheer him. Maybe it's the jet lag making him feel like this, as if there's been a sort of death. But it's not that, he knows. It's her, Magda. Haunting him like a ghost.

In the beginning, he'd been naive enough to believe his work could make a difference. That he could present a version of the truth, his own, that would stir something in people. Maybe even change the world, one photograph at a time. It didn't take him long to figure out that truth was as various as light itself. It shifted and brightened depending on the circumstances. There was the man in the palace and the man in the cardboard box, and while they might have the same criteria for happiness—shelter, safety, a modicum of privacy—their realities couldn't be further apart. The truth was fluid. *The truth shall make you free,* the Bible said. But if the truth was different for everyone, freedom was equally as elusive.

His early pictures were pure, unedited. He missed that.

People on the street, in bus stations and factories, on farms. You saw hope in their eyes, courage. You saw deliverance.

He'd made his own money. But he'd been around money all his life. He was raised with a certain sensibility. His parents had been educated, adventurous, charitable. His father was a builder of bridges. He used to say that a bridge was an apt metaphor for life; you had to get from one side to the other, you had to conquer your fear of heights. You couldn't depend on abstractions. You had to engineer your own destiny. You could trust the reliable logic of physics, the exclusive equation of design. His father sometimes took him to the site of a new bridge, where a hundred men were working. He'd witness the amassed collaborators, the survey crew, the engineers, the masons, and even at the age of seven or eight, he marveled at the scheme of metal that whipped across the water like the tail of a diplodocus, shimmering in the sunlight.

They had a sprawling house in Marrakech, its paint white as sugar, with a tall front gate through which you could see mosaic floors and archways and numerous potted plants. His mother was famous for her parties. The rooms crowded with diplomats and entrepreneurs, artists, eccentrics. As a child, he'd wander below the eye level of the adults. He remembered the scent of clove cigarettes, the naked shoulders of the women, the air crammed with words, the charged momentum of a good story—and the sudden burst of laughter that followed.

From the time he was a boy, his mother encouraged him to engage with strangers. As a result, he had no fear of people, which had served him well in his work. She'd send him out into the streets with his father, through the dust and clatter of the street vendors, his father's gait hunched and labored as if his pockets were full of heavy stones. His first camera was an Olympus, a gift on his fourteenth birthday. Like some sudden preposterous deformity, it rarely left his hand. He photographed everything he saw: the rippling tents of the market, his mother's Sphinx-like Weimaraners, the peacocks his father raised from birth. For high school, they sent him to boarding school in Massachusetts. It was like going back in time, the historic village, once a frontier settlement, the yellow leaves of autumn, the green fields; he came to respect history, the simple practical beauty of the buildings, the spiritual pull of nature. His years at Columbia were a blur of drugs and guilt and protest. The summer he graduated, he drove out west to Yosemite in a used VW bus, alone with his camera and his ambition, intent on finding the views Carleton Watkins had made famous in the 1860s, some of the most notable platinum prints of landscapes in existence. He'd wanted to do that: to make images that had the power to inspire and to change.

He remembered that first morning at Yosemite, when he'd set out alone, trudging through the cold shadows up the trail to Glacier Point, eager to see with his own eyes the views Watkins had captured of Half Dome. It was a strenuous climb, and he could only imagine the difficulty Watkins must have had getting up to the point with all his equipment, including an 18 x 22 inch–plate camera that likely weighed a hundred pounds, which he'd had specially built for the expedition, not to mention the heavy glass plates he needed in order to make the exposures. When he reached the top, Rye discovered a much different plateau than Watkins had set his tripod on over a hundred years ago. Instead of raw land, there were a snack bar and restrooms and a platform built as a lookout. But it didn't diminish the magnitude of the view, the triangular rock jutting into blue sky like the bow of an ark. Standing there alone, with all his senses fully engaged, he realized how small he was. How inferior to the splendor of nature.

Instinct made you a good photographer. It was like the scent an animal followed. You followed the light, looking for your shot. There was something sacred in it. And you knew it when you saw it. It was just there. Waiting for you.

You had to teach yourself how to see. How to see people and the lives they led.

All that summer, he was alone, which was all right with him. He drove around in his van, taking pictures of the people he met. It was a kind of campaign, to set down his vision of the world. There were all kinds of people out on the road. Travelers. Families. Drifters. The drifters had the most beautiful names. They could have been anything else, but they chose this life. They chose to drift. Some wouldn't tell him their names or where they'd come from or where they were going. Some of them didn't know. They wanted to remain anonymous, that's how they put it. That phrase had stayed with him a long time.

Along the interstate he found cheap motels with big neon signs and soda machines, squat ten-room establishments where you could see the canyons reflected in the picture windows. The sunlight woke him in bed, a golden light on the white sheets, his naked hands. He shot the people getting into their cars or standing outside, marveling at the sunrise, the open plains, their windbreakers ruffling in the desert wind. Even in July it was cool at daybreak, the wind a shimmer of light. He remembered this one woman squinting in the brightness as she smoked her first cigarette, the red canyons in the distance, the pale green of her top.

That summer he learned there was something intoxicating about transience, when you are in between, moving from one place to another, unscheduled, open to the day before you, open to the land, unafraid of the passing of time. The beauty of the land washes over you. It forgives you. It says: Start here. Begin.

All that open space could change you. It had changed him.

Some of those pictures were in his show at Brodsky. It occurs to him now that it was the night Simone and Magda had met.

Who's that girl?

He told her Magda was a fellow student.

She wants something from you, she said.

What does she want?

Simone shook her head, as if there would be no stopping her. Everything.

Simone

It used to be good here.

They lived off a desolate road where no other houses were visible, only fields and trees. Their driveway ran a mile into obscurity. You came upon the house like something in a dream, an early Dutch Colonial, circa 1670, built of stones, with original twelve-over-twelve windows and dormers and a wooden roof. From upstairs you could see the creek and the grassy hill that ran down to it, and the orchard with its twisted black trees. Their home had a quiet beauty, the wide pine boards covered with Turkish kilims, the primitive antiques, the paintings by newer artists—large, bold canvases—and sculptures, a few of them significant, the metal one in the field that turned slowly in the wind, and the things they'd carried back from trips, artifacts of their life together. It's what you did in a marriage—built a life—or at least collected evidence that you had one.

They lived a secluded life. On occasion people from the city would make the trip to see them—Rye didn't do house calls, as he called them—although they seldom came anymore. Even from the very beginning, he was a loner. She always made excuses for him—he was exhausted, jet-lagged, overscheduled. But in truth he wasn't good at friendship. He wasn't really interested in people, even though he spent the majority of his time photographing them with the invasive precision of a surgeon. She was the one to make the calls, to send the invitations, to organize the parties—this was back when they still had friends, when relationships were easier and a little reckless. They'd arrive in taxis from the train. Many were poets, a few actors. The rare photographer—most were too competitive, or too needy; those who could tolerate Rye's success were critics, academics. With their week-end bags at their feet, they'd stand looking up at the house. There is something about an old house that inspires reverence; it has withstood the vagaries of history—the regimes, the controversies, the brutal changes—and has endured, with its unyielding stature and design—the lath and plaster, walls thick as cinder blocks, the archways and floors, the windows—for centuries, a home that allows for beauty and light, a celebration of trees and open space, peace. They'd have dinner out in the garden at a long table laid with cloth, some block print from India, and ornate, mismatched china and unpolished silver, all from a consortium of dead relatives, and sit in half-broken chairs with failing cane seats, and in the glow of candlelight they drank wine retrieved from the damp cellar, good wines, the heavy green bottles powdered with dust, and smoked for the simple pleasure of smoking, and if they drank too much, which was often the case, they sang. They sang the songs of their youth, their voices lifting in unison to the sky, and some-times someone or another would rise from his chair and recite one of the old poets that nobody read anymore, Yeats or Milton or Dickinson or maybe even Neruda, and they would discuss and argue and drink a bit more, then shuffle finally to their rooms and their waiting beds, their heads filled with the promise of new ideas, and fall asleep in the hours before sunrise, only to forget them by the next morning.

They hadn't had any guests out here for a couple years. Nobody seemed to have the time. She didn't hear from people all that much anymore. It seemed to her a commentary on society. Nobody needed to go out. From the confines of your little world you could present the brightest colors of your existence, like an ad for the product you were selling, your very own happily-ever-after.

In truth, aside from her colleagues at the college, she had few friends left. It didn't really bother her. Everything was different out here in the country. For one thing, you couldn't always depend on the Internet. You had to be able to let go of technology. You had to know what to do with time on your hands.

She woke earlier than usual that morning and, leaving Rye to sleep, put on whatever she could find lying around, his old flannel shirt over a T-shirt and leggings. The field was calling to her through the window. She hurried downstairs and found her boots by the back door and her old shearling coat. Her boots were cold, crusted with mud. The dogs rushed to the door; they were ready to go out.

They went up into the pasture. She could feel the cold sunlight on her face. The dogs ran ahead. She loved this field, this land. The air smelled of woodsmoke, and she could see her neighbor's cows up yonder, the few old barns in the distance, broken, leaning. There were wagon trails, demarcated by crumbling walls of stones under ancient trees, their branches strung like canopies of lace.

When they lived in the city, in the tiny apartment on Leroy Street, her sense of space had been finite, contained, and she, too, had been contained. She'd had a limited capacity for disorder. When they'd first moved up here, the wide openness had intimidated her. Confidence to wander was an acquired skill. She might encounter a lone fox or a quintet of deer, aloof as her neighbors in the city had been. Once you lived in the country, you couldn't go back. You were drunk on space. Free in your body as you moved across the land.

She was known for her garden, the dahlias she pulled from the ground every November and nurtured through the cold months in the cellar. Now it was winter, but in the spring she would crawl on her hands and knees into the brambles, pulling and twisting, choreographing flowers like dancers on a stage.

She worked in isolation. The room was dark, even in bright daylight. She would sit at her desk and watch the trees, and the trees, she knew, watched her, peering through the window, indifferent as nuns. From an early age she'd had an ear for language. Words were her life, her music. Her precision as a translator had earned her a reputation. Occasionally, rarely, she published a poem of her own, but they were generally impersonal contemplations of nature, and in truth she was more comfortable translating the work of others than conveying her own particular perspective, although she told herself that one day she would. One day, perhaps when she felt freer, or less afraid of revealing something that could have a deleterious effect on her marriage, their daughter—those private thoughts were not accessible to her yet.

Her husband was rather famous. His photographs hung in museums and galleries around the world. He was especially known for his portraits. He'd been called a visionary, which, of course, was no small thing. In the few photographs that existed of Rye in the media, he was portrayed as a mythical icon, distinguished by his graying hair and light blue eyes, wearing the usual blue work shirt, old khaki trousers, white tennis shoes, and the thin twine bracelet Yana had made him, sitting in a black leather Eames chair, smoking—this was before he quit. Apart from the mythology, he was actually a very shy man, surprisingly cautious and even conservative when it came to more localized adventures, like going to the supermarket—he often stayed in the car. Simone had always sensed that, for Rye, it was hard to be home, and yet, when he wasn't shooting, he didn't want to be anywhere else. As proud as she was of her husband, she saw him as a man who hid behind his success; his ego, healthy as it was, sustained his luminous enterprise. He wore his cameras draped on his shoulders, around his neck, like artillery. Ironically, while his pictures conveyed an intimacy with his subjects, in his private life he was distant and enigmatic, the sort of person who might have worked in intelligence, who even under strenuous torture would never reveal his secrets.

He was a realist. In his work, he captured life as it was. Of course, in the name of art, he exploited his subjects—it was an inevitable outcome—although he would argue otherwise. In the beginning, she accused him of being careless, taking advantage of people for his own benefit, but Rye argued that he was only an objective observer; improving the lives of his subjects was not his responsibility. She had decided that he needed to believe this in order to work, in order to contain the visceral reality of his subjects' lives. And yet, while his photographs displayed a keen perception, his insight into his personal life was lacking—of course, for all of the years that she'd known him, she'd kept these thoughts to herself.

In fact, their work was not all that different. They were similar people, visual people. They made images, he with pictures, she with words. Beauty was important to them. They savored time. Moments. They utilized the same materials, light and darkness, texture, pathos. They conjured scenes. The empty street, a single waiting car. A fleeting emotion pulling the edges of a woman's face. The worn soles of a husband's shoes. The farmer's hands. Purple carrots in the wooden trough. Children running, laughing, crying.

From the start she'd found his pictures troubling—and yet so compelling. Their powerful effects came later, not unlike the dizzying revelations of dreams. He refused to be put into any category and bristled when people called him a celebrity photographer. I photograph famous people like anyone else, he'd argue. Some of his competitors accused him of having it easy, of being connected, but connections were like gossip, they guaranteed nothing. It all came down to the work, and Rye worked. Harder than anyone she knew. He shook off his background, his pedigree, like tight clothes. They lived a solitary life.

Socially they were outcasts. Much of her time was spent alone, working, cleaning, tending the dogs. She walked the great fields behind the house. At night, when Rye was away, she wandered from room to room, a little afraid, shivering in her long nightdress, her feet bare. She knew where to look for the moon. When she let out the dogs, she stood on the cold porch, listening to the night, the language of the country, the animals, the insects, the distant train, then the edge of quiet that came at last, like the final sentence of a novel. When he was home, she cooked elaborate meals. They'd dine in candlelight, the dogs sleeping at their feet. They made love cautiously, a well-rehearsed dance. It was still moving, still satisfying. And yet—

She will soon be fifty. A certain corruption has frayed the seams of her heart. The news frightens her, the government, the widespread complacency. She doesn't know how to think about the future. If the planet can heal, if the species can continue.

She is a professor, revered for her expertise and intelligence, her bewitching optimism. Her students flock to her, for she is the warrior from the real world, protecting their ideas, their fragile ambitions. She is a visiting lecturer, which means they are getting away with paying her less. They are getting away with not paying health insurance. And they don't have to deal with her, not really. She comes, she teaches, meets with students, and leaves. It is amazing to think that, even with her stellar education, the PhD, the honors and awards, she is, in truth, a glorified temp. No matter. There are positive aspects to the arrangement. She can be less committed, less anxious. And there are no administrative responsibilities.

Twice a week she drives to the college, to her classroom in a house built by Shakers. She and her students sit around a large oak table on stiff ladder-back chairs. She is one of the older professors and dresses accordingly in long skirts and handmade sweaters in the colors of the earth and sky, clothes that drape on her thin frame, and her lucky half boots and a scarf woven by her daughter and presented to her as a gift on her last birthday. She has stopped coloring her hair. Her eyes are clear and gray.

She doesn't let them have their phones. They are kept in a basket for the length of the class. At first, when she'd decided on this rule, they were fidgety, their fingers so accustomed to fiddling with their devices, the small screens, the tiny buttons, their ears pitched to intermittent pings and chimes. They were distracted, anxious that perhaps they were missing some essential message. They stared at her blankly, with the glazed eyes of addicts, not listening. Now they are better at it, more engaged. Even so, when the class ends, they scramble to retrieve their phones, relief in their eyes, the color returning to their cheeks, each of them a little weary after the forty-two minutes she has asked of them, the strain of thinking.

She meets the new hire for lunch. His name is Caspar Ahmadi. He is a little younger than her, a man from Iran, with smallish, elegant shoulders and eyes that can be described only as pretty, the lashes thick and glossy, the lids sleepy, almost lavender. His hands are lovely and square. His wife, he tells her, is an oncologist. They are renting a house near the middle school. It's been an adjustment, he says, but does not elaborate. There is something attractive about his mouth, the uncertainty of his smile. As he speaks, she wonders what it would be like to lie next to him naked. She wonders what he dreams about. She imagines the ghosts of his dead parents standing over him while he sleeps.

You have to love books if you are going to write. This is what she tells her students. She has too many books for one house, and they seem to be occupying every surface. She loves her poetry collection most. The care demonstrated with every book, the slender binding, the ecru pages, the elegant font designed by someone from another time. The words are all that matter. They lead you through the dark wood of the poem. The words wait in her house, and the house waits, and the house has been waiting for hundreds of years. Waiting for what, she does not know. Only that it is coming sooner than anyone thinks.

It was the denouement of their marriage; she could feel the slow descent.

He seemed preoccupied, muddled. Peering into the screen of his phone, transfixed by the cryptic dispatches of strangers. He was sitting at the kitchen table, wearing the old gray sweater she'd knitted for him twenty years ago. She can still remember the fresh, taut wool under her fingertips, the wooden needles she'd bought in Hudson when they'd first moved up here.

What are you looking for?

What?

You keep checking your phone.

I have a meeting tomorrow with one of my editors. I'm waiting to see where he wants to meet.

Which one?

Someone at *Esquire*. He's new.

It all sounded a little odd to her. Rye didn't shoot much for them. They had limited funds. But you never could tell. She had learned to stay out of his work.

But still. She always knew. It was some voice out in cyberspace worming its way into his consciousness. She could read his body. Non-committal. Shunning her. Like: I'm not really here with you. Don't expect anything from me.

There were always excuses, the work, the travel, and she forgave him—

In spite of herself, she forgave him.

Because his work was everything to him.

She couldn't intrude on it.

It was an unspoken condition of their marriage.

And because deep down she knew, as all spouses know such things, that he loved his work, his freedom, more than he loved her.

She'd accepted her role, she supposed. She was his wife, his conservator. She maintained the order of his days.

She unpacked his bags, started the wash. Gathered his oxford shirts for the cleaner. Tossed out receipts in Japanese, scraps of paper scrawled with notes. It was love that ran through her fingers as she folded his trousers and T-shirts. She took special care with his things, stacking his mail, his books. Wiping the dust from his desk. It was women's work, yes, but it didn't diminish her. Her care, her tenderness, her watchful insight was what she gave to him.

And yet, she felt this loss, for what, she did not know.

She watched him like a detective. She was critical, suspicious.

She hated herself like this.

At dinner, he seemed distracted. The meal she'd made, his favorite. He ate purposely, like an inmate. He complained about the work, the younger editors who had different ideas. People thought differently now. Their sense of timing, their tolerance, their patience. People *saw* differently too.

It was no longer the viewer's gaze that found his pictures, but a flash of judgmental eyes. Moreover, he couldn't surprise the viewer as easily, simply because there was too much visual stimulation to compete with. Thus, the medium had changed. And there was no going back.

He was overwhelmed by it all, he told her. It wasn't fun anymore. His adventurous spirit gone.

He was too young to retire, plus they had compelling expenses, Yana's rent in Santa Monica, which they helped her with, and her car insurance, and basically whatever she needed; she was only an intern making minimum wage—this after four years at Berkeley with a 3.8. Additionally, there was the upkeep on the house, the barn, the land, the taxes, the new furnace they'd installed to be more energy efficient, the new refrigerator, since the old one had gone kaput, and all the things they'd acquired—the photographs he collected, the art, the jewelry he gave to her, guiltily, perhaps trying to make up for rarely being home, for not loving her enough. Or the gifts from his travels—woven scarfs, leather boots, everything exquisite, handcrafted, her taste—she was particular. He had earned her, she had taught him, they had grown together, and now, finally—after all—they had grown apart. It could happen in a marriage, she knew this. And it had happened to them.

Sometimes she would stand at the window, looking out through the wavy glass, and it was enough. The green fields of summer, the yellow leaves of autumn, then, for months, nothing but snow and white sky. She loved the hill down to the creek, the orchard with its wormy, deer-eaten apples, warped, fragrant.

Her life was a gift.

She was translating a new book by the Israeli poet Maya Ronn. The poems gave her courage. They argued for change, peace, resilience, love. In the end, she wrote, that's all we have. Love.

Unlike a lot of the American women she knew, Israeli women didn't question their worth. They fought, they protected their country, they relied on intelligence; they didn't distinguish themselves from men. They seldom questioned their own abilities. They believed they could do anything.

In comparison, Simone felt like her own neurosis was American Made.

For a year, during college, she'd attended Tel Aviv University. She'd learned Hebrew by reading the poems in the Old Testament. She was most proud of the fact that she'd memorized the bus system and mastered her bargaining skills at the *shuk*. When she went to the wall to pray, whispering into its ancient cracks, up close like a lover, her fingertips tracing the yellow stone, she somehow knew God was there. There was no doubting it. There were times during the long months without Rye when she thought of making *aliyah,* but, alas, she had not been willing to leave her own country behind. One day, perhaps. Yes. One day.

* * *

That night—their last night together. He'd made a fire and they shared a bottle of wine. At one point, the screen of his phone brightened with a notification and she asked him what it was.

Nothing, he said.

Why don't you turn it off? You just got home. You have a life, you know. You need your own time.

With disdain, he tossed his phone onto the coffee table.

Thank you, she said, feeling like his mother, not wanting to feel like that. It's important for us to be together. To really be together, you know. When you're home.

He nodded but didn't look at her.

They're intrusive.

What?

The phones. I feel like they're spying on us.

I get it, Simone. And I agree. But you have to remember the business I'm in. We can't function anymore without texts. That's what people want. Nobody wants to talk anymore.

She nodded. I know. But—

But what?

I feel like your work is coming between us.

That's ridiculous.

You're always looking at your screen.

You know that's not true.

I'm just telling you how I feel.

He shook his head. I'm sorry.

What time are you leaving?

Early.

I was hoping we could—

He frowned. I'm beat, Simone.

She nodded. Okay.

He rose and started up the stairs. Just as he reached the top, she heard the chime of a text.

She went up a little later. He was already asleep. The bedroom windows were blue-black. Outside, there was nothing, only darkness. She stood in the shower under the rushing stream, the sound of so much water filling her ears.

Before the sun rises, he is up, getting dressed. She watches him in the half dark as he pulls on his shirt, his trousers, standing at the window, looking out. The trees are bare, they move in the wind, and the glass trembles slightly. She can hear the birds calling to one another.

She closes her eyes, drifting. The smell of coffee nudges her awake. She pushes off the covers and rises, naked, from the bed. The tiles in the bathroom are cold. She washes her face with cold water and the black soap, like tar, he brought her from Africa, and runs a brush through her hair. She considers her changing reflection, the new lines on her face. Her history. You can see her wisdom now, fierce like Athena, but no, not so fierce. Not fierce enough.

Outside, the dogs are barking. She pulls on sweatpants, an old sweatshirt, and hurries downstairs. He's sitting at the table, drinking coffee. Even at this hour, ragged with sleep, he is still hers. You are mine, she thinks, and I am yours. She wants to take him back to bed, to wrap his arms around her, but he is already thinking of the day ahead. He is thinking of the special winter light, the wind, the possibility of snow.

Good morning, she says.

He only glances at her, drains his cup, rises from the table, and sets it in the sink.

He pulls on his coat. I should get going, he says.

When will you be home?

I don't know. I'll call you.

She sits in the broken Windsor chair. She can hear the bare branches scraping the window and wonders now why they never bothered to trim them. Maybe they like the sound, she thinks, a reminder that, in nature, there is a time for everything, for being bare or bursting with blossoms, the pageantry of spring.

Is it for work?

Of course, he says with annoyance.

What are you working on?

He only looks at her, as if the answer is impossible to explain.

He gathers his usual accoutrements—the black nylon knapsack, his camera bag, a small, canvas duffel full of clothes—and heads outside. Shuffling into her boots, her coat, she follows him. The cold finds her like a stranger's hand. After a moment it bites her ankles, the backs of her legs. He tosses his things into the truck and gently positions his camera bag on the passenger seat. He is a man who resents attachments and commitments. Over the years she has come to accept this. Secretly, she knows she's enabled him—perhaps he is enabling her as well. While she stays behind to guard the fort, he ventures out and does what he wants. But she has come to a point.

We need to talk, she tells him.

About what?

Everything. Us.

He looks at her hard. What about us?

Something doesn't feel right—

Soon, he cuts her off irritably. We can talk all you want.

She nods like a scolded child. Then he touches her cheek and kisses her. Goodbye, Simone.

She stands there shivering as he pulls the truck off the grass into the long driveway. Just before he turns, he raises his hand out the window in a tentative wave. He is looking at her in the rearview mirror. She can see his eyes, bright with the early light. And he can see hers.

And then he is gone.

They are already strangers. She takes the blame. She is always blaming herself, as though she's never been enough for him.

The sky is white. The wind gusts around her legs. She pulls her coat around her and walks back to the house, the waiting dogs.

She makes herself go to yoga. Every time it's hard. There seems no improvement. Each pose is as challenging as it was the day before. Still, only fifteen minutes in, she is already better. Grateful she can move like this.

At the very end, when they are lying on their mats in the near dark, she twists toward the woman beside her. Simone sees her hair knotted at the back of her head, her long neck, her grace. The sweat on her arms. They are so close, she thinks, sprawled beside each other like sated lovers.

She drives home. The fields are white with snow. The barns are brown, blood-colored. Rudy and Pal are waiting for her. They wander into the field as the sun steeps like tea in the copper dusk.

They had made love. She thinks of it now, how he'd reached for her in the night. She still marvels at his intelligent face, his knowing eyes, how his shoulders slump just slightly in the wrinkled blue work shirts as though there is always something upon them, some weighty urgency, some world problem to solve. He is, she knows, generous to a fault. Generous with strangers. With people who need him more than she does. Still, she does not deny her status. She loves him perhaps too much. Even though they are damaged. Even though they are standing there, peering into the abyss, their hands bound.

Rye

When he is working, he is better. They are better. They are better apart than together. They are better as an idea than the reality. He doesn't believe in marriage. Not that he has an appetite for other women, it was never about that. But his freedom, being free in the world, that's what matters to him.

He doesn't have to be this person. He doesn't have to be the carrier of all faces, the one who sees. The one who can read a face or see the promise inside a person like the pit of their own fruit.

The grim light suits him, this hour of before. Before the day happens and becomes after. As he turns onto the Taconic, the morning sky opens, and he indulges in optimism, at least for now. It'll be good to see Magda, he tries to convince himself, and yet it feels more than a little strange, the same sort of queasy apprehension that comes when you discover you've mislaid an important document, one that distinguishes you somehow and cannot easily be replaced.

He'd come to know her through her photographs. Her pictures had been technically proficient, black-and-white prints of the people in her neighborhood, mostly women, most of them immigrants. Neighborhood girls in tank tops with charcoaled eyes and bad skin. Wives and mothers in the supermarket, handbags over their arms. An old woman with a crooked back, walking home on the littered sidewalk, the metal wheels of her cart catching the late sun.

He hadn't found any evidence of a career online. Even with all that talent. But it isn't easy for women. No matter how good they are. And it was even harder back then.

He remembers the early days, hustling quarter-page magazine assignments. Trying to meet the editors. Your work had to stand out. He'd gotten a lucky break with National Geographic. They'd sent him all over the world, covering all sorts of stories about all variety of people. He'd seen a lot and he'd learned that there were innumerable ways to live a good life. He'd seen joy in people who were living in squalor. And despair in some of the wealthiest.

He'd done a lot of street photography back then. Simone used to accuse him of being irresponsible when he photographed the indigent or homeless. He would hear their terrible stories and learn of their misfortunes. He would get to their truth, and make it beautiful, and walk away.

He's a different person now. Over time, out of necessity, he'd segued into more commercial work, getting assignments with some of the major magazines. He had a reputation for knowing how to put people at ease during a shoot. As a result, he'd witnessed a wide breadth of the human experience. In his more introspective moments, he was deeply humbled by it. He was the first to admit that his own success had turned him into someone else. His raw vision was gone. Now the camera owned him. It was the camera that decided what and how he saw.

At 34th and Ninth he pulls into a garage, then walks a block east. It's an old Irish pub, two o'clock in the afternoon, the sun wobbling in the windows, drunks hunched over the bar. Places like this, they stop time, he thinks. You step out of the world for a few hours. The bar is their time machine. At this hour it's nearly empty, the windows bright above café shutters, their slats thick with dust. He glimpses the people on the sidewalk walking by, their heads covered in hats, their faces wrapped in scarves as they brace against the wind.

He takes a seat and orders a Dewar's. Waits. The bartender sets down his drink.

Thanks, man.

He holds the glass in his hands. Sips. It's a cold day and the scotch tastes good. Medicinal, he decides, with this guilt he's feeling. He thinks of Simone, how she fussed over him, making the meal, ever solicitous of his needs. He'll call her, just as soon as—

Hello, Rye.

He'd know that voice anywhere. He turns, and there she is. Magda, he says.

No longer the girl he knew but a grown woman. Still beautiful, yes, but broken somehow. It's not the years that have done it, he thinks, but something else, some temporary saboteur.

He opens his arms like a peddler showing his wares. He holds her a long time, longer than he should.

You look the same, he says.

No, I'm old now.

Not old. Hardly. You look well.

She nods, accepting the compliment. Been a long time.

Yes, it has.

She shrugs her coat from her shoulders and hangs it on the hook next to his, then unwinds the scarf, revealing the pale beauty of her neck. Her movements are methodical, restrained, as if she is remembering the steps to a dance. Her clothes are expensive, the black cashmere sweater, the long gray skirt, worn leather boots. Mexican silver on her wrists. As she pushes her hair back behind her ears, he notices her wedding band. Not that he's surprised. Women like her are always married.

How are you, Rye?

All right, I guess.

He can see the window's reflection in her dark pupils, the cold white sky. She rubs her hands together. I didn't think it would be this cold.

Winter, he says softly. Already here.

Feel my hands.

He takes her cold hands into his own. You weren't kidding.

I forgot my gloves.

What are you drinking?

The bartender comes over.

Red wine, she says. Do you have something French?

He nods and pours her a glass and sets it carefully on the bar.

Na zdrowie, she says, and he watches her taste the wine. It's good.

Good. Cheers.

Outside, the green awnings clatter in the wind. The sky is very white, very bright, but only for a moment. Then it shifts and darkens, coaxing the worry out of her eyes. For some reason that he cannot explain, he feels a bitter nagging jealousy over the husband she has left at home. She looks at him carefully. He wonders what she sees. An old man, he thinks, hardwired, a little ragged.

You're very famous, Rye. Your work, it's very good.

Thank you.

You've had a remarkable career.

I've been lucky.

No, that's not luck. I saw something recently. About that actor. With the gold ceiling?

He doesn't feel like talking about his work. Not with her.

Some people don't know what to do with all their money, he says.

I'm sure you've seen plenty.

Yup. Movie stars, politicians, rock stars, gangsters, but when you come down to it, they're all just people. It was his stock answer.

No, she says. They're rich people. Big difference.

Is she suggesting he's sold out? He's worked hard, and he's proud of his work. But now, sitting here with her, pride isn't what he's feeling.

And you?

I work here and there. She smiles a little. Twenty years is a very long time, she says.

Yes, it is. Where do you live?

Westchester. But I've never felt at home there. It's convenient. My husband is in the advertising business. He makes commercials for the pharmaceutical companies; it's his niche. He's been very successful. I'm sure you remember Julian.

Julian Ladd?

He tries to hide his surprise. Ladd is about the last person on the planet he would have chosen for her. Although he hadn't expected her to be unattached, hearing this is disappointing news.

They'd been roommates that year in Philadelphia. After only a few weeks of living with Julian, Rye had come to the conclusion that he was a rather odd fellow. Type A didn't quite cut it; obsessive compulsive was more like it. He'd seemed overly preoccupied with Rye's lifestyle, down to how many beers he drank, or the little boxes of takeout that languished in the refrigerator, or how often he changed his sheets, which was not often. When he'd come home, Rye sometimes had the feeling that Julian had been in his room, going through his things. He'd notice the slightest aberrations, the drawers slightly open, the clothes pushed around, the book on his nightstand open to a different page, as if Julian's fingerprints were all over his life. These covert violations troubled him, and yet he never mentioned them to Julian or questioned him. He was like an overlooked child—too good-looking and well behaved to incite alarm, innocently ignored. He was always watching, lingering on the periphery like someone who didn't speak the language and had to rely on careful observation to understand what was going on.

They'd been living together for half a year before Rye asked him why he never photographed people.

Julian sat up a little taller and defended himself. I'm not interested in people, he said, as if he'd prepared the answer to a long-awaited question. People get in the way. They change the story.

What's wrong with that?

I've never liked people very much. Even as a kid. My mother used to worry about me because I was such a loner.

But isn't the medium itself designed for people? To show who we are? Where would we be without Strand's blind woman, or Arbus's twins? Or all of Frank's Americans?

Like I said, people don't interest me. I don't like them very much. They've never been very nice to me.

You don't have to like them to photograph them, do you?

Maybe *like* isn't the right word. You have to appreciate humanity for what it is. For all its filth and deception. I guess I just can't. I think when you look at a picture without a person in it, you think about why there's nobody there. You see it as a lonely place. The window of a tenement takes on a new significance. It becomes something else. In my pictures, the story is in what you don't see.

Rye thought about that for a long time. Julian had a kind of brilliance, but it seemed misguided. His photographs were empty, even morbid; he found their ambiguity disturbing. They seemed to reveal something about Julian, but he couldn't quite figure out what it was.

He was always hanging around. No matter where Rye went, he would turn his head and see Julian. Watching him. Listening. Seeming to memorize anything he ever said. More than once, Rye heard him repeating, almost word for word, a comment he'd made himself, and when he finally called him on it, Julian cracked a strange grin and said, I guess it's like that old expression: Great minds think alike.

One night, Rye made the foolish mistake of inviting Magda back to his room. He knew it wasn't right. It wasn't fair to her. For one thing, he had a serious girlfriend. And when he was totally honest with himself, he also knew that, as much as he liked her, once the workshop ended, it was unlikely he'd ever see her again. Still, he couldn't stop himself. They were just getting into it when he heard Julian's key in the lock and his feet stomping into the apartment. Magda was pulling off her top when his door suddenly opened. Horrified, she covered herself with the sheet, but Julian just stood there, staring at her, in no particular hurry to leave.

Sorry, he said, finally. I didn't know she was here.

Now he is looking at her in a new light. He can't imagine how she's stayed with Ladd all these years. The idea of the two of them together, intimately, makes him feel a little sick. How is Julian?

Her face changes as if a shadow has crossed it. Her eyes go dull as she constructs a lie. He's been very good to me.

Rye can see there's more to it, much more. His phone rings, and he glances at the screen, Constance. I need to take this. It's my assistant.

Of course.

But that's not the reason he gets up. Because he doesn't plan on answering the call.

He walks to the back of the bar and pushes through the door of the men's room. He turns off his phone and puts it in his pocket, then pees and rinses his hands, avoiding his reflection in the dirty mirror. There's something about all this that feels underhanded and strange, and he worries about his capacity to leave it alone. He decides it's time to go, and soon. Whatever she's come here to tell him is not his problem. He wants nothing to do with her, he decides. Nothing good can come of this. The thing to do is to leave the bar as soon as possible and go home. He'll erase her contact information from his phone and forget he ever saw her. But when he returns to the bar, that's not what happens, that's not what he does.

Instead, he orders them each another drink and wonders how long it will take to get her alone.

Sorry about that.

No problem. I know you're busy. How is Simone?

She's well, thank you.

Such cordiality feels forced, he thinks, the casual scrutiny of an interloper.

You have a daughter, don't you?

Yana. She's twenty-three now.

I remember reading about her in the *Times*.

It always surprises him when people seem to know things about him, things they've read. One of the drawbacks of becoming known for what you do. It certainly wasn't his intention. He has been guided only by a desire to do good work.

She's pretty special, he says. What about you? You have any kids?

Magda nods. A son, she says, and her eyes brighten with sudden tears. He's twenty.

Hey—

She shakes her head. Look, I need to go.

What's wrong?

I'm sorry, I shouldn't have—

He reaches for her hand as tears roll down her cheeks. She pulls away and wipes her eyes, irritably. This doesn't feel right, she tells him. I shouldn't have—

We're old friends, he says.

We're not friends. But that's not important. It's not relevant.

She pulls her leather knapsack onto her lap and starts digging through it. I brought you something, she says. That's really all I wanted. To give you these.

She retrieves a manila envelope and slides it across the bar. For you, she says, then rises from the stool and puts on her coat.

He stares at the envelope. Please, Magda. Sit down.

She sits but doesn't remove her coat. Her eyes are cold, a little desperate. He holds up his glass, signaling for another, and the bartender comes right over.

Rye opens the envelope and pulls out a stack of photographs. He's not surprised that it's the same boy from her Instagram feed, a chronology of childhood milestones: the first day of kindergarten, the toothless second grader, the school play, the braces, the girl he took to the prom—and more. He flips through them quickly, like a deck of cards, an unpromising hand. What is this, Magda?

He's yours, she says.

He sits there, trying to think. For some reason he can't seem to move.

His name is Theo.

Why didn't you—

I tried.

He looks at her, waiting for an explanation.

I went to your apartment, but you had already moved out. I tried to get your number. It was unlisted. Anyway, it wasn't something I wanted to discuss with your wife—

He can't look at her. Magda, I'm—

But she isn't interested in his pity. I tried to contact you through the magazine. They said you were somewhere unreachable.

Slowly it starts to come back to him. I was in Somalia, he says.

They said they'd try to get you a message, but they couldn't—

Couldn't what?

Promise anything.

He shakes his head. He'd never gotten any message.

So I wrote you a letter.

Well, I never got it, he says irritably. So, what do you want?

It comes out too fast and sounds harsh; he doesn't mean it to be. But maybe he does—this intrusion into his life. He watches it take effect. She looks offended but not surprised. She stands and yanks her bag from the floor and digs around for her wallet.

This was clearly a mistake, she says.

Hey, put that away, I've got this.

She looks at him with finality. Goodbye, Rye.

Then she's walking away, turning through the door.

The photographs of the boy seem to jeer him. He shuffles them back into the envelope and shoves it into his pocket, then lays two twenties on the bar.

The cold hits him. He scans the street. For a turbulent moment she is gone forever, and then he spots her, crossing Eighth Avenue, heading east in her long coat. It has begun to snow, thick flakes floating through the air. He jaywalks against the light, missing a cab's fender by inches, and jogs to catch up, sensing that time has already swallowed her, that she has retreated to her place in history, where nothing changes.

Let her go, a voice in his head is telling him. He slows down, breathing heavily, watching her brown hair swinging across her back.

Magda! he shouts. Magda, wait!

He's just about to touch her shoulder when she turns on him, fiercely. Turn around, Rye, and walk away. That's something you do very well.

What are you talking about?

The letter? I sent it certified. You signed for it.

No. I didn't.

Well, somebody did. Maybe you should ask your wife.

He stands there, unable to speak. The thought of this is too much for him.

I assumed you wanted nothing to do with me, she says.

He shakes his head. No, Magda. You know that's not true.

It doesn't matter now. She looks at him coldly. Don't worry, I got over it.

She starts walking. He follows. They walk for several blocks without talking, he a few steps behind her. She shifts her heavy bag from one shoulder to the other, and there's the sound of her boots hitting the ground. Her hair is long and thick, a little wild. She walks with the brusque impatience of a woman who knows her own beauty. Who has learned to expect nothing from people like him.

Look, he says, catching up to her. Magda, wait.

She turns.

I have to ask—and forgive me. Why didn't you get an abortion?

But the question only makes her angrier. She turns again but he grabs her hand a little roughly and pulls her toward him. Why didn't you find me?

You didn't want to be found.

You didn't try hard enough.

Maybe you're forgetting you were married.

It shouldn't have mattered.

She looks away, as if she despises him, tears rolling down her cheeks. But it did.

They are too close, he can smell her, a hint of fragrance, sweat.

Does Julian know? I mean about—

She just looks at him. Doesn't answer. Theo, she says finally. He's gone.

What do you mean?

She shakes her head. Gone—there are many ways to disappear.

Drugs?

She nods. I only contacted you now because there's no one else.

The girl in the picture? Who is she?

I don't know. A ghost—

She can't seem to finish. I've lost him, she says. I've tried—

She shakes her head. I've tried everything.

She looks at him now, the determined gaze of a predator. Will you help me, Rye?

Just now, he is not prepared to answer. Instead, they stand there like the opponents in a strange, dangerous game, their eyes negotiating the rules and how far they will go before one of them falls.

They walk up Fifth Avenue under the falling snow. They pass the Christmas tree at Rockefeller Center, the tourists snapping pictures, the holiday a week away. People rushing through the streets with their bags of wrapped gifts. They don't speak. They are like refugees after an arduous journey, clutching each other. Come with me, he says finally, when they reach the awning of a hotel across from the park.

I shouldn't. I need to go—

Just to talk. Just to sort this thing out.

It's an older hotel, elegant, Old World. They ride the elevator to the ninth floor. They don't look at each other; they say nothing. The room is large with big windows and wood floors. The walls are pale blue.

Here, he says, sit down. Let me get you some water.

He finds her a glass in the bathroom and fills it at the tap.

Thank you, she says, taking the glass. He watches her drink.

Better?

She nods.

It's almost four, the sky gritty. I'm going to order something for us to eat, all right?

Again, she nods, avoiding his eyes.

From room service, he orders a bottle of wine, a plate of cheese and olives. He helps her remove her coat and hangs it up in the closet. She uses the bathroom and he can hear her washing her face. An older waiter brings a cart, sets the plates out on the table, the olives and the cheese and the basket of bread, then uncorks the wine and pours some into two glasses, necessary as blood. Thank you, sir, he says, handing the man a generous tip.

Magda returns as the man leaves. Thank you for this, she says.

Of course. He hands her a glass, and they sit at the small table by the window. The sound of the street rises up. It's a comfort somehow, he thinks. A reminder that there's a whole world out there. That they are not responsible for everything.

We didn't know he was using, she says. For a while we didn't know. She shakes her head. The girl. She's the one who got him started.

Did you call the police?

No. Maybe we should have. I keep thinking there's still a chance he'll come back, you know, to the world. That he'll come back and stop.

What does Julian say?

He's very upset. Theo won't talk to him. We've been having—

She doesn't finish the sentence. It's been very difficult.

He senses there's more to the story—much more.

She covers her eyes. It's all my fault.

Look at me, he says.

No, I can't.

Magda—

Ashamed, she looks at her hands. I was in love with you, she says quietly. Stupid, right?

No. He can barely speak. Not stupid.

He kisses her face, her hands, but she resists him.

I'm sorry, he says. I'm sorry.

Then he shakes her a little and tells her, I was in love with you, too.

They lie together, fully dressed, facing each other, staring into each other's eyes. The windows are dark now. The room is very quiet.

I'm a little drunk, she says.

You're beautiful.

No.

I was afraid of you, he tells her. I took that job because it would get me on a plane, away from you. From how much I wanted you.

They cannot wait any longer. Their lips find each other.

It begins with her face, the time that has shaped it. The grief in her eyes.

This feeling of *being* as she allows him to touch her, to discover her as he pulls off her clothes, one garment at a time—this feeling of *being alive* with her. With *her*. At this moment.

This moment, he says.

She understands. Yes.

The sheets are white and cold. They hold each other.

He remembers when her photographs were pinned up in class and everybody would stand back a little. The strength of her vision. The tenderness she brought to every shot. The world pulls you to it, he thinks. You see it, and you take it. You *see* it. You show it all, you hold nothing back. You give everything to the image.

You give everything, he says.

Inside the crowded rooms of his memory he finds her again, the girl he knew and feared. For all of these years, they have lived in alternate worlds. He can almost smell her younger self, the patchouli scent she'd leave behind in the darkroom, her photographs hanging on the line, mocking them all. He hadn't known her feelings for him. She hadn't shared them. They talked about their work, and that was all. He didn't think she was the kind of girl who wanted someone like him. Someone who would leave.

Magda, he says. Where have you been?

I don't know. *Lost.*

You're not lost now, he tells her. You're right here.

They lie there a long time without talking. There is the sound of the street, the traffic, a symphonic lull, and the slow shadows of passing cars on the ceiling. He looks over at her. What are you thinking?

I don't want to think.

Are you hungry?

Yes. But I don't feel like eating.

I can order more room service.

I don't even want to talk.

We don't have to, he says.

Just hold me. That's all I want.

She turns away and he lies against her warm back. His stomach aches with hunger—hunger for her, this woman, this stranger. This bed is our country, she says.

Yes.

Where can we go? I would go somewhere—

Where?

Away. She decides, Canada. She whips off the sheet. There's no escape.

No, he says.

She walks naked through the dark, through blocks of window light, and pours herself more wine and stands at the window with her back to him, drinking it. I want to get very drunk now, she says.

He wants to tell her something essential, some philosophical truth, but he can't find the words. Come here, you look cold.

She sets down her glass and puts on his shirt, sits on the edge of the bed. It's like a plague, she says. People are sick. The world is sick. The planet. It's only a matter of time, you know. What do they even have to look forward to? Nothing, that's what, I don't even blame them.

It's very difficult, he says.

It's like a war. Worse. There are no bombs dropping from the sky. There are no troops marching in the streets. But there are dead people, dead kids. You never think it's going to be yours. You think things like that can't touch you. But they can. They do.

Ravenous, they go down to the street and find a café. It's a neighborhood joint, bustling, noisy, white tablecloths, waiters in black vests. They are seated at a quiet table in the back. They order oysters and fresh trout cooked in butter and a bottle of Albariño. He watches her closely. Her eyes are at once hesitant and resolute. He hasn't yet earned her trust. And as close as he feels to her right now, he knows she has not forgiven him.

The colors in the restaurant seem to radiate, the people who have come to dine, the determined waiters, the gleaming white dishes.

She is watching him intently, a rare smile brightening her face. The waiter brings the wine and the oysters.

I'm dreaming, he says.

She reaches across the table and touches his hand.

Again, he feels a surge of anger. He wants to tell her that she should have tried harder. Tracked him down. Shown up at his door with the boy. He wants to tell her that he's furious she didn't. That marrying Julian Ladd was a terrible mistake. He wants to tell her he hates her for it. That he'll never forgive her. But he knows better. Because what if she had found him? What then?

He remembers now: he couldn't wait to get on that plane. To start his life as a real photographer. But it came with a cost. Because to do that, to really *be* that, you had to be free. You had to be okay with hurting the people you loved.

He thinks of the boy, Theo—his son—out on that highway ramp with the girl, but somehow now it's far worse. What he's feeling is anger, no longer at her, but at himself for being reckless, for assuming that their brief relationship, as undefined as it had been, was less important than his ambition. That in all honesty, she'd meant no more to him than any other of his subjects. He'd used her, as harsh as it sounds. He took what he wanted and left.

Back at the hotel, they sit at the small table, finishing the bottle of wine. It is their impromptu home. The light is dim under the yellow shade.

People change, she says. The world hurts.

Yes, it does. But not everybody feels it.

I feel it. Too much.

She tells him about their son, the boy he does not know, her face alight with pride. She is a mother, a warrior, whose only armor is love.

He's a sensitive person, maybe too sensitive. He sees things. He sees too much. I suppose he takes after you, she says, and smiles. And he smiles too.

I don't know why he started, she says. I'm a good mother. We gave him everything we could. Julian has his flaws, but he's not ungenerous. I take the blame. It's my fault.

Don't blame yourself. People do things. You don't always know why. He opened a door and walked through it.

That girl, she says. She lured him to it. And now he's trapped.

No, Magda, Rye says. He's not trapped. He can walk out anytime he wants.

He holds her in his arms. While he regrets the lost years, time that could have been theirs, the son they might have raised together, he knows this is pure fantasy. It is not his nature to be paternal. Even with Yana, he was rarely there. He knows this. Regrets it, perhaps. But wouldn't likely change it. He thinks of Simone, alone in that house, at this very moment waiting for his call, the small gestures that make her happy, the gifts he brings her from his trips, their time together, rare as it is, the meals, the occasional sex. Over the years, Yana has been a good foil. She distracted Simone from fully seeing him. He never wanted that life in the country. That was her dream. But he knows, even for his wife, the reality has worn through. She has finally discovered who he is, a man who prefers to be alone, who has better things to do than stay at home with her.

They sleep a little and wake in the night. The wine has worn off. She wants a drink of water. He runs the tap till it's cold and hands her the glass. She is like a child who has woken from a bad dream, her hair like a nest, her lips full and pale.

They lie under the white sheets, facing each other. The watery light of the city washes over them. What are we doing here, Rye?

He doesn't answer.

Who are you?

He tries to think. He is muddled, enervated.

Did you forget?

Yes, he says. I forgot.

Me, too.

No. I know you—I *know* you. And you're—

He can barely speak. Very beautiful.

Not beautiful. Nothing is. Not even this.

She meets his eyes, a dare, an ultimatum. Will you find him? Will you do that for me?

Yes, he promises at last. For you, I will do that.

Finally, she sleeps. He stands at the window, looking out at the empty streets. For the first time in years, he feels no impulse to take a photograph. He simply stares out, enlisted in a silent vigil, a vigil of the self.

When they wake a few hours later, snow has fallen, muffling the moving parts of the city. He showers alone, his body thrumming, as if he has been brought back to life. He doesn't know how long he can exist without her.

They dress in silence. They are like soldiers preparing for battle. She scrubs her face and brushes her hair. They pull on their coats.

The hotel lobby is empty. They leave, entering the cold darkness just before daybreak. The streets are desolate. They stop at an all-night diner and drink coffee and order breakfast, although neither feels like eating. He watches her across the table. Their hands still touching. Already, he feels the weight of his longing.

Outside, he holds her very close. Just for a few more minutes. For a few more minutes, it is just the two of them standing there in the cold wind. And then they part.

On the drive up the Taconic, he thinks about what she said. How the boy is like him. For a moment he allows himself to feel almost proud. But then he understands the reality of his own recklessness.

He imagines her now, walking downtown to the train, wrapped in her scarf, concealed, his. It begins to sleet, and for a moment he can't see, and there's the sound, like a thousand pins hitting the roof of his truck. It feels like a warning. No matter, he drives straight into it, toward whatever may come.

Magda

The train is nearly empty at this hour. These are travelers, not commuters, a few tourists. She leans her head against the window as they leave the city behind. The river is black. The sky like smoke. She tries not to feel guilty. She feels grateful, mostly. That he is willing to help her. That she can try to forgive him now, that they can move on.

She allows herself to remember his hands. She is still wearing his scent.

She didn't want to love him, but she did. From the moment he turned to her at the bar and uttered her name.

She wanted to hate him, to punish him, but he followed her out onto the street, and they kissed, a Doisneau kiss, with people all around and the heavy snowflakes melting on their faces. They stumbled along, looking for someplace to go. He knew a hotel on Fifth. She didn't argue, her finger in the belt loop of his trousers. They were like drifters, nomads, new to this foreign city. The people around them strangers, aliens. It was only the two of them, that moment in time—a place in between what was real and what was imagined. The past was useless. Their lives meant nothing.

She stood behind him as he checked in. The concierge was fastidious, assured. He didn't raise his eyes as he slid the key card across the marble counter, and Rye thanked him with a nod.

It was an old building, the elevator slowly rising. He took her hand. They hurried into the room and removed their coats. She told herself that they were just going to talk. To maybe drink a little and talk and she'd tell him all about Theo. But that's not what they did.

In the grand room with the endless ceiling, she gave herself over to him. This time, this place, was theirs. They were removed from the world. Nothing outside mattered. Not the streets or the snow falling. Not the sky, even, or the moon. They lay in bed fully clothed, looking at each other. Her hand perched on his cheek, his on the small of her back. It was like being inside a cloud, as the light crawled across the walls, one hour, then two, in the lull of early afternoon.

He talked about his work. He said he loved to look at people. He loved their faces, their eyes, the color of their skin. At first, he would observe them. How they sat in a chair. How they crossed their legs or arms. He would look at their hands resting or clenched in their lap. He could read them, he told her. Some were very famous. It didn't matter; they were still shy, still insecure.

We're all children, no matter our age. We wear our childhoods in our faces.

There's so much in a face, she said. My mother stopped looking at me when I got pregnant. She couldn't accept it. She thought I was lazy. She wanted me to be an accountant. She never told me I was smart. Maybe she thought I would stop working so hard if she told me.

My parents thought I was a bum for not going to law school, he said. My father threatened to cut me off. He told me he'd made an appointment with his lawyer—then he died. Cerebral hemorrhage. My mother was devastated. I took her into the darkroom with me. I asked her to watch me process. I had taken some shots of my father with his birds a few days before his death. She watched one come up, and she saw—

He stopped talking a minute, shaking his head. It was a moment we had, you know? Where I knew I'd never have to apologize to her again. She accepted it, my work.

You were lucky, Magda said. She allowed you to be yourself.

Yes.

I've never had that. Ever.

No?

Maybe because I'm a woman. We don't get that choice. Not really, we don't.

He smiled at her knowingly. I thought we were a liberated society.

Right. Not quite. At least not in my neighborhood.

What about your work? What happened?

I got quiet, that's what happened. Once, my mother saw a few of my pictures—she said they weren't nice. They made her friends look bad. The wrinkles, the bad teeth, the big stomachs. I photographed some of the women I knew from Port Richmond, most were immigrants. I took a picture of two adjacent yards, split by a chain-link fence. There were two parallel clotheslines and one woman on either side, one black, one white, same hands, same clothespins, same clothes—their husband's respective uniforms—hanging there in the cold like ghosts.

That's a good shot, he said.

Some of the men were making their own wine, like they'd done in the old country. They grew their grapes on tiny plots of land. They would dance. They would stumble out of their chairs and clap. They would laugh, showing their crooked teeth. The women around the kitchen table, drinking this homemade wine, their cheeks flushed. They were so beautiful. And nothing mattered. Because they were here.

Yes, he said, and told her how many times he'd wanted to kiss the ground when he returned from some other country where he'd felt unsafe.

I photographed some of the young girls on our street, she said. Girls like me. First-generation Americans. From all over. Just kids. Bad skin. Bad teeth. Poor. But you could see the light in their eyes. The light of their dreams, you know? That hope?

He took her hand, then the other one. He kissed them both. You are kind, he said. You have kind eyes.

No, I am too frightened to be kind.

She told him about Theo. By nature he was impulsive, giving, noble, and terribly bright. He had heroic qualities. He'd grown taller than she'd expected, and had the face of a young prince in an old German fairy tale, the high forehead and cheekbones, the square chin, the light brown hair he'd taken to pulling back with an elastic. He was built like a medieval soldier, someone Michelangelo would have sculpted. And he was a good person. He never spoke ill of anyone, even the ones who hurt him. He seemed to understand from a very early age that the world was imperfect, and so were the people who inhabited it. He was open to people, he let them in.

Too much, she told him. He trusted too easily.

Rye took her into his arms. Then he will trust me, he said, and said it again, as if to reassure her. He will trust me.

The train pulls into Philipse Manor. For a moment she considers not getting off, riding north, leaving all this behind. Escaping for good. But then she's up, walking toward the door, buttoning her coat, wrapping the scarf around her neck, and stepping outside into the shattering cold. In the parking lot she finds her car and sits there awhile, letting it warm. She looks at herself in the sun-visor mirror, takes out her brush, her lipstick. There's something in her eyes—a wildness. She feels like she's capable of anything.

She opens the glove compartment, finds her cigarettes, lights one, cracks the window. She can hear the wind as it gusts against the glass and, somewhere in the sky, the cries of birds. The light is sharp, fragile, and, as the train pulls out, it breaks and breaks.

They lived near the river, on Farrington Avenue, in a white clapboard Colonial with glossy black shutters and a trellis that clamored with wild roses in summer. The house was a fortress built in the twenties. They'd been renovating since they moved in. High ceilings, elegant moldings, plaster walls, wood floors. Julian had cool, impersonal taste. The Italian-leather sofas, vintage rugs. She often thought it resembled the theater set of a Pinter play, down to the bar cart from his mother's house, stocked with expensive whiskey.

They were the Ladds. They lived a privileged life. Julian worked for it. From the very beginning, it was all about proving to her that he was better than Rye—smarter, more successful, a better husband, better at everything, better for her. She'd catch him looking at her across the table. He was possessive, devoted, demanding. He expected certain things from her: a clean house, dinner on the table when he came home, her tolerance in bed. When they made love, he was distant, impersonal, like he was paying for it. He rarely looked into her eyes. It troubled her, but it was a subject she could never bring up. Still, she tried to love him. She loved the sad, hidden boy inside of him. The boy his father had ignored. She saw who he was in his old photo album, the longing that bled through the snapshots like too much light. The one on the field after a track meet. Just him on the dark, late spring grass, tall and slender and elusive, the empty stands behind him, his hair sweaty over his brow, the lithe, deerlike stance.

Over the years, she'd stopped trusting him. He had a secretive manner that excluded her. She couldn't break through it. She sensed he was capable of unspeakable things. On some level, she didn't care. It was like an ailment, a compulsion. She didn't think it had anything to do with her. Maybe she'd convinced herself that it was part of the bargain. That she deserved to be betrayed. Once in a while, some man came on to her, one of the fathers at Theo's school, one of the men she knew from town. She'd flirt back, sometimes even exchange numbers, typing into her contacts digits she knew she'd never call. She was a mother first. Her own pleasure was secondary. At night she would cling to his back, waiting for him to open his eyes, to see her, but he never did. He was a sound sleeper. He told her he never dreamed.

Mornings, he'd leave the house before six to catch the express train. He was finicky about his clothes, the Tom Ford suits, crisp blue shirts, the sleek Ferragamo loafers. Even the sandalwood cologne, which he'd found in some boutique in the village, was part of his costume. He'd come a long way from the malcontent camera nerd in polyester shirts and Wallabees that she'd met in the Brodsky Workshop. He was moody, particular, intolerant. Women noticed him. His arrogance appealed to them. Once the money started flowing, there was little she could do to stop him. She'd concluded that a man's failure to communicate could be his best asset in the boardroom, so often mis-interpreted as a poker-face strategy. In Julian's business, being cagey and enigmatic was tolerated and even admired. It was a small price to pay for results.

Like the accidental genius of his old photographs, he left out the essential clues and counted on others to draw their own conclusions, which were almost always more complex and intriguing than any he'd intended.

She'd never told anyone about Brodsky. He'd let her into the workshop with next to no experience. It was her eye he accepted, he explained. There were only two other women; the men ignored them. They were polite during critiques, but Magda knew they didn't think much of her work. Even Rye rarely commented. Once, he went up to her in the hallway on a break and told her how much he'd liked one of her shots. She can still remember how she'd felt, the stupid grin on her face, the warm feeling rushing through her. It was a kind of sex, this sanctioning of her potential. She hated herself for letting them decide.

Over the years, she had learned not to care. She wasn't a typical American girl, begging for approval. She could be fierce. She knew how to fight.

Brodsky liked her; he encouraged her. Her pictures had a darkness that verged on noir, infusing an ordinary moment with a casual disturbance, intent on disrupting assumptions, like Winogrand's work in the sixties. A nun in a long habit on roller skates, a homeless man lounging on the sidewalk reading Chaucer. She constructed her photographs like small plays, using street people as her players. The juxtaposition of people and things impelled her to see beyond the curtain of routine and express an ironic, almost playful, irreverence.

She grew up fatherless; he'd died in an accident when she was six. After that, it was just her and her mother. They came from Lodz. Her mother's brother lived in Port Richmond. He was a Latin teacher in the high school, a surrogate father to her. They believed in only tangible things. Dreams, her mother said, were for fools, and rich people. They worked. They never complained. Her mother was ambitious. She did the books for a company that printed textbooks. And she owned the two-family house they lived in, the first floor rented to a butcher and his young wife. They'd bring them cuts of beef wrapped in brown paper.

Her mother could cook. She made her own yogurt, her own wine. Even on the tiny plot of land in their backyard she made a garden. You have never seen such a garden, vines with the fattest purple grapes, flowers as big as your fists. They came to the U.S. when Magda was a toddler. Her mother was aloof, a person of secrets. In one of Magda's earliest memories, she'd spied her parents alone in their room, her mother sitting on the edge of the bed, half clothed, dabbing her neck with cologne, her father buttoning his shirt. The casual separation that could happen after lovemaking, a kind of reckoning. It was her first photograph, she thought now. Taken inside her brain. Even as a child, Magda recognized it as intimacy. As soon as she could hold a pencil, she began to draw, but her mother refused to encourage her, claiming that artistic pursuits were impractical. When she started high school at St. Anthony's, her uncle, an amateur photographer, gave her an old

Pentax with a broken light meter. Figure out how to use it, he told her. You'll find in life that you can't rely on anything but your own instincts to tell you when there's enough light.

She started taking pictures at recess, of the sisters in their gray habits, smoking on the playground, and Father Mullahy combing his hair, the back of his sandy head, the tortoiseshell comb, his freckled hands. After school, she photographed the children on the street, the stray cats. The row houses of Port Richmond, with their solemn brown stoops puddled with sunlight. When she went to pick up her first roll of film at the photo store, the man behind the counter, who had developed and printed them, handed her the envelope and looked at her carefully, like a scholar or a judge, and said, These are good.

It was the first time anyone had ever told her she was good at something. But her mother insisted she get an accounting degree. She went to a community college and earned her associate degree, then started working for an accountant, helping out during tax season. Brodsky was a client. He came in one day around lunchtime with a folder of receipts and notes scribbled on mustard-stained napkins. Everyone knew Brodsky. He had a thick accent. He came from Prague. He found an envelope of some of her recent photos on her desk and sifted through them, shaking his head with amazement. You took these? She nodded. You must come to the workshop, he said. It is where you belong. Come, I will tell your mother.

Her mother made him tea with mint leaves and kiffles with apricot filling. He licked his fingertips and flattered her, and she waved him off like she did most men, staring bashfully at her hands, already resigned to giving him whatever he wanted. Brodsky explained that her daughter had a talent that could not be ignored. So her mother relented and agreed.

Brodsky would give her advice. You can't be sentimental in this life, Magdalena, he told her—he was the only one who called her that. Not if you want to get anywhere. If you want something, you have to take it. You have to feel it here, in your belly. Like fire.

They understood each other. He would invite her to his apartment. He lived in city housing. The elevators took forever. He said it was like Dante's Hell, all nine floors. He would give her vodka in a pickle jar with half a lemon floating in it, and they'd talk with the windows open, and she could hear the men playing chess in the courtyard and the wheels of strollers, and sometimes the babies cried or their mothers would argue or laugh. He was an old man with a bad leg by then. White hair curling out of his ears. He would lie on his dead wife's crocheted quilt and smoke and talk about the old days, when he was a student of Alexey Brodovitch. He told her he would come back in his next life and marry her.

Once, halfway through the year, he asked her to take off her shirt. He just wanted to look. She told him no. He said, Just this once.

It was early in the afternoon. She felt like she owed him. She unbuttoned her blouse, pulled up her bra. He held her breasts in his hands. So beautiful, he said. His fingertips were yellow. He brought his mouth to her nipples. He sucked on them noisily. When he looked at her, his face was flushed with shame. Go now, he said.

She never told anyone. It was something that happened. An accident. But she didn't regret it. She knew he meant no harm. She forgave him.

Brodsky taught them: if you want to be a true artist, you cannot be afraid. You have to push forward, without fear. You have to be open to failure. You should not fear it, he advised. Failure is your butter and your bread.

When she first saw Rye, something pitched in her heart. She couldn't move. She was afraid of him—because he looked right at her. He *saw* her.

He was different. He was himself. Some people accused him of being an elitist because he didn't always join the conversation, and often during a critique, he'd sit in the back and say nothing.

He had a kind of darkness about him. A darkness because he knew people.

He was very tall and slouched a little. His arms were long and sculpted and his hands had a particular grace, like the wings of a hawk or some such majestic bird, his fingers tapered and square at the tips. She'd hold his hand in both of her own, and it was big and warm and alive.

He shared an apartment with Julian, but they weren't actually friends. It was obvious to her that Julian despised Rye for reasons he'd never reveal, private reasons. Rye seemed almost cavalier in his indifference to others. He didn't run after people. People came to him.

He asked to photograph her. She told him yes, but in her mother's house. Just standing next to him made her nervous. He came when her mother was at work. They drank some beer and sat at the little kitchen table by the window. She met his serious blue eyes. He was a few years older. He said he had a girlfriend from college with a beautiful name, Simone. They were engaged. She was a poet at Columbia. She was very smart, he said, the smartest woman he'd ever met. It made her jealous, and she told him she had a boyfriend, but it was a lie. She'd never actually been with anyone. Then he asked if they could start.

He had a Leica M6, an expensive camera. She envied it. It made her hate him a little. She watched him load it with Tri-X, his fingers agile as a surgeon's. Could you maybe let your hair down?

She removed her barrette and let her hair fall down over her shoulders. And then she took off her shirt. Why did she do it? She wanted him to see how beautiful she was. More beautiful than his studious girlfriend! Maybe she thought he'd leave the girlfriend to be with her, something stupid like that. She could feel the light on her face. Her eyes were wet; she was already in love with him. It was a love that couldn't be. And she glanced out beyond the sheer curtain to the street, the dark line where the buildings met the sky, the faraway clouds, and heard the sound of the shutter as he took the shot, forever trapping her in his gaze.

And then they were kissing. It was like an opera in her head. She brought him to her room. He stood in the doorway. There was her narrow bed with the iron headboard. Her tall dresser, the music box with its turning ballerina. The quilt neatly folded at the foot of the bed. There were the familiar sounds of her neighborhood, voices on the street, cars.

Afterward, he said, I don't think I will ever forget you, Magda Pasternak.

They lay there, side-by-side, in her childhood bed, smoking like the couples do in movies. It was a little awkward.

One weekend in the spring, he took her to his summerhouse on the sea. He'd invited a small group of them. It was a musty old house, what they called a saltbox. They walked on the beach, picking up shells. He found one, pink and perfectly formed. Here, for you. She held it in her hand. It seemed to signify something. She carried that little shell around in her pocket for a long time for good luck, but after a while, after they'd gone their separate ways, she lost track of it.

His real name was Denis, but everybody called him Rye. He said it was a family name. For a few brief months they were good friends; they were lovers. It was a secret. It was like a hole she had dug in the ground, a grave for their love, full of whiskey and cigarettes and sex that she loved and made her sore and tears she cried alone later and his smell and his old, dirty clothes and his hands and how he looked at her, like she was beautiful, like she was everything, deeper and deeper and still deeper, knowing all along she should fill it in with dirt and walk away. But she didn't. Couldn't.

They'd go for drives together. He had his mother's old station wagon with the fake-wood siding that always had something wrong with it. He was working on this monograph called *Working Class,* and he liked the dirty old car because he said he could be anonymous. She suspected he felt guilty for having money. He didn't like people knowing it. She also knew money wasn't important to him. I'd rather be poor, he once told her.

He wanted a simple life. Just him and his camera.

He said he spoke in pictures, not words.

He could be gloomy, quiet.

He was interested in people. He liked that moment of connection, that tense interaction, when you looked at someone and they didn't look away. Two strangers setting eyes on each other for the first time. Magda's mother had taught her to look away. *It's not polite to stare.* But Rye looked right at you. Maybe because he'd grown up overseas, the son of eccentric socialites, he'd been encouraged to look, *to see.* To pull people in with his gaze. He didn't care what you had or what you did. You could be a bum or a junkie or some main-line aristocrat. He treated everybody the same.

Outside the city, you could find country, farms. They'd roll their windows down and blast the radio. There was this waitress he started photographing, Joyce. It was one of those places off the highway. You'd see the pickups in the parking lot at six in the morning. Farmers. The plaid-flannel shirts lined up at the counter. They'd go in. Everybody always looked at Rye. Maybe because he was tall, like Abraham Lincoln. Then they'd look at her. Now, Rye had never told Magda she was beautiful, or even pretty, for that matter—he wasn't generous like that, at least not back then, not with her. She didn't think of herself as particularly beautiful. She was sturdy as a peasant, breasts like her mother's, too big. She'd been born to figure numbers, to make her own bread and wine, to sew her own clothes. This waitress, Joyce, was older than them, her face already lined, a timidity in her eyes, like she knew fear. Her name stitched in frayed red thread on her breast pocket. You could see in her face her whole mixed-up history. The farmers liked her. They felt comfortable. She was their sister. Rye asked her this one time if he could photograph her. She asked him why. And he said: Because you're beautiful.

Toward the end of the year, Rye put up a photograph of Joyce in class. Everybody stared at it hungrily, instantly transported to a field somewhere in rural Pennsylvania. Joyce was sitting on one of those old metal lawn chairs, naked, her skin very pale against the green metal chair and her nipples very pink, her black hair cut short. Her pubic hair was very black, black as a skunk. She was smoking, and the sky was almost lavender, and in the very far distance you could see the late sun flashing off the cars on the interstate.

He never told her how he'd managed to get Joyce to take off her clothes, and she never asked.

That final month of the workshop, Magda started to believe in her own work. She loved the world inside her pictures. Her ambition roiled inside her like a ravenous appetite.

As a photographer, she never had a problem with being female, but other people did. Other people: the whole world. She was quieter, maybe, than the men. The fact that she was outnumbered only made her work harder, made her want it more. She admitted that some days she was intimidated. The men were standoffish, superior. Julian. He'd watch her from afar. She thought he was good-looking but strange, as if his tidy, immaculate appearance was a disguise and the real person underneath was entirely opposite, repressed, wildly discontent. They were all of them a little odd, in fact. Some didn't like her work. They'd say things. It was too female. You could practically smell the menstrual blood! She'd walk home alone on the dark streets, clutching her coat around her, tears running down her cheeks. But she never doubted her talent. She knew she was good; they knew it too.

They'd go to the VFW. You could drink cheap. They had these red-leather stools and a black-and-white-tiled floor. They'd sit at the bar next to men in wool coats with watery eyes and red faces. Hands that worked in the factories and mills. Sometimes she was the only girl in the place. They'd get drunk, and he'd walk her home, and they'd fool around in the backyard on the cold grass under her mother's laundry. She liked to pin him down and say things to him in Polish. You are the love of my life, she would say; he never knew. She'd be on top of him and he'd run his hands through her hair and clutch it in his fists like the strings of a dozen balloons.

There is nothing better than that, when someone is holding you, looking at you, seeing *you*.

Love comes to us. It arrives unannounced; it swarms you like a hundred bees. Then you fumble around like a stung person.

She was one of his subjects, nothing more. He saw her. Captured her. And then he left.

She wrote in her journal: *What makes the photograph work? Is it a technical accident? Yes, sometimes. Is it how you take the shot? The angle, the light, the frame—or what you take? The subject? Or is it what comes later, in the darkroom? How you manipulate the image. How you make it yours.*

The people give themselves to you. They are saying: This is me. Look. I dare you to see me.

They remind us who we are. Why we're here.

They remind us that we're human.

She was going to tell him. She'd gone to the drugstore, done the test. He wasn't the type to be a father, she convinced herself. And he'd warned her about Simone. They saw life the same way, he said. They wanted the same things.

He didn't love her enough.

He didn't love her at all.

That last day. He brought Simone to the show. Magda watched them across the room. Simone was smaller than her. Confident in her expensive clothes. Magda could feel her skin growing hot as they came toward her. This is my fiancée, he said to her, blameless, beyond reproach. This is Simone.

She left and walked through the streets, looking into people's windows, the yellow lights. She'd lost track of how she fit in. These other people had options. They weren't like her, stuck.

Later, there was a party at Rye and Julian's apartment. Everyone was going. Some people brought their spouses, partners. She was nervous, climbing the stairs. The small space was jammed, and there was a lot of smoke and loud music, and she wanted none of it. She only wanted him to hold her and tell her it would be all right. But she didn't see him anywhere. Julian was in the kitchen, pouring everybody drinks. He caught her eye as she started for Rye's room. The look said: don't. The door was ajar. They were in there, the two of them. Simone was taking something out of a paper bag. It was a white tulle veil. She held it up for him to see. It had been trimmed in lace, she told him, by a blind woman on Bainbridge Street. Here, she said, and took his hand. Close your eyes. And he did, running his fingertips along its fragile edge.

Magda retreated silently. She found something to drink. One and then another. Why not just take the whole bottle. She would drink herself sick, she decided. And maybe all her trouble would go away.

It was Julian who walked her home. She threw up in the grass. He helped her, clutched her. At her door, holding her arms, he made her face him. Stop being stupid, he said. You're wasting yourself on Adler. He's just using you. He doesn't care about anyone but himself. You're a beautiful girl. You deserve better. And then he kissed her. A hard, hateful kiss, and left her there.

She never saw Rye again. A few days later, when she went over to their apartment to give him the news, she found the place empty. They'd both moved out. She lingered a moment at the bay window, taking in the view as Rye might have done, understanding for the first time how alone she was. Nobody could protect her, nobody was going to take care of her, and everything that came next was up to her.

They'd left behind a big, leafy plant. She took it. It seemed like a metaphor. Well, she would bring it home and water it and put it in the sunshine. And it would grow. It would grow.

The next morning, she broke down and told her mother, who offered only shame. Who was this man? Where had he gone? If he loved her so much, why had he thrown her away like garbage? All the usual things a mother would say. You can forget that career you're in, she said. You'd better find yourself a real job. You're going to need every penny.

She took her mother's advice and started sending out her résumé. She went to the clinic and met with the doctor. They talked about terminating the pregnancy. The first appointment was in two weeks. She didn't know, she wasn't sure. There were a lot of reasons not to have it. It cost a lot; she'd have to borrow money from her mother. How stupid she was, how impulsive! Like some girl in a movie, rolling through the grass, never considering the consequences. And where was he? Off living his life!

She was beginning to feel desperate when she got a call from an editor at *Seventeen,* who'd received her résumé and wanted to interview her. Brodsky was her reference. Her mother tried to talk her out of it. Even if she got the job, she couldn't take it, not in her condition. But Magda wasn't going to pass up an interview like that. The morning of their meeting, she dressed carefully in a black skirt and silk blouse that she wore only on special occasions and borrowed her mother's church shoes, patent leather pumps. When she looked at her troubled face in the mirror, she could only think what a good shot it would make, how her reflection represented so many other women like herself, fearless, relentlessly capable.

The editor was an old friend of Brodsky's named Alice Fuller.

She was wearing a flower-patterned dress with a blazer, her bifocals hanging on a chain around her neck. She had a deep smoker's voice, and Magda could tell she'd been in the business a long time. In lieu of a husband and family, she'd given herself to her career. They talked for a few minutes about the workshop, how Magda, as a woman, had been outnumbered, and Alice admitted that in her own experience, she too had suffered for being female. Magda felt like they were fighting for the same cause, but when she handed Alice her portfolio, the older woman flipped through it quickly, like a perfunctory exercise, never once lifting her eyes.

These are good, she said at last. Very fresh. I like how you capture the lives of these women. The sort of routine repression.

Thank you.

Alice handed her back the portfolio. It's good work, and you should be proud of it, but unfortunately I can't hire you as a photographer.

Why not?

Well, for one thing, the models won't trust you. They're used to men. They won't believe you know how to use a camera. They won't believe you can make them look good.

That's outrageous. I'm well trained.

The girls are young. They're very insecure. They won't want to act sexy in front of a woman.

They'd rather have a man salivating over them!

I don't make the rules, Alice said. It's very unfair, I realize.

It's discrimination. Magda got up. She was ready to go.

We do have an opening for a secretary. Can you type?

In despair, she rode the elevator down. When the doors opened and she stepped into the lobby, she saw a familiar face. It was Julian Ladd, in a suit and tie. Julian!

Magda!

They hugged. What are you doing here?

I had an interview upstairs.

How'd it go?

Not very well. She asked me if I could type.

Can you? Julian cracked a smile.

No. But I take a hell of a picture. She held up her portfolio. What about you?

I'm with Hopkins and Donne. Advertising. Fourth floor.

Impressive. How is it? Do you like it?

More than I expected to.

You look rather dashing in that suit.

He smiled. It's good to see you, Magda.

You too.

You look—

She waited as his eyes roamed around her face.

Really beautiful.

Do I? No—

She was suddenly self-conscious.

Have dinner with me tonight?

My train. I should—

I know a good place right up the street.

It was a pretty little restaurant called Harry's, with white tablecloths and candles and a piano player. They ate steak and potatoes and shared a bottle of wine. She drank a little of it, even though she knew she shouldn't. She could tell he wanted to impress her. He had good table manners. He knew how to use his silverware. He had sharp features, dark perceptive eyes. He was patient, polite; he listened to her. She heard herself telling him exactly what he wanted to hear. It was a defense mechanism, she knew, generated by her suspicion that he was the kind of man who had little patience for small talk. A man who, under particular circumstances, could snap.

He asked to see her portfolio. Begrudgingly, she showed it to him. He turned the pages slowly, with care. These are beautiful, Magda.

Thank you, she said gratefully.

Good luck with them.

What about you? She asked if he was still taking pictures.

Not really, he said. I sort of gave it up. I knew I'd never make it.

Why do you say that?

I'm not good enough. Not like Adler, for example. He looked at her uncertainly. You heard about him? He's somewhere in Africa.

She nodded. I never thought much of his work. His pictures are shallow and totally superficial. No wonder he's making it so big!

Of course, none of this was true. But Julian's eyes brightened, and she could tell he was pleased.

But your work, Julian. You shouldn't give up. I always liked your pictures. They're provocative. It's much harder to take pictures of nothing. Open spaces. You never guided the viewer. You simply asked for their consideration. You posed a question; the answer didn't interest you.

She was a little drunk. Maybe she wasn't thinking clearly. They went back to his apartment. It was clean and organized. They drank some more, she wanted something strong. He gave her whiskey. He took off his jacket, his tie, his shirt. He was fit; assured. She stood there as he unbuttoned her blouse, unzipped her skirt, unhooked her bra. Her breasts felt heavy and sore. He watched as she removed her stockings and underpants. Naked, she stood before him. He looked her over from head to toe.

I've wanted this for a long time, he told her.

They held each other tentatively, like teenagers, fully understanding the promise of their future together now that Rye was gone.

When she finally told him she was pregnant, she neglected to mention that the baby wasn't his. It was something she let happen. It wasn't right, she knew, and yet she couldn't stop herself, the detour she took in that moment.

And Julian was elated.

You've made me very happy, he said, and kissed her. They were married a few days later in the city clerk's office and had a small party on the terrace with some of his friends from work. Her mother did all the cooking. At one point, she cornered Magda and squeezed her hand. He never has to know, she said. It is what mothers do for their children.

She never heard from Rye. Not that she expected to. She supposed he was too busy becoming famous. He wasn't shooting starving children anymore. He had swiftly moved on to more lucrative subjects, and his pictures seemed to be everywhere, in magazines, advertisements, on the sides of buses. He'd done the new This Is Me campaign for an organic clothing company, huge studio portraits of regular Americans standing against a gray backdrop, a spirited celebration of diversity and inclusion. She knew they were special and political and great, but she looked at them only with contempt. She had no business admiring his work. She had taught herself to hate it, to hate him, to trust her anger. Her anger was more reliable. It was like an animal tethered to her heart, ravenous, determined to survive.

They moved into a larger apartment in the same building, one that had a tiny second bedroom for the baby. The doormen called her Mrs. Ladd. While Julian was at work, she painted the nursery, the lightest blue of a summer sky. Sometimes she'd take pictures from her window. She was like Steichen, who'd glimpsed his neighbor reading the Sunday papers in a tenement window across from his. All of the greats had taken photographs from their windows and she would too. There was the dark crease of the curb, the black street. The people crossing from one side to the other in the sharp river light, their shadows stretched long and thin. Sometimes she'd take her camera and venture out. She'd walk into the park and sit on one of the benches, watching the people. She'd shoot a roll and print out a contact sheet, review it with disdain. The shots were just okay, she thought.

Once, Julian looked over her contact sheet. He took his time; he seemed to enjoy the minutes of suspense as she sat there waiting. Finally, he gravely set down the loupe and offered his opinion. They're good, honey. But don't give up your day job.

He wasn't home very much. He was building a life for her, he said, for all three of them. They'd already promoted him at the agency. There were dinners after work. Entertaining clients. If she felt up to it, she'd join him, but she got the distinct feeling that nobody wanted a pregnant woman around.

In those last days of her pregnancy, she felt more alone than ever, even a little terrified. She'd stand naked before the mirror, running her hands over her belly. How could she not be thinking of him now? One night when Julian was out at a party, she called information. She'd seen their wedding announcement in the *Times,* the two of them dressed in their ceremonial clothes, barefoot, on a farm somewhere upstate, a little town called Ghent. It all sounded nauseatingly storybook. The operator had the number. With shaking fingers, she dialed. It rang and rang. She was about to hang up when she heard his voice.

Hello?

She couldn't speak. Her heart was pounding.

Anyone there?

There were voices in the background. Laughter. Music.

Rye, she thought. Oh, Rye.

Last chance?

Mute, she hung up. It was like she'd ripped open the air into another dimension, hearing his life on the other side.

She gave birth that first snowfall. Julian was right by her side. They named him after her father—Theo—and he had rosy cheeks and broad little shoulders and the clearest blue eyes you've ever seen. Rye's eyes, she knew.

But she told Julian, He looks just like you.

If she'd learned anything from her mother, it was how to survive. A perfect life wasn't an option; it wasn't an expectation. You did the best you could. If you had to tell a lie once in a while, God would forgive you. You were grateful for what you had and didn't question it. Like her mother, she accepted her life as it was, unconditionally. In the quiet of her hospital bed she held her baby to her chest and gazed out at the snow-covered treetops, knowing that Theo was the only thing that mattered now, raising him right, giving him the best life that she could. Her work—the person who made her pictures, the person inside her who saw everything that was wrong and beautiful and true—would have to wait.

And it waited.

It waited while the snow fell and she nursed her baby and rocked him in the old rocking chair, and it waited while he cut his first teeth and had his first fever and cried all night, and it waited while she bundled him up in a snowsuit and walked him all around the city, saying *cat* and *dog* and *cookie* and *taxi,* and it waited while she read to him, or sang to him, or sat on the floor and built towers with him, while she cleaned the kitchen or wiped up another mess or gave him a bath. It waited while she started him on cereal and boiled carrots or peas or squash and pureed them in batches to pour into glass jars, while she collected toys or did the laundry or took him to nursery school or Suzuki, where they'd made pretend violins, or exercised at the gym with all the other mothers or had lunch, standing over the kitchen counter, or picked him up and took him to the playground or to someone's house for a playdate, where she sat politely in another mother's kitchen, someone with an MBA or a doctorate and countless other achievements who was now, by choice, in this wind tunnel of pause, raising her child, and they'd drink tea or lemonade or sometimes, though rarely, white wine. It waited while she figured out what to make for dinner and took him to the market and set him in the cart and rolled the cart all through the store, buying ingredients for a recipe she'd been wanting to try, and it waited while she cooked the meal and served it to Julian, drinking a little wine together just to feel like adults, and it waited while she lay in bed beside him, too exhausted for sex, just listening to him breathe. Always her work was right there, the countless shots she took inside her head. There was so much beauty. She saw beauty wherever she looked. Even in the ugliness she saw beauty. She'd hold her camera in her hands and feel the rush of happiness come back to her. It was her phantom limb.

When Theo entered first grade, she started doing weddings.

What for? Julian asked.

I want to work.

You don't need money.

It's not about the money.

Like all the other Brodsky snobs, he thought she was wasting her time. She didn't care what he thought, or anybody else, for that matter. It was work, and she was damned good at it.

Before long, she had a fully booked schedule: weddings, bar and bat mitzvahs, Communions, baptisms, baby namings, graduations, and once she photographed a woman who was turning one hundred. There were anniversary parties, couples who'd been together for sixty years or more, and it was on these occasions, focusing on these older faces, that she witnessed a kind of love she did not have with her own husband, a love she feared she'd never have, deep and rare and true. *All true things are equal,* she'd tell herself, repeating Stieglitz's famous words like a prayer.

How to show devotion in two sets of entwined hands, or the sacred connection to something greater than one's self in the face of a boy reading from the Torah? She thought of Salgado's famous photograph of Brazilian children on the day of their first Communion, dressed like angels.

After all those years of Catholic school, she'd become numb to God. However, she was not altogether agnostic. She wanted to believe. But something kept her from it. Maybe her own guilt. Maybe she felt she didn't deserve God.

Still, sometimes in bed at night, she'd pray.

And now all this time in churches, temples, commemorating the occasions that supposedly gave life meaning. The landmarks of existence! During a service, she would watch the people, how they gazed so thoughtfully, and when it was finally over, when the couples were united in marriage, or when the boys and girls had completed the requirements to become a bat or bar mitzvah, or when a baby had been consecrated unto God, everyone stood and meandered out, their faces soft with joy, as if their faith in humanity, in life itself, had been restored.

Her pictures served as proof that people had a great capacity for goodness, that they could be kind, and reverent, and generous even when the rest of the world seemed full of darkness and tragedy. With pride, her clients displayed their photo albums on coffee tables in their living rooms. They'd flip through them from time to time, trying to remember the taste of the cake, the happy rush of conversation circulating the tables, the bride's spectacular gown, the flowers, the marvelous food, the love that shone in people's eyes, the hours of suspended joy.

She was a time thief. She captured it. Time was a butterfly pinned to a board.

It was time people wanted to save. Before it all ran out.

Her work was her dignity. It defined her. She took her own photographs whenever she could. She was inspired by other women photographers: Cindy Sherman, Lorna Simpson, Nan Goldin, Corrine Day—and so many others. Their photographs whispered to her during her darkest moments, when she felt like there was no point, when she wanted to give up. They said: Keep going. Don't stop. *Raise your voice!*

She'd go out into the streets and find her subjects. Women doing what women do on an ordinary day. The woman at the Fairway, molesting the cantaloupes to find the ripest one, the look of ambivalence on her face, or the young lawyer on the playground after work in her rumpled suit, standing in the grass in her stockings, handing her fussy toddler a juice box, or the new mother, dozing in the shade of a park bench, with her baby sleeping on her chest. Or the woman just like her, sitting at a window in a café, drinking a glass of wine, content to be alone, a dreamy expression on her face, the rain streaming down the pane of glass.

Dorothea Lange once said, *I am trying to get lost again.*

When Magda first heard those words, she cried. Because she understood that feeling, that insistent need, very deeply, and she knew it in her own work.

You have to disappear in order to make good work.

You have to leave your life, to let go of it completely.

You have to travel far into the woods, alone, and be willing to lose your way.

You have to be willing to be forgotten.

Magda understood what it meant to be caught in between the life you always wanted and the life you had. It was, she knew, a common predicament for a young mother, finding herself doing what everyone said was more important, and while she was not ungrateful—she had all the requirements of a comfortable existence—she could feel the darkness unfurling its black flag.

Part Three

Act Natural

The most beautiful and simplest reflex of all is the spontaneous desire to preserve a moment of joy destined to disappear.

—Robert Doisneau, *Master Photographers*

Theo

Like that time she took him to the Met, his very first visit, he was maybe five, to see the photograph. He remembered all the steps, how she'd held his hand as they climbed, counting, counting, following the backs of people's legs, the stockings and trousers, the hems of coats, until they reached the top and shuffled through the narrow door into the balmy hush of the lobby with its towering ceilings and archways. They rode up in the elevator, her hand sweaty. She looked down at him and smiled, her earrings dangling, and he could tell it was an important day, that she was going to show him something that mattered to her. He remembers the long hallway, like the kind in dreams, where you can't get to the end, and she was hurrying, her shoes clickety-clacking, her hand a little slippery as she pulled him along. They came to a big room with pictures of people in frames on the walls, and the first one you saw was of his mother with her big dark eyes. She wasn't wearing any clothes.

Mommy, you're naked!

It was just for the photograph, she told him, and picked him up so he could see. She held him and kissed his cheek and her eyes were glittery. A very important man took that picture, she said.

After the museum, she took him out for ice cream. He got a chocolate sundae. He could still almost remember the taste of it, how sweet it was, and how, even though he didn't really want it, he ate the whole thing.

Maybe that was the day he'd become an addict, he thought. Long before he'd started shooting heroin. Or maybe it was back in middle school, when he was still kind of chunky and the kids sometimes made fun of him. They'd moved out of the city that year into this big house in the suburbs so he could go to the public school and have more space to quote, unquote run around. Sixth grade was pretty rough, and he felt bad about himself because he was bigger than the other kids and always really sweaty and he didn't think the teachers liked him and his grades were just okay, but then in seventh his voice changed and he started smoking a little pot with some of the older kids and people respected him because he knew things and was an only child and basically his parents treated him like an adult, plus they had money and his father was in advertising and his mother was pretty hot for a mom and they drove nice cars. So nobody cared that he was kind of overweight and no good at sports, and the coach usually let him sit on the bench instead of going onto the field and messing up. Theo wondered if the coach was trying to save him the embarrassment or just wanted their team to win. He didn't mind it so much, but it pissed off his dad, and this one time when the coach didn't put him in, he went up to him after the game, fuming, and threatened to call the principal or even the superintendent. In the car on the way home, his dad reasoned, ever so gently, that Theo lacked the appropriate coordination (since he was a little overweight), and that's why the coach didn't let him play, which of course Theo already knew, but somehow hearing him say it out loud made everything a lot worse, and then he offered to get him a coach, like somebody to work with him in private to improve his skills, and Theo thought that just sounded weird and told him so. To be honest, Theo found soccer incredibly stupid. The whole enterprise was stupid, the kids trying to be so great, and the parents in the bleachers who were all pretty creepy, the bossy mothers sucking up to the coach, and the dads shouting Let's go! or Bring it home! or some other crap. Beyond the bleachers you could see the edge of the field and the little white houses lined up on School Street with their chain-link fences and Virgin Mary statues and the German shepherd who never stopped barking and the guy who had a mental disorder who sat out on a lawn chair counting cars, and then you looked back at the kids in their soccer uniforms and it all just seemed to say something about the world and how uneven things were between the people who had money, like the spoiled brats in his school, and the ones who didn't.

Around that time, his mother took him to see someone because she thought he was depressed. People called her Dr. M, and she was supposedly good with teenagers. She had a nose ring and looked pretty dykey, and he had zero interest in talking to her about anything remotely related to his life, but when he looked at his mother's worried face, her eyes flitting around the room like flies, landing for a second on his face, then flying off again, he went along with it. They all sat down on worn, dirty couches, and his mother sort of crumpled into her chair like a horse in a chair, if you can picture that, her legs kind of jagged and crossed, and her eyes already teary, and this so-called doctor asked Theo what was wrong, and he shrugged and said nothing, but tears were streaming down his face, and his nose was running, and he kept saying, Nothing, nothing's wrong, but the tears kept coming, and it occurred to him that maybe he really *was* depressed. Dr. M kept her cool, watching him like he was a lab monkey and jotting down notes, and Theo looked right back at her, conducting an evaluation of his own, noting the barbed-wire tattoo around her wrist, the multiple piercings, her putty-colored pallor, and wondered how happy *she* was. It seemed to him that people were way too preoccupied with being happy all the time, and obviously no one liked seeing somebody cry, especially a boy. They sat there, staring, waiting for him to divulge some grotesque horror, when a little buzzer sounded, indicating that her next patient was there. On the way home, they filled the prescription; it felt like the goody bag after the birthday party of a kid you hate.

As it turned out, taking meds made him more popular with his friends because they were taking them too. Prozac, Lexapro, Wellbutrin. Everybody was on something to make them less depressed, and why shouldn't they be depressed, his mother liked to announce, pacing around the kitchen with all the cabinets open and the TV blaring, with the world full of gunslinging freaks and a melting planet. He'd take his pill at dinnertime, pushing the tablet far back on his tongue and drinking a lot of water, and his mother would smile at him like it was some kind of panacea (one of his SAT words), and now she didn't have to worry so much because the pill was working to fix the problem, when in fact there really wasn't any problem except that Theo was his own person and not really interested in doing the things everybody else was doing but wasn't smart enough or articulate enough to put that into words. Once he swallowed the pill, he thought about it breaking down and pictured these little white angels floating through his bloodstream, and he tried to believe it was making him feel better, but it really didn't, when he was totally honest with himself, change anything, and it actually made him more anxious because he'd heard that one of the side effects was weight gain, and that was about the last thing he needed. He would look in the mirror and compare himself to some of the other boys in his class who already had six-packs and hard shoulders, when he was soft and still had his baby fat and a sort of round chin and was really hungry all the time and wanted Doritos with melted Velveeta all over them. His mother wasn't the most ambitious cook and mostly fed him pasta, and he'd shake out half the container of Parmesan cheese on top and drink a huge glass of milk, then go down to the basement to play Call of Duty until it was time to do his homework, which was generally some form of moronic busywork, and go to bed.

After a while, it started becoming clear to him that everybody was super-medicated and in any house on any street, there was somebody taking some kind of antidepressant, and that became normal, and being somebody who didn't take drugs was actually kind of strange, and when he looks back at his life and tries to analyze how he got here to this awful fucked-up place, he doesn't really think it's his fault. And maybe he refuses to take responsibility for it because he is a product of his upbringing and maybe even of the times. Because everybody enabled his addiction. His parents and their fucked-up marriage enabled him. The blank, sort of dazed expression on his mother's face as she'd remove his father's place setting from the table after he'd text to tell her something had come up at work and he wasn't coming home. The stupid politicians on TV enabled him, with their blue and red ties like athletic pinnies, arguing endlessly about the misdeeds of others while systematically indulging their own interests, and all these people in other countries roaming around in black and white robes with explosives strapped to their bodies, and the assault weapons and the bombs and the fucking wackos killing people or hacking into the Internet—all that enabled him. And the movies he'd see with his friends on the weekends at the cineplex, where he always went to Five Guys beforehand and ate two mega-burgers with fries, then during the movie these strange sugary pecans that came in a paper cone, not because they tasted good but because his parents would never allow him to consume so many calories in such a short period of time, like, probably enough to feed a small village in Africa somewhere, and in the movie on the screen everything was at total fucking stake, and the world was going to end, and only one guy could fix it. Those, too, enabled him. And his father driving off every morning at, like, six a.m.

in his Beemer to the train station so he could spend the day coming up with new ways to screw over the American consumer, and the first call he made was to his assistant, who was also his girlfriend, and his mother standing at the counter, waiting for the coffee in her silk bathrobe with her skinny shoulders, looking like at any minute she might start crying. How the first thing he'd do when he got to his homeroom was look at the black, twitching hands on the clock, and it was the last thing he did at the end of the day when the bell started ringing. Time passed ever so slowly, and none of it mattered; the whole day was, like, pretty pointless. There was no escape from the tedium of life; that was the first lesson he'd understood as an adult. Time fucking had you. It fucking had you. It was your master, and you were its ignorant slave.

His mother tried. She wanted to be a good mom. She had a hot temper, and when she was angry or disappointed, she'd start speaking in Polish, and nobody knew what she was saying. She was demanding and impatient and expected a lot. Not just of him, of Julian too. Like all the times she made Julian pick him up from practice, and he'd come straight from the train, and you could smell the beer he'd drunk on his breath. They'd drive home through the village when all the stores were closed and all you saw were the big dark windows and the blotches of the streetlamps on the lonely sidewalks, and Julian would be talking to someone on the phone, someone who was obviously more interesting to him, more necessary, than Theo. Then they'd all have dinner together, and Julian would try to ask him about his day, but it was so obvious to Theo that he wasn't the slightest bit interested and was doing it only to avoid talking to his mother or breaking into another argument about how fucked-up a husband he was and what a lousy father he'd turned out to be.

In high school he hung out with the music and theater people, and he took up the saxophone and he was pretty good at it, and the girls liked him because they said he had good lips and he was a good kisser. He was pretty happy about that. He started running and lifting and had a growth spurt, and suddenly he wasn't fat anymore, but he still felt fat and worried about the fat coming back, even though his mother was continually telling him he wasn't fat, and he looked great and he knew some of the girls liked him and thought he was good-looking, and yet every time he looked in the mirror, he saw his old chubby self, who he kind of hated but felt sorry for, which was almost worse, and that's when he started writing on a stack of yellow pads he found in a closet, and he liked the feeling he got when he wrote, because he was in his own little world where he felt safe and nobody could bother him. Meanwhile, his English teacher, Mr. Rosendale, made them write poems, and Theo's were pretty intense, and he knew there was, like, this pit of bones deep inside him, and he couldn't get to the bottom of it no matter how hard he tried. Mostly he wrote about what it felt like to be fatter than other people and not great at sports and have bad skin and have to go on Accutane and the problem of being hungry all the time and there never being enough good food in the house because his mother had started drinking a lot and was forgetting to shop and he usually ended up eating a peanut-butter sandwich or something bad for him instead of having a regular meal like most of his friends, where they sat around the table with their parents and talked about their day and stuff, and it made him feel really lonely and abnormal. His mother would sit at the table, drinking her wine and reading the newspaper or watching Chris Matthews, and his father would call at some point and say he was staying in the city because he had too much work, when they both knew he was seeing his girlfriend instead of coming home to them.

And then, in his senior year, he met this girl India. And, like, bells went off in his head. It was classic; she was the new girl at school, like in those Disney movies. And she had long blond hair and kind of a soft, tubular shape, and she looked like somebody's cool favorite sister, only she didn't have any siblings, it was something they had in common, being Only Children. And how fucked-up was that expression, *only child*? Like, how sad for him, you know? Like, it was just a really sad situation for everyone involved, his parents, who didn't want to have more kids, and him, being the only one they got. India's family had moved out of the city, and her mother was in a hair commercial, and her stepfather was some kind of banker and had a fund that literally festered with money, and she was always rolling her eyes behind her stepfather's back because she thought he was an idiot, and she said her life was incredibly boring, when in fact they had an exotic sort of lifestyle, like the people in magazines. They lived in a ten-thousand-square-foot house that had been built by the architect Frank Lloyd Wright, and it jutted out over a creek like a fist punching the air, and he always imagined when he stood at the floor-to-ceiling windows in the living room that he was inside a terrarium. She called it the terminal, as in airport, and said her life was terminally boring and she hated everybody in the school except for him. At the end of the day, they'd go into town and get a slice and sit on the bridge in the park, eating it and talking, or they'd walk down to the library and hang out in one of the tutoring rooms and eventually get around to doing their homework. They were in the same AP classes, but India was noncommittal about academics and said she didn't really care how she did. I deliberately don't apply myself, she told him once, taking off her shirt, letting him touch her breasts, which were fairly nonexistent. It's not like I'm stupid or anything.

She did ballet. One time, when he was walking through the village, he saw her through the storefront of the ballet studio in her pink tights and black leotard and ballet slippers, and this guy who was apparently pretty famous and danced in the city with some offbeat company had come to teach there, and she was all excited about it and said she thought her teacher was sexy, this tall black dude in gray tights and a white T-shirt, and at one point, this so-called famous dancer was holding her from behind, his two hands around her waist, and it was hard to discount the sort of obvious triangular proximity of his dick, and then he lifted her in the air and carried her around in a circle. Anyway, that was her. India. Tough. Spoiled. She had ADD. She loved to curse. In India's world, everything fucking sucked. She'd get depressed and they'd up her meds.

She let him try her Adderall. It made him feel driven and crazy, and he liked the feeling, and they kissed so hard for so long, his jaws ached. He still thinks about the first time he put his tongue inside her. She was so soft and sweet and smelled a little sweaty, like when he used to go camping and he'd wake up at dawn all sweaty in his sleeping bag and it was really cold out and the air sort of stung your nose and the whole sky stretched out and he felt really alive.

It was around this time they started looking at colleges, trying to narrow things down. On the weekends, his parents would drive him here and there, all throughout New England. It aggravated him that they assumed he was smarter than he was. Like they had all these handy excuses for why he wasn't getting better grades or why he'd gone down on a test: he was tired, he had bad sleep habits, he didn't study enough, and if only he had, he would have aced it, which wasn't necessarily true. Plus, his parents were always covering for him, always stepping in to pick up the mess, to take a crisis and turn it into something potentially workable, like he was better, smarter, like basically a genius, when in truth he had no clue and couldn't really talk about anything of real importance, and thank God he had his phone, it was especially convenient when the chime interrupted the awkward bloom of nothingness at the dinner table and he could get up and leave the room for a minute.

But he couldn't really fault his mother, because all the mothers were like this. It was like some kind of contagious disease they all picked up when their kids were juniors. Like this savage competitiveness. And the bottom line was, you had to be really fucking spectacular to get ahead in life or forget about it. It was ALL OR NOTHING, because nobody wanted a mediocre kid. No one wanted a kid who took their time, trying to figure out his options. Not really, they didn't. Because that was boring. You had to know, like, right the fuck now what you were doing with your life. You had to, like, excel at calculus or speak Mandarin or fucking Aramaic, and you needed some offbeat hobby, like stamp collecting or sorcery. Your essay had to be fucking eloquent, and what did that really mean, anyway? They wanted to hear you were a good fucking soul. That you were willing to go to fucking Honduras or Vietnam or pick up trash along the highway or hand out plates of turkey dinner at a soup kitchen, because that meant you were a good fucking person, even if it was all just a lie and you weren't in fact so good and you did things you didn't tell anyone about, the fucking real things that defined you. The *real* things. Like how he preferred being alone to being with people, but if he admitted to this, they'd call him anti-social and put him on more drugs, or how parties actually annoyed him, the games the girls played, and how they'd fuck you over if you neglected them, or how friendship with guys was based on a couple unspoken parameters, like how much you could bench or what sports you played or how far you got with somebody when you did Ecstasy. It was all just trickery, and you were doomed from the start because everybody knew you just didn't have the goods. You were nothing special.

In his own defense, he believed he was smart, but not the kind of smart you saw in movies, like the Matt Damon character in *Good Will Hunting,* who was so fucking smart and sat around in his shitty apartment reading all these esoteric books but chose to reject his brilliance because most of the kids with real brains were assholes like the ones Theo had grown up with.

Truthfully, by the time he'd sent in his college applications, he didn't even want to go anymore, and when he got rejected from his first choice, Julian nodded diplomatically like he'd expected it. Rejection is a fact of life, he told Theo. Get used to it.

That summer he worked at J. Crew, which was a slow form of torture mostly because they played this pounding shitty music at an incredibly deafening volume, like, *all day long.* There was no escape from it. Kids would come in with their mothers and try stuff on and leave everything heaped on the floor, and he'd have to fold it all up and put it back on the shelves. There were these gigantic pictures on the walls of really good-looking people, and the customers would want to look just like them, but obviously nobody did, so, like, at the end of the day, it kind of reinforced how inferior people felt, how imperfect. Other than that, he didn't mind getting a paycheck, driving home in his mother's old Passat through rush-hour traffic with all the other working people. He liked having a purpose, making his own money instead of grubbing off his parents.

His father was apparently extremely busy doing this commercial for some miracle constipation drug that was all of a sudden big news, and the company had gone public and the stock had split or something, and it was like this big deal. He would call and leave messages in a weary, pedantic tone, explaining why he wasn't coming home. Theo thought it was seriously anticlimactic, selling a product whose claim to fame was that it made people shit. The whole situation basically embarrassed him, and he didn't tell any of his friends what his father was doing.

They didn't see much of Julian that summer. On the rare occasion that they were together, his father never looked him in the eye. Never. He found it confusing, as if Julian didn't trust him, or assumed he was doing bad things, which he wasn't, like he had some exclusive inside knowledge about Theo. It was sort of like being accused of a crime you didn't commit. That same frustration, and Theo found it unsettling. Like this *shame* he felt. Deep inside. For what exactly, he didn't know. That was the only word he could think of that seemed to fit. And he knew he didn't deserve it. It made him sort of hate his father. And that made him feel really bad.

All that August, his mother seemed really distracted. Like if he asked her a question, he could see her deliberating all the possible answers for the one that would worry him the least. They did a lot of school shopping. She took him to Target, where they roamed the aisles, pushing the big red cart. They bought extra-long sheets and a new comforter and a wastebasket and a little gray bathmat and a toilet brush and an alarm clock just in case his phone died and a light for his desk. He'd gotten into the honors college at the state university, and even though his father could easily afford the tuition, they were giving him a scholarship, and he could tell how relieved his parents were that he'd actually gotten in because even if you were, like, Einstein, there were no guarantees.

Then, like a week before school started, India came home from Florence, where she'd spent the summer studying art, and told him it was basically over between them. They were standing in her kitchen, and he felt something lurch in his stomach, and it was almost like being punched, and he stood there a minute, getting his bearings, hearing the annoying sound of her mother's high heels clacking back and forth, back and forth, from the hall to the mudroom to the living room, clacking, clacking, in her little blue suit.

India had changed those few months in Italy. Her hair had gotten longer, and it was really blond, and her chin wasn't puffy and babyish anymore, it was square and important and sexy, and her pimples had pretty much gone away. She said she'd met somebody over there, and he was older and, like, studying economics, and they'd *been together,* a phrase he found annoyingly shallow, and, well, she'd gotten HPV and vaginal warts, and it was very upsetting, and anyway, it was over with him, *over,* the word like a bad taste, like she wanted to spit it out, and now she sort of hated men and was, like, really confused, maybe even queer or pansexual, she didn't know, she was still trying to figure it out, and she was really sorry, like, really, *really* sorry to be breaking up with him.

They stood there, looking at each other, and she lit a joint and sucked on it and smoke came out through her nostrils. She said her pediatrician had given her the shot when she was, like, thirteen, and it wasn't fair because she still got it and apparently everybody had it, and she was really pissed because she'd made every guy she'd ever been with wear a condom. And to be brutally honest, she didn't even like sex, and as much as she tried to come, she never did except when she was alone, having these weird and scary fantasies, and there was obviously something wrong with her, and every time she watched a couple having sex on film with all the noise and theatrics, it annoyed her because it didn't happen like that in real life, at least not for her.

Life is a big fat betrayal, she said.

I don't think that's true, he lied; of course it was true.

You don't know anything, she said in a gently patronizing tone, and her solemn, beautiful face turned ugly, like melting wax. You can go now.

But—

I have nothing more to say to you.

It was like a line from a movie, he thought.

He left her house and walked home, and there was the cat-piss smell of the rain and the sky was almost yellow, and then it started, first a pitter-patter on the leaves, and then this amazing deluge, and steam hovered over the pavement like smoke. He started running with this pressure in his chest, like he couldn't breathe, and tears streaming down his face, and he was alone in his misery and he hated India and he never wanted to see her again. He kept running, and when he finally made it home, his mother was on the phone, and there was some big-deal terrorist event playing out on TV, and they ate dinner together, watching all these dead bodies getting lifted into an army plane, and she asked him about India, and he said she was fine, she wanted to be a curator, and they'd had a really good time.

Julian

Brodsky was particular; he favored Magda. When her pictures were up for critique, he'd stroke his beard, thoughtfully, parsing the various comments, the shards of passive aggression, and proceed to defend her, emphasizing the brilliance of a photograph that the others had failed to see. As a result, they were all a little afraid of her. Because she was good, and she was beautiful, and she had a power he envied and wanted to crush. You couldn't describe exactly what it was that made someone's work better than another's, except to say that, like the weather, the consequence of viewing it shifted your sense of well-being.

It was around this time he started seeing a therapist and admitted to her that he was obsessed with Magda and sometimes thought about hurting Adler, or at least doing something to screw him. Sometimes he'd lie in bed at night, dreaming up eloquent scenes of sabotage. When Julian saw them together, he explained, it was a physical response. The only word for it was *animal*. Like he could kill for her.

This last thing, he kept to himself.

Sometimes he followed her. After class, when she was going home. She would walk for a while and then catch the bus. She never saw him. He was good at it. The buses were crowded, people standing in the aisle. He'd lurk in the rear and watch her. He was content to just gaze at her, swaying a little with the movement of the bus. She'd grip the strap, staring out the window. Always so curious. Drinking in the streets. Scavenging for images. Her stop was Allegheny Avenue. From there it was a few blocks to Salmon Street. He'd watch her hips, the little gully where her back got small. The sway of her long brown hair. The wooden shoes she wore, clomping along. She would vanish through a rusty metal gate with a NO TRESPASSING sign.

He would linger a moment on the sidewalk, waiting for her to turn on the light in the second-floor apartment.

It wasn't love that drove him. It was something far baser, something he couldn't control. It occurred to him that she was his connection to Rye, for whom he'd developed disturbing feelings, a compulsive envy that wouldn't go away.

About a month after the workshop ended, he ran into her in the city. She was stepping out of the elevator of the building where he worked. He'd been so dazzled by the surprise that he hadn't noticed the few pounds she'd put on, or the radiant flush in her cheeks. He took her to Harry's, his go-to place with women. Unlike most of the girls he dated, who were neurotic about food and perennially dieting, Magda ordered a steak dinner and cleaned her plate, using her bread as a sponge to sop everything up. When she finished, she looked across the table at him, glassy-eyed, and grinned. I guess I was hungry, she said.

How about some dessert?

Should we look at the menu?

He convinced her to come home with him, and they walked uptown arm in arm. He casually asked if she'd seen Adler, and she said no, they'd lost touch. In fact, she never wanted to see him again. That's when he kissed her. They had a few drinks in his apartment, and though he'd anticipated a certain degree of hesitation from her in the bedroom, she was in fact more than willing to oblige. A month or so later, when she told him she was pregnant, the thought occurred to him, vaguely, quietly, that maybe it wasn't his. He never said as much; he never asked. But he couldn't help thinking: if it's not mine, whose is it?

There was only one answer to that.

Julian wasn't, as the saying goes, the marrying kind. It was his mother who had told him that. He would never forget the look on her face when he and Magda told her they were getting married. They sat there in her living room on the fancy, uncomfortable couch, drinking a toast out of crystal glasses that hadn't been used in years and tasted like the inside of the china cabinet where she stored them. She'd put out a dish of herring with sour cream and some Ritz crackers with toothpicks that looked like swords. It was the sort of thing his father used to eat. Magda was out on the front walk when his mother grabbed his arm and pulled him aside. Are you sure about this?

Of course.

She's a very nice girl, Julian, but is this what you want?

He had only nodded. The question seemed impossible to answer.

He tried to be a good husband—even the word *tried* felt worn, like the heaviest of suitcases. But his wife sometimes made him feel bad. Like he was just another task she had to deal with, like clearing the table or washing the dishes.

The thing with Vera just kind of started. She was young and wanted to move up at work. That's what he liked about her. She understood the principle of a means to an end. She was calm. Easy. They'd spend an afternoon in bed. Sometimes they'd just lie there, talking. He didn't think there was anything wrong with it. And for a couple of hours, he'd feel almost free.

Once, his therapist asked if he felt responsible for Theo's addiction. He said no, no, he didn't. But now, in retrospect, maybe he did.

What was the word she'd used? *Present.* Was he present in his son's life?

I tried to be, he said weakly. I did what I could.

Did you?

His therapist didn't believe him. She cocked her head to one side, gazing at him like he was some sort of sociopath, waiting for him to admit to something.

In truth, he didn't know why Theo went off course. So many kids had—it was a national crisis. He resented his therapist's insinuation that it was his fault. Maybe he hadn't been the best father in the world, but he'd been there as much as he could. Julian didn't know where to assign the blame, but he'd get this feeling in his chest when he thought about it, like a burning there, like a fire you couldn't put out.

They had their outings. She wanted him to attend Theo's soccer games whenever he could. It's a dad thing, she'd say. But it wasn't easy with his schedule. It meant catching an early train. He was out there busting his butt for her, entertaining multimillion-dollar clients, and she'd complain if he couldn't get home for a stupid soccer game. Like she was setting him up, you know? Already assigning the blame for all the ways that Theo might fail.

So, he'd get the early train—for her—and drive to the school and jog from the parking lot to the farthest field, where the seventh graders played, and he usually found Theo sitting on the bench. Basically, the coach was an asshole. It was no secret that Theo wasn't the most athletic kid, but how was he supposed to get any better if he never got to play? Obviously, the score of the game was more important to the coach than the experience the kids were having. In Theo's case, he was learning more about what he lacked, how he had failed at being a normal boy—whatever the hell that was—and it pissed Julian off because there wasn't a thing he could do about it.

He'd sit there in the bleachers with the other parents. Not his favorite people. In an effort to be inclusive, one of the mothers told him she'd hired a fitness tutor for her son, suggesting that Theo might also benefit. It was totally worth the two hundred dollars an hour, she told Julian. Another woman had the gall to suggest taking Theo to a nutritionist. They were seeing great results in their overweight daughter by giving her these special milkshakes so she could skip meals.

He found it all very sad. In Theo's defense, he told the same woman he was taking Theo out for burgers and fries after the game.

He doesn't even like sports, Julian said. Why are we making him play?

It's a school requirement, Magda told him. And he's burning calories. We both know he needs that.

It was a Greek diner in town, but they served everything, and the food was good. Julian let him order whatever he wanted, usually a burger and onion rings and a shake. Let him enjoy himself, he thought.

Afterward they'd drive home, not talking very much. He felt like it was okay with Theo, like they didn't need to talk. Instead, Theo would sit back and look out the window, and when they pulled into the driveway, he always said, Thanks, Dad, before getting out of the car and going inside to find his mother.

First question out of her mouth when they were alone: What did you two talk about? And he'd feel the heat rising up his neck. Women don't seem to understand that men don't require conversation like they do. It's just not important. He and Theo had had a perfectly good time without uttering a single goddamn word.

He couldn't really blame the university. But maybe a smaller campus, in a more rural area, would have been better for Theo. Still, it was hard to know, because he was kind of a quiet kid. In truth, they knew him only peripherally. Theo was a thinker, an observer—he didn't necessarily jump into things. He'd stand back and watch for a while before he decided to take part. So this heroin thing had really thrown them.

It occurred to Julian that in other areas of his life Theo was still sitting on that bench. It wasn't his grades that were the problem— he was a good student, especially in math. But ask him how to think, how he felt about all the bad things going on in the world, and he'd just shrug and stare into the stupid game on his iPhone, frantically exercising his thumbs. Julian had hoped college would change that. In all those classes they made them take, you'd think he would wake up and figure things out. But Julian hadn't seen much evidence of that. He was still kind of a big, clumsy kid, kind of a dreamer. Julian had to wonder who he took after. Someone on her side, he decided. Some aberrant limb on the family tree.

Theo

Two parallel lines that never meet. It was sort of an elegant proposition. This was his freshman math tutorial, eight a.m. Monday morning, sixteen of them around a table and the old geezer who looked like an ostrich with a name Theo couldn't pronounce. He actually liked the class, and he was a little obsessed with Euclid and his parallel postulate. It was like this girl he always saw on the path, walking in the same direction at the same speed, both of them with their hands in their pockets and their heads down, looking at the pavement and the grass and the wet leaves instead of at each other. But he could feel something between them. He could feel how very alike they were. Her name, he had learned, was Lucia, *Loo-chia*.

He would daydream about her in class and end up missing large chunks of important information. You could see the treetops through the window and the gray clouds. He admired his professor's dedication, and he could picture old Euclid in his toga and sandals, writing down his postulates by candlelight, and it occurred to him that people didn't actually sit around thinking or postulating anymore and maybe that was the problem, because now you had Google, which was super-convenient, but trying to think on your own, say, as a social imperative, as part of some essential discourse, was a lost fucking art.

Freshman year was all about getting his bearings. His roommate was from Lebanon, and they got along all right, except Pierre was tidier than Theo and it sometimes caused problems. On Pierre's side, you could see the floor, and his desk was strategically organized, but on Theo's side, the floor was like a sea of dirty clothes, and his desk was covered with papers he was currently or had at some point been working on and empty bottles of Lifewtr and Gatorade and crumpled-up bags of chips and books he was supposed to be reading for class.

He felt kind of down.

There were a lot of people at the school, and basically, outside of his classes, which were tepidly interesting, it was like being back in high school, only nobody was telling you what to do, plus the campus was kind of strange, and he walked around sometimes feeling like he was in a science-fiction movie or a bad film based on a Kafka novel, where things were recognizable but not actually real. The sky was usually gray or maybe white and often it rained, and all that September it was muggy and annoying.

He worried about his mother. He knew how alone she was. Not really because of Julian and all his bullshit. It was something else. Like a howl trapped inside her. She wouldn't let it out. They never talked about it. But you could see her loneliness. He tried to call her every day, and she always put on her happy voice for him, which he definitely appreciated, but nothing really seemed the same anymore.

He had a few friends, nobody special. He preferred to be alone. He spent most of his time in the library. It was nice, because you saw people but you didn't have to talk to them. He would simply nod and settle into his favorite carrel near the art books, and once in a while, when he was too bored to study, he'd pull one out and flip through it.

Meanwhile. The world was ending.

It was all anybody talked about. The melting planet, the dying polar bears, the rising oceans. There was scientific evidence! There were pictures! There was proof! And yet people still didn't get it. They couldn't seem to process it. Like you still saw all the wrong stuff in the trash, and you heard stories about the plastic bags on the bottom of the ocean, and that was just really depressing. Because at some point you come to the conclusion that nobody really cares. They're still going to use plastic bags and dump their trash wherever it's convenient, and he read somewhere that the recycling plants were just a big scam and threw everything out anyway, so why even bother?

He worried about these things.

He worried about the corruption in Washington, the so-called civic leaders championing the tenets of democracy! Marching down the slippery marble hallways, making deals. Your elected representatives at work! Theo understood his ambivalence toward others as a result of the pervasive deception of the times. He was unable to trust that they or anybody else, for that matter, really gave a shit, and therefore he trusted nobody. And everything was just kind of dead to him, kind of pointless, but when people asked him how he was, he automatically replied, It's all good. Even though it wasn't all good, not at all, and he doubted anyone else thought so either. Life was like this big covert operation, and nobody could say the truth, because if you did, like if you admitted to how fucked-up everything was, you'd have to fucking deal with it.

And then one day, by pure chance, he intersected with Lucia on the path outside the campus center. They started walking together, their shoulders almost touching.

She was an English major from the city, a dark-haired girl who didn't shave her pits and her hair was very thick under there, thicker even than his, and her pubes were really thick, too, like the back of a small furry animal, and honestly at first he was a little afraid of it. It doesn't bite, she said. But I can wax it off if you want.

They would lie next to each other on her bed, reading this book

Nausea out loud because she was a little dyslexic and it helped her understand it better, and she thought its author, Sartre, was a genius. From what he gathered, it was about a guy whose life made him feel really sick, and the idea of existence and whatever the hell it meant. Her room was next to the lounge, where some of the gamers played from dawn to dusk, and you could hear the sound of the world destructing, the explosions, the gunshots, the menace and wrath of aliens, and the sound thundered right through the wall and made the bed vibrate. They had a lot of sex. They had sex to the screams of people running from burning buildings. They had sex to the sounds of submachine guns and the cries of people getting shot. Sex had become his version of an antidote for all the fucked-up things going on, and for a few nearly perfect seconds he could totally disappear. Her smell drove him crazy, the hairy underarms, the oils she dabbed behind her ears, always with this thoughtful expression on her face, a drop of some exotic potion on her fingertip like something out of Shakespeare, and he'd marvel at her routine of beautification as she stood before the mirror, gazing at herself or posing for a selfie to post on Instagram.

Lucia, he would say. *Loo-chia.*

She had a casual beauty, like a hostess at a restaurant, a girl who shrugged her shoulders, noncommittal, as if you didn't actually matter to her. Like if she never saw you again, it wouldn't faze her. A lot of the girls were like this. He figured it was because they didn't want to get dumped or screwed over. He liked to watch her read in the library, when they'd sit across from each other at one of the tables, and her lips were moving ever so slightly, like someone praying.

Around that time, he started hanging out with Carmine, from his creative-writing class. Carmine was an Albany boy, with dark hair and bright black eyes that knew you, and he wore this St. Christopher medal that he'd tug on and slide back and forth on its chain when he made comments in class about somebody's poem or story. For some reason Theo trusted him. One night, Carmine brought him home to the house where he'd grown up. This was downtown somewhere, a row house in a long line of them, each painted a different flavor, lemon-yellow, mint-green, pumpkin-orange. Theirs was chocolate, with heavy drapes covering the windows. But inside was all this fancy furniture, like crazy ornate chairs and a marble coffee table with gold curlicue legs. The house smelled of whatever his mother was cooking, eggplant parmesan and spaghetti carbonara, and she served everything on these thick white plates, and everyone had a napkin made of cloth. She lit candles, too, like they were celebrating something, only it was just an ordinary day. His mother spoke mostly Italian. She was a seamstress and had this sewing machine set up in her basement, and people from all over brought her their clothes. Carmine's father was a mechanic. In his spare time, he was fixing up this old Jaguar in his garage. That's all he wanted to do. Practically every time Theo saw this guy, he was on his back on one of those little carts that slide under your car.

Carmine had a kind of bounce to his step and walked around in a long black coat he'd picked up somewhere, and he had a Keats fixation. Out of nowhere, he'd start reciting some random poem he'd memorized, some ode to this or that, his voice booming. They'd smoke a little weed and get lost in this used bookstore downtown that had these narrow passageways that wound around like a maze through towering stacks. He always felt like he'd entered the Matrix, like you were leaving the real world behind for this other one, and all you had to do was read to understand your purpose in life, to know whatever the hell it all meant. Somewhere in those cryptic lines you found the answer. It was just sitting there, waiting for you to wake the fuck up.

He went home for Columbus Day weekend. Within seconds of his stepping into the kitchen from the garage and setting down his bag, it was pretty obvious that his parents were having difficulties. They were basically ignoring each other and fixating on Theo, firing all these questions at him, like how was he sleeping at night and did his roommate snore or how was the food and what exactly did they serve and were there a lot of drugs in the dorms and how were the kids and were any of them nice and did people clean up after themselves and had he made any friends. With all this attention, he found himself sitting a little taller and trying to sound articulate about his quote, unquote college experience and how enthralling it was, which was basically total crap, and in reality he was pretty uncertain how he felt about it all and wasn't actually making real and true friends that, like, you wanted to keep for the rest of your life, and he had absolutely no idea where he stood gradewise. Coming home was really stressful, he decided, and probably not worth the effort for any of them. For his mom, who had troubled to make a nice dinner—chicken and rice and roasted vegetables, and they all drank some pretty decent wine—and his father, who had to sit there listening and looking interested when in fact his mind was obviously elsewhere. Later that night, he smoked a joint out his window, remembering all the times his mother drove him to school and played her Cat Stevens or Don McLean or Neil Young CDs, all the same songs she'd listened to growing up, and they'd end up singing together the whole time.

Funny, the things you remember.

The next morning, his father woke him early to help clean out the gutters. They hauled out the ladder from the garage and brought it around to the back of the house, and Julian told him to climb up to the top while he stood at the bottom with his hands on the sides, securing it. Theo liked doing things for Julian because afterward Julian was always a little nicer to him and almost seemed proud of him.

From the top of the ladder you could see the Hudson. A long, brown barge, slow as a caterpillar, was making its way upriver. Once he'd cleared out all the leaves, he climbed back down, and they moved the ladder to the other side, and he climbed up again and did the same thing. At his parents' window, he could see his mother lying on the bed on her side with her hands pressed under her cheek. She was just lying there, staring across the room. *Despair* was the word that came to mind. He knocked on the window, and she looked caught. She rose and came toward him, making an effort to smile, and put her hand on the glass like in those prison movies, and he put his up to meet hers, and they stayed like that for a couple seconds with their hands on the glass, almost touching.

Later that afternoon he went for a run. The streets were empty. He felt like the last man on earth after the Apocalypse, when everybody else was dead. Sometimes he'd feel like crying and have to tell himself to man up and not be such a loser.

It occurred to him that there were things about his parents he didn't know and would never know. He supposed they were private. He didn't like to think about it.

Ever since he was little, he could sense when something bad was about to happen. It was like he could hear on a whole different frequency. Like in the movie version of his life, he'd be the guy with super hearing who knows danger is closer than anyone else realizes. When he was little, he'd be up all night, worrying about the sounds he heard, like a car slowly passing the house, its radio thumping, or the creepy swaying of his window shade, or the breathing sound coming from his closet. He'd hear his mother walking around, doing mother things, watching TV, talking on the phone, and he'd finally fall asleep, and in the morning, there'd be the sunshine and breakfast and his mother's smile, and everything seemed all right again. But when night fell, it started all over, this routine terror, the thing out there that wanted him.

Sunday morning their fighting woke him. They were shouting at each other in the kitchen. He got up and washed and pulled on his jeans, hearing them going back and forth, with her saying he was a selfish person, thinking only about himself, and him saying she was a cold, spoiled bitch, and if it weren't for him, she'd be back in that shitty row house of her mother's, not here in this fucking mansion, and at least Theo had benefited, and how dare she open her mouth to complain to him, she had no right, and who did she think she was? And then she was crying and in the voice of a tolerant fourth-grade teacher reminded him that she'd been a very good wife, and what had he given her in return, lies and deception. She said she was totally humiliated. She said she had too much self-respect to keep going. I can't do this anymore, she said decisively, as if, unlike all the other times, there'd be no talking her out of it. She was done, she said. Just done.

Theo descended the stairs. He took his time. He could see them in the kitchen. He could see Julian's guilty red face. I don't have time for this bullshit, he said, and grabbed his keys and walked out.

That's when she saw Theo standing there. She crumpled into the chair and put her head in her hands. Sorry, Theo.

All good.

He poured himself some coffee and a cup for her and set it on the table in front of her. You okay?

She nodded. Thank you. We're just—

Theo held up his hand. You don't have to—

Having some issues, she said. She looked at him. I'm sorry we woke you.

I was up.

He sat there, drinking his coffee. There was a lot he wanted to say to her. He wanted to comfort her somehow. But all he could muster was I need to go soon.

She nodded. I'll get dressed.

In the car, driving up to Albany, she confirmed that it was over with Julian.

He's cheating on me with a girl from his office.

That's so fucked-up, he said.

How can you trust anything in this life, she said, if you can't even trust the person you live with, like, on a very basic level?

It felt like a rhetorical question. He couldn't find a suitable answer. He didn't really want to think about it. It was one of those things in life that made no sense but kept happening.

Halfway there, she pulled off at a rest stop. They both used the bathroom, and she said she wanted another cup of coffee and did he want anything, and he said he'd have an iced tea.

They found a small table near the window, and she looked at him carefully and said, Look, I need to tell you something.

He waited.

I wasn't going to. I didn't think it was important. But now I know it is. Do you know why I wanted to become a photographer?

He shook his head.

Because I believed in the truth. As a concept, you know. As a political right. The truth is our freedom. Do you understand?

Sure, he said, but he didn't think he did. Not like she wanted him to.

But people lie all the time. Everybody does. And it finally dawned on me that it's why we're all trapped. All of us are.

He watched her, her dark eyes, the face he knew best, even better than his own.

Freedom. It's not something you can buy. I don't care how much money you have. You can be living in this supposed democracy with laws that protect you, and maybe you're safe and have a good life, but that doesn't mean you're free.

She sighed and wiped her tears. Now listen. I should have told you this a long time ago, but I didn't, and I'm sorry.

Told me what?

I guess I was afraid. I guess because I was trying to give you the best life I could. A happy childhood and all that—

You did, Ma, he insisted unhappily.

I didn't think I could do it on my own.

Do what?

Be a single mother. She reached out and took his hand. Julian—he's not your father. I mean he's not your biological—

What? What are you saying?

Your father is somebody else.

Somebody else?

Theo couldn't say why, but he took this information personally, like a deep insult. He tried not to show it. He tried to control his face. Does Julian know? That I'm not—

She shook her head. I wanted to tell you first.

He sat there, sort of amazed. You lied?

She nodded. I know. It's unforgivable.

She cried and said that at the time when she was carrying him, she was very young and very alone. I tried to find him, your dad, but he'd left the country. He was a photographer, she explained, and (by the way) already married to someone else.

She put her head in her hands. I'm so sorry, Theo.

Ma, he said.

He wanted to say that he was the one who was sorry, but he couldn't bring himself to speak, so he reached out and took her hand and she smiled a little. They were sitting in this vast cafeteria with tables that resembled spaceships or some ride at Disney World, white metal, round, and screwed into the floor so you couldn't steal them, and the light coming in through the windows was dull and white.

Please don't hate me, she said. I did it for you.

He went into the bathroom to look at himself in the mirror. He felt like he needed a moment to collect himself. He studied his face. There were guys stepping up to the urinals, the sinks, the sound of the hand dryers, but he was someplace else. He suddenly realized that his whole life was sort of based on a lie. And he recounted all the pain and agony of putting up with Julian's shit, always trying to please him or make him proud, wondering how it was even possible to be related to a guy who was such a supreme asshole.

When he came out, she was standing outside, smoking a cigarette, with her hair blowing all over the place, and it was suddenly distinctly and emphatically clear to him that he needed to start his own life apart from her, and that he never wanted to see Julian again.

Back in the car, he stared out the window at the nothingness on Interstate 87 and tucked his head into his hoodie and tried to sleep. His mother kept glancing over at him like she wanted to make sure he was still breathing, then stared back out the windshield with glazed eyes, her jaw set, some sort of master plan grinding through her head.

When he got back to his room, he swallowed a couple of Carmine's Oxys because he was suddenly feeling very anxious and the pills made him a little calmer and sort of distracted him, but not really. When you were doing Oxy, you were giving yourself an excuse to do nothing, stepping outside yourself for a couple hours, like you're buying time. The whole thing about drugs was connected, he thought, to being sick when you were little, when you needed extra time to figure something out, when you needed to step out of your life for a few days so things could calm down. Back in middle school and even in high school, he would lie sometimes about being sick just to buy a little time. His mother was always extra nice to him and let him watch TV and spend the day in his pajamas, doing pretty much nothing. It was on one of those days that he noticed the bird's nest in the pine tree outside his window. He saw the mama bird with her babies. Every day after that when he came home from school, he'd run upstairs to look out his window, and they'd still be there. But then, finally, one day, it was empty, abandoned. He still kept checking, but it seemed they were really gone, and it made him a little sad, and a few days later, the wind blew the nest down and it fell apart.

Pierre showed up and said he needed to study, so Theo left. He went outside and walked across the parking lot to the outskirts of campus to a package store that didn't card him, and he bought a can of Foster's and opened it and drank half of it, and it was cold and tasted good. He was starting to feel a lot better. He took the long way back to campus, through this neighborhood of narrow streets lined with tiny houses. You could see into people's windows, into everybody's little life with all their stuff, their tables and chairs and couches and plates and lamps. All the trash cans were out on the curb, and he saw this one dude taking bottles out of the recycling bins and putting them into a shopping cart. It was dark and cold, and he shuddered a little, but he was all right, he wasn't scared, and he was almost back to the dorm. His phone rang, his mother.

Hey, he said.

Hey, Theo. You okay?

Really busy. I have a lot of work. This, he realized, was true. Not that he planned on doing it, at least not tonight. How about you? You okay?

Don't worry about me, she said.

He tried to picture her in the kitchen, with everything out on the countertops, whatever she'd found to eat for dinner, maybe some crackers and cheese, olives, and the bottle of wine already half empty.

Theo?

He waited.

Are you worrying?

No.

We're going to be fine.

Uh-huh.

I'm sort of regretting that I told you.

Don't. Like you said, the truth is always best.

She didn't say anything for a minute, and it occurred to him that the truth as a concept, as something to live by, wasn't even a remote possibility for either one of them.

Do your work, she said. That's why you're there.

I know. I will.

He wanted to tell her he knew he'd been a burden to her. He knew she'd married Julian for all the wrong reasons. And he was sorry about it. He was really fucking sorry. But the words wouldn't come.

Instead, he listened to the noisy quiet of his mother's kitchen, the faucet that was always dripping, the willows scratching against the windows every time the wind blew. And the drone of the TV, reminding everyone how fucked-up the world was.

Theo? You there?

Yeah, Ma, I'm right here. I'm not going anywhere.

Magda

The girl was a friend from school, Theo told her. She was just stopping by; she was in the area over the break. They were going to the movies.

It was Thanksgiving Day, already cold, the lawn covered with brown leaves. They ate their meal in the early afternoon. She'd made all her usual dishes and even baked an apple pie. She'd bought the turkey from a local farm. And it was nice, just the two of them sitting at the dining room table with her mother's special china, one of the few possessions she'd brought over when they'd immigrated. They talked a little about Julian, and she told him how, under the circumstances, he'd elected not to come, and how she'd filed for the divorce and how Theo didn't have to worry, they had plenty of resources, meaning money, and basically things would go on like they always had. Your father will be staying in the apartment, she said.

He's not my father.

Well, Theo. As angry as I am with him, he's still your dad. He's still the man who raised you.

I don't want to talk about it.

Everything's going to be okay, I promise. Your life will not change.

But sitting there, looking at her son's troubled face, it occurred to her that it already had.

Everything she'd done up till now—her photography, her ambiguous professional status, the outrageous lie of her marriage, and now her impending divorce—had cast a gaudy spell on his destiny.

Roger that, Theo said.

In the few months he'd been away at school, he'd changed. He seemed distant, indifferent. She found she couldn't look at him. Somewhere inside his eyes was the truth she wasn't ready to face.

He seemed fidgety, restless, like someone about to be stung by a bee. He got up and crossed the room and sat down and got up and stood at the window and sat down and got up and opened the refrigerator and poured some milk and put it back and drank the glass and set it down and took out the ice cream and ate some out of the carton, then put it back, then walked to the table and sat a minute looking out at the birds, then got up again.

What's wrong with you?

Nothing.

You seem kind of nervous.

I'm not. I'm just waiting for her to get here.

What's her name?

True.

That's an unusual name.

Well, she's an unusual girl.

It occurred to her that he'd broken off from the mother ship. They were no longer on the same course. He'd chosen his own direction, navigating some obscure region of independence. She didn't want to be one of those helicopter parents. It was appropriate for him to be his own person, making his own choices and decisions. But her motherly intuition told her something wasn't right, and she suspected the girl, whoever she was, had something to do with it.

Is she a student?

What? No. She was going to be a nurse.

What happened?

He shrugged. Something. I don't know.

How'd you meet her?

We met at a party.

By then the car was pulling into the driveway.

We'll be back in a couple hours. It's not her car, so—

Don't you want to—

But he was out the door. She watched from the window as the girl got out of a dented blue Honda and gave him a hug. It was a hug of understanding, a hug that said, I'm here now. She was as tall as Theo and very thin, and her long black hair whipped across her face. They seemed in a hurry as they scrambled into the car and pulled out.

It would have been nice of him to introduce her, she thought, trying not to feel insulted. She stood there at the window, half thinking of jotting down her license plate number—just in case. In case of what? she wondered.

They were gone a few hours. It was almost dark when the car pulled up. Magda had heated up all the leftovers in case they wanted something to eat. She went to the door and opened it and stood there behind the screen, waiting for them. The girl got out first. Even from far away Magda could see her beauty. She waited for Theo to get out. Slowly, he stood and stretched to his full height, holding on to the car as if for balance. Immediately Magda could tell something wasn't right. Like his attendant, the girl held his arm as they started up the walk. He was taking slow, cautious steps, like someone with an infirmity, his posture slightly hunched, his face peaked. Then he staggered onto the lawn and threw up in the grass. The girl just stood there, watching impassively, her hands on her hips.

Magda hurried out the door. Theo, honey, what's wrong?

I'm a little sick, he muttered.

What is it?

A bug, I guess.

He stepped inside and ducked into the powder room to throw up again.

The girl followed Magda into the foyer, and they stood there together, listening to the awful sound of Theo getting sick. The girl crossed her arms over her chest and stared at the ground, avoiding Magda's fury, complicit, Magda decided, in whatever it was that had made him ill.

Oh, you poor thing, Magda said when he came out. Let's get you into bed.

She helped him upstairs to his room and into bed and pulled up the covers, aware of the girl's presence downstairs in the foyer.

Look at me, she said. And when he did, she knew.

His eyes were strangely translucent, as if they were made of glass. His pupils constricted. What have you been doing, Theo? What's going on?

Nothing.

You don't look right.

I'm just a little sick, he said. Calm down.

You're on something. I can tell.

He closed his eyes and turned away.

Try to rest, she said, and shut the door behind him.

The girl was waiting downstairs.

He's sick, Magda told her.

Yeah. She kind of shrugged. She was around Theo's age but looked older, sunken cheeks, dark, bitter eyes thickly outlined in pencil. She smelled like dead flowers. I'll go.

Listen, Magda said quietly. Is he doing drugs?

The girl looked her in the eye, with practiced intention. Not that I know of.

But Magda wasn't satisfied. Are you?

She jerked her head back, indignant. I don't do drugs.

Magda withdrew. She felt bad, like maybe she'd insulted her. Would you like something to eat?

That's all right. Her phone chimed. I should go.

Where do you—

But she had already stepped outside and was talking to whoever was on her cell phone. She walked unhurriedly to her car and got behind the wheel and sat there for at least five minutes before starting the engine.

Magda stood at the window, watching, infuriated. She wanted to run out there and tell her to leave and leave now. The girl's passivity seemed deliberate, like she wanted to let Magda know she'd go whenever she damn well felt like it.

Later, when she went to check on Theo, he was lying there in the dark with his eyes open, staring at the ceiling. He seemed possessed, altered. The thought occurred to her that he was gone forever, that she'd never get him back.

You need to drink some water, she told him.

He picked up the glass and took a sip, then set it down again. He wouldn't look at her. He settled back on the pillow, and she saw in his face the boy that he was. I'll be all right, he said.

He slept through the night, and in the morning he was up, walking around a little restlessly, like nothing had happened. Now his pupils were the size of peas.

Something's not right here, she said.

What are you talking about?

What have you been doing, Theo?

Nothing.

You don't seem like yourself.

Mom, you're so paranoid. I'm not doing drugs.

In the car, driving him back to school, she said, Tell me about this girl.

She's just someone I met.

Where?

She came to the Halloween party.

She's not your usual type.

What do you mean?

I'm your mother, I can tell.

That's what I like about her. She's a good person, Ma.

Is she?

To this, Theo said nothing. He pulled up his hoodie and closed his eyes, and they didn't speak for the rest of the drive.

She took the Fuller Road exit and pulled onto campus. He'd gotten into other schools with nicer campuses far from home, but SUNY had given him the most money. Theo was good at math, it's why they'd taken him into the honors college, but she knew he secretly wanted to be a writer. In high school, he'd had an English teacher who'd encouraged him and made him believe he had talent. A voice, Theo explained. I'm trying to find mine.

He had a stack of yellow pads somewhere, clamoring with sentences.

She pulled into the circle that led to his dorm. You okay?

Yeah. I'm fine.

Get back to work. That's why you're here.

I know, Ma.

Listen to me, Theo. Whatever you're doing, it's got to stop. Do you understand?

No, he said. I don't know what you're talking about.

Was it a lie? She wasn't sure. He opened the door and looked at her, waiting to be released.

Try to be careful, she said, resigned to some abstract negotiation. That's all I'm saying. I'm always here for you, you know that.

I know, Mother, he said with a hint of sarcasm. It's a big ugly world out there.

She watched him head down the path to his dorm, his shoulders slightly hunched, the easy swing of his arms and legs projecting a kind of cavalier indifference that was, she knew, pure bravado—there was nothing cavalier about Theo. He was a worrier, and ultrasensitive. But maybe this was *her* perception of him, and maybe that was the trouble. Maybe he'd shed that image long ago and she was the one clinging to it for some reason, out of fear, perhaps. Maybe it made her feel more in control in a world that was entirely out of control. And maybe she was hanging on to it because it was a handy explanation for his behavior, the lurking malaise that had seemingly taken possession of him.

But then, maybe she was exaggerating. Magda tended to do that, she knew. It was hard not to think of the worst with so many reminders, an overabundance of bad news in the papers and on TV. And how could it be possible that those awful things hadn't had an influence on her son? Not to mention what was going on in their lives right now— Julian, the divorce, what she'd told him about Rye. Of course he was off! What was she thinking? What did she expect? Theo needed her support, not her judgment. She felt bad about everything now. Guilty. Like whatever was going on with him was her fault. It had to be.

He started up the steps of the dormitory. He was wearing his fuzzy old Patagonia jacket, the sleeves too short, and his jeans were so baggy they'd drifted down below his hips, revealing the thick waistband of his boxers. It was only now that she noticed how thin he'd gotten. He turned suddenly, as if reading her thoughts, either annoyed or amused that she was still there, and waved to her with a goofy smile on his face. She waved back, like she had done so many times before throughout his life, and he stood there a moment longer, just looking at her, then pushed open the door and went inside.

Julian

He was in the lunchroom with Vera when one of the secretaries came and got him. There's some guy here to see you.

He was a beefy man in a cheap suit. He handed Julian an official-looking envelope. You've been served, he said.

In truth, he never thought she'd go through with it.

I'm tired of living this lie, she'd told him when he'd gotten to the house. I can't stand to be in the same room with you.

She was in her bathrobe with her hair a mess, and he could smell the wine on her breath. Her face looked a little greasy, and there were circles under her eyes, like inky thumbprints. Why aren't you dressed? he asked.

I'm taking a sick day.

There were dishes in the sink, crumbs on the counter. The garbage stank.

If he didn't take his shit, she'd throw it out, she told him.

Cunt, he thought.

So here he was, packing. It occurred to him that he was at odds with the world—an expression that had never quite made sense until now.

When he'd called his mother from the car to tell her they were getting divorced, she came to his defense. I never liked that girl, she admitted to him. Let her go back to where she came from. You gave her too much. You spoiled her.

The phone started ringing, and Magda wasn't getting it. He could smell her cigarette—an increasingly annoying habit—and knew she was out on the back steps.

He picked up the phone. Hello?

It was a girl named Lucia, who said she was Theo's sometime girlfriend. He's using, she said.

Excuse me?

Heroin? I thought you should know.

I'm sorry, who is this?

Look, you don't have to believe me. I'm just doing you a favor.

The girl waited for him to say something, then grew impatient. I have to go now.

Wait—what should we do?

Make him stop, she said. Before he can't.

He hung up. He went downstairs and opened the door. Magda put out her cigarette like a teenager who'd been caught. There was a call, he said.

Who was it?

A friend of Theo's.

He told her what the girl said. She made him repeat it several times.

I knew he was doing something, she said, shaking. I mean, I suspected something. At Thanksgiving. I figured he was maybe smoking a lot of pot. I mean, who isn't smoking pot these days? I figured maybe he was stressed because of all the work he had. Or maybe because of us.

Us?

Yeah, she said with annoyance. Us. As in you and Vera. She looked at him openly with hate. Because we're splitting up. Because it was the first time—

Yeah, I get it. This is all my fault. Because I wasn't home for Thanksgiving.

I didn't say that.

Right. Okay. Of course, you didn't.

Look, Julian. We have to deal with this.

I know.

I never figured on heroin. Anything but that. I never even imagined—

I know. It's terrifying.

We have to go up there.

He nodded.

We have to, Julian. Like right now.

I thought you couldn't stand to be in the same room with me. How are you going to survive being in the same car?

I'm sorry I said that. I didn't mean it.

Oh, yes, you did.

We're still friends, Julian. We have a child together. He needs us. That's more important right now.

All right, he said. I know. But we're not friends.

She looked at him, her face pale. Yes, we are, she said, and reached for his hand. I'm afraid.

He nodded.

Should I call him?

No. Let's just go.

They took his car. All the trees were suddenly bare.

I'm in complete shock, she said, her voice trembling, her teeth chattering, as if her spirit had risen out of her body and were floating around in the deep cold of her despair, unable to return.

In all their years together, there'd only been a few things that had caused his wife to tremble like that. The time Theo had gotten hurt at the playground and they'd rushed him to the emergency room. While they sewed him up, she'd sat on the plastic chair, trembling, unable to speak. And there were the rare instances in bed when he did things she liked, and she'd let herself go, and she'd lie on the bed afterward, drenched in sweat, trembling, or the night she'd seen Vera's texts, and he'd broken down and admitted to it, and she'd sat there on the bed, not looking at him, her face stricken and wet, and had thrown his phone across the room so hard it cracked the screen.

We must be terrible parents.

To this he said nothing.

We must've missed something. Some deep unhappiness. Why else would he resort to this?

I don't know, he said. Maybe there's no reason.

It's my fault, she whispered.

Stop, Magda. It has nothing to do with you.

Then, what? What caused it?

He made a bad decision. It's a mistake. People make them all the time, he said pointedly. Not that he'd ever considered his infidelity a mistake; he'd needed something she wasn't giving him. That's how he rationalized it. Now that it was ending, he was glad he'd had the other women. Even with a stranger, he'd sometimes felt more appreciated.

Two hours later they were pulling onto campus. His head was starting to ache and he felt a little nauseated as they drove around, looking for a parking space in one of the vast visitor lots.

I'm sort of regretting sending him here, Magda said. We thought it would be good for him, being closer to home, remember? But look at this place.

It's not the place, Magda. Nobody is forcing him to do drugs.

They got out and started walking toward his dorm in the Colonial quad. The campus was devoid of personality, a concrete wasteland. It was the magic hour, the golden sunlight slanting down, turning the people in the distance into shadows. They crossed huge blocks of cement in the wind, their jackets blowing open like wings.

You couldn't get into the dorm without a swipe card, so they waited for someone to come out, and caught the door before it closed.

He's on the second floor, Magda said. We can walk up.

Due to complications at work, he hadn't been able to be there on moving day, and although Magda had assured him they would be fine on their own, Julian knew he'd forfeited one of those parenting milestones.

It was a perfectly adequate building, if somewhat sterile. They climbed the stairs and turned into a long corridor. They were obvious interlopers, as if the word *parent* were imprinted on their foreheads. It was surprisingly quiet. Unlike his own college days at Rutgers, there was no music spilling out of the windows. He supposed these students were all hooked into headphones, a kind of modified version of life support, he thought.

They came to Theo's suite and hesitated. Should they knock? But Magda bustled ahead of him and pushed open the door. They stepped into a tiny rectangle that represented the common room, with a stained couch and an old bean-bag chair with its stuffing spilling out. There was trash scattered across the floor, fast-food containers, napkins smeared with ketchup like the bloodied bandages after a fistfight. In the corner a metal trash can overflowed with empty beer bottles. A dubious puddle that might have been Mountain Dew or urine glinted on the linoleum in the late-afternoon sunlight. The air was overheated, circulating a faintly unpleasant odor of aftershave, Doritos, and vomit.

In there, she said, pointing to the room next door. Julian knocked, no answer. Then one of the suitemates sauntered out of the other bedroom in workout clothes. He reacted when he saw them, standing taller and remembering how to behave, reaching out to shake Julian's hand. Sorry it's kind of a mess, he said. I'm Todd.

We're here to see Theo, Julian said.

Go on in, it's not locked. Catch you guys later. Eager to escape, he grabbed his coat and walked out.

When they opened Theo's door, they found him lying in bed on his side with his eyes closed, facing the wall. They could hear the spit-static of some rap song coming through his earbuds. Julian shook him a bit roughly, and Theo awoke, alarmed.

Hey, buddy, get up.

What?

He sat up and wiped his eyes and pulled out his earbuds. Hey, he said, like somebody coming to. His eyes scanned the room, making sure there wasn't anything incriminating out on his desk. Mom. What are you doing here?

Magda sat down on the bed and put her hand on his shoulder. A friend of yours called us, she said gently.

What? Who?

That's not important.

What the fuck?

We just want to talk to you.

He seemed furious. What? I have exams this week. I have to study.

What do you think we should do, Theo? What would you do if somebody called to say your child was using heroin?

Who was it?

That's not important.

That girl, Lucia—don't listen to her. She's just jealous 'cause I'm seeing someone else. And anyway, it's not such a big deal. It's not like you read in the papers.

What do you mean?

I did it once. I'm not fucking addicted.

Good, Magda said, managing to keep her cool, understanding the sensitive nuances of negotiation. She was her mother's daughter, Julian thought, a woman who refused to tolerate the stupidity of others, especially when it compromised her own fragile status in the scheme of things.

I'm glad to hear it, she said. Then it should be easy for you to stop.

Julian put his hand on Theo's shoulder. Why don't you splash some water on your face and comb your hair?

Theo frowned and shrugged off his hand. You guys should leave.

Not till we have a talk, Julian said. We need to discuss this.

We think you should come home for a few days, Magda said.

Home? What? I can't. No. I can't do that. Do you have any fucking idea how much work I have?

Theo, honey, Magda said. This is really serious.

Mom, listen. There is nothing fucking wrong with me, all right? I'm just trying to get my work done.

Okay.

I need to—clean up a little. Sorry it's kind of a mess. I didn't know you were coming—

That's all right.

I'm just going to use the—

Sure, buddy, Julian said. Take your time.

They were starting to feel a little guilty, like maybe they were wrong. Like maybe the girl who'd called was mad at Theo. Like maybe it was all just a rumor.

Shaking his head with annoyance, Theo left the room. They could hear the squeaking of the shower faucet in the bathroom next door and the sound of running water.

Julian looked around the room, comparing the two sides. The roommate's side was neat, the bed tightly made, a few photographs of his family back in Lebanon thumbtacked to the wall. Theo's side was messy, disorganized, the desk layered with books and notebooks, half-eaten bags of Cheetos, empty cigarette packs, wayward pens and pencils—it seemed a telling disparity. The kid from Lebanon was clearly more on top of the situation. These American kids were awfully spoiled, he thought, although he'd never say it to Magda. Just look at her now, he thought, trying to clean the place up, tossing things into the trash. Stop, he said. You're not cleaning his goddamn room. Here, let's pack him a bag.

He opened the closet and found Theo's duffel bag up on the shelf. He brought it down and put it on the bed and unzipped it, and she started filling it with some of the new clothes she'd bought him that summer, before he started school, just like she'd done every year of his life—to set him off on the right foot. What a crock, Julian thought now. Opening the desk drawers, he was dismayed to find such chaos. In the bottom drawer was a brown paper bag, kind of crumpled up. He took it out and opened it. Inside were a couple bags of white powder, no larger than packets of sugar, and a few brand-new needles in sealed plastic wrappers. Here we go, he said, and showed his wife. Her face blanched and she looked ill. He's not addicted, right?

Oh, my God. She sank onto the bed and put her head in her hands. How has this happened?

I don't know.

Then she looked up at him. What's taking him so long?

He went to check the bathroom. He could still hear the shower running, but when he knocked, Theo didn't answer. He opened the door and pulled back the curtain—there was no one there.

She took out her phone and called Theo, but of course he didn't pick up.

They ran down the stairs and pushed through the metal door and out into the dark of evening. Together they ran around the building, slaloming a sudden onslaught of students, but they didn't see him. In just a few moments he'd disappeared. Just beyond the lighted path was the endless ocean-size parking lot. She looked at Julian desperately. Should we wait?

I don't know, Magda.

They tracked down one of the campus security guards and told him they couldn't find their son. They said they'd had an argument and Theo had gotten upset. He may be doing drugs, she said.

Lady, the guard said, welcome to my world.

He assured them that Theo would likely return later that night, after he had some time to decompress. It's pretty cold out. He'll be back.

He urged them to go home and promised he'd stay on top of it. They made sure he had their number, and he told them he'd call once he'd talked to Theo and assessed the situation.

They drove around the campus, the dark parking lots, the neighborhoods that surrounded it, lined up like teeth. The night seemed very dark. Magda was shaking, trembling all over.

Are you cold?

She didn't answer. Her eyes were fixed on the dark, boring through it to find their son. As Julian turned onto the interstate ramp, they passed a boy standing on the embankment holding up a cardboard sign. Magda put her window down to get a better look, but they both knew it wasn't Theo.

When they got home, they sat in the kitchen, in the dim yellow light of the small table lamp. He poured her a glass of whiskey and they drank in silence. They were on their third glass when she looked at him and said, He's not yours.

What?

Theo—he's not your son. I've been meaning to tell you.

You've been *meaning* to tell me?

She started to cry. She wept, as if she'd been saving up the tears for a long time, all the years of their marriage, he guessed, and for some reason he thought of his mother on the day of his father's funeral, how she'd sat in the kitchen and he'd gotten her a Kleenex and how even such a small gesture like that had made all the difference. He walked robotically into the powder room and grabbed the box and brought it back to her and sat there, waiting for her to calm down. In the high corner of the bay window he saw the nearly full moon, bright enough to cast jagged shadows of the trees on the grass.

Magda tugged a Kleenex from the box and blew her nose. I should have told you, she said finally. I wanted to. I'm sorry. I don't expect you to forgive me.

In a matter of minutes, she'd become a total stranger to him. He didn't know how to feel.

If he's not mine—

But her expression silenced him, her frown of shame. And he knew.

Maybe he'd known all along. Maybe he knew every time he looked at Theo and saw those blue eyes. He'd been reminded of Rye the day he'd hauled out his box of photographs from the workshop, for a very brief moment entertaining the idea of going back to photography as an art form, a sacred avocation, and Theo had studied each of his pictures carefully, laying them out side-by-side on the dining room table, squinting like an expert, and asked why there weren't any people in them, and when Julian told him, repeating the same excuses he'd given to Rye all those years before, Theo nodded like he understood, and muttered, Interesting, with a casual superiority that seemed all too familiar. In his heart, underneath all the matrimonial posturing, maybe he *had* known. And if he had, so what? It didn't mean he wasn't Theo's father. It didn't mean he didn't love him.

I don't care, he heard himself say. It doesn't matter. He's still my son. And you're my wife.

But she wouldn't look at him.

You're still my wife, he repeated. Magda, do you hear me?

She couldn't seem to move.

Look at me, he demanded.

She wouldn't.

He was angry now. He rose from the table and jerked her out of her chair and slapped her as hard as he could across her face. And she shrank back. But she didn't cry. She was done crying. I've never loved you, she said.

That can't be true. His voice cracked, and his eyes glazed over. He stared at the floor, the yellow linoleum they'd always planned to replace, and then he hit her again. And she went down.

He knelt beside her, stroking her hair, blood running from her nose, and she whimpered a little, and he opened his belt and fumbled into her, and her fists beat against his back, and his hands entwined her hair. When it was over, he held her for a long time, maybe hours. And they waited there like that on the floor in the dirty yellow light. They waited, for what, exactly, he didn't know. But it was coming. Something terrifying and real that would change everything.

Magda

When she woke the next morning and faced herself in the mirror, she saw what he'd done to her.

She'd allowed it, she decided.

That last part, how he'd gripped her hair so hard he'd pulled out a chunk of it, how he'd held her down.

Call the police, the little voice said.

But she couldn't. She couldn't bear it, the cruiser in her driveway, the flashing lights. Neighbors peering out their windows. No.

No, thank you.

It wasn't how she'd been raised.

There were things that didn't leave the house.

He had left her there on the floor. Stood there, buckling his belt. Watching her without even a shred of remorse. She was like some kind of animal in the road, the blood smeared on her cheek. She didn't move till his car pulled out.

She hadn't spoken to him since that night. She was still bruised, and her cheeks were puffy. There was the red mark on her neck where he'd held her.

She hadn't left the house in a week.

Theo hadn't called either. The security guard had left a message saying he was sorry he'd never caught up with their son, though he'd tried. Pierre had reported to the R.A. that Theo hadn't returned to the room. A few days later, the dean of students called to ask what was going on with Theo and why he hadn't been going to classes. She lied and said he'd come home with the flu; they were getting a doctor's note. She promised to get back to him. But more days passed, and Theo still hadn't called, and now it was almost the winter break.

Maybe he would come home for Christmas, she told herself.

She made herself get dressed and put on some makeup. Then she drove a good twenty minutes outside town to a Christmas tree farm and bought herself a tree. They tied it to the roof of her Range Rover, and when she got home, she had to bring it into the house by herself. It was heavy and cumbersome and it scratched the car a little, but she was determined. And like all the years before, she set it up in the front window where everybody could see it. Let there be no doubt, she thought bitterly, that in the Ladd house it would be a very merry fucking Christmas.

All afternoon while the snow fell, she decorated the tree, something she and Theo usually did together. Some of the ornaments had been her mother's and some were from her own childhood, and a few Theo had made over the years in school, a snowflake, a reindeer, a star— even now, after all these years, the glitter came off on her fingers.

The next morning, she hired a private detective. He drove all around Albany, looking for Theo, and finally found him in a not-so-great neighborhood, huddled with the girl in the doorway of a Chinese takeout. He said her son was living on the streets with a group of kids, all of them addicts. He'd approached Theo and explained who he was and asked him to get in the car, but her son refused.

She didn't know what Theo was thinking. Or what sort of emotional catastrophe, if any, had prompted his addiction. She only knew that, as his mother, she was somehow culpable. She had to be. And it made her very sad. She didn't know why he'd chosen this. She had tried very hard. She had given him everything she could. She was a good mother!

But it wasn't enough. Obviously she'd missed something.

She sat in the kitchen. It was late afternoon. The windows were almost black. It had snowed all day and it was very cold. The sky was a deep, punitive blue. Under the full moon the snow-covered ground seemed to sparkle. But she couldn't appreciate its beauty. She couldn't appreciate anything, because her son was out there somewhere, cold and alone and fucked-up on drugs.

She found she couldn't eat. She went into the living room and fetched one of Julian's bottles of whiskey and brought it back to the kitchen and poured herself a drink, her hand shaking just a little, and sat there at the table, drinking it. She drank one glass and then another.

Clean up, she told herself. Look at this place. Don't just sit there.

Julian had left a message that he was putting the house on the market. Start packing, is what he said. Translation: if you don't want to be my wife and sleep in my bed and do my laundry and take my suits to the cleaner, you don't get to live in my house.

What power did she really have? Her lawyer had assured her she'd be all right, she'd get the house if she wanted it, and Julian would continue to support her. But Magda wasn't smart about this stuff. She didn't want the house; she didn't want anything from him. She just wanted to be free. She'd come to the marriage with nothing. She would leave with nothing.

Where would she go? She didn't know.

Back to her mother's place, which they'd been renting out. She thought of her mother now, gone already ten years; she didn't miss her.

She looked around at the mess. She'd let things go. She didn't care about this house. It had never felt like home.

She turned on CNN and winced at the president making more excuses. She turned the sound off and stood at the sink and stacked the dirty plates in the dishwasher and wiped down the counter and the table and swept the floor. There she was, her whole rumpled self, in the black glass of the French doors. She was broken, weary, unforgivably middle-aged—softer, rounder, less defined, and at the same time more defined than ever—and she was angry, very angry, with herself more than anyone else.

She made herself go up to Theo's room. Maybe this time she would find the one clue she'd overlooked, some stupid thing that accounted for this nightmare. She turned on the light and sat on his bed. It was a really nice room, nicer than most, and everywhere she looked were reminders of all the nice things they'd done for him, the shelves cluttered with souvenirs from all the places they'd taken him to, the circus, Broadway musicals, Disney World. His books. His dresser. Some of his clothes he'd outgrown. The old sneakers in his closet. The long-ignored tennis racket.

He wasn't this person anymore, she realized.

She thought she'd been strategic, the extra activities outside school, the pottery classes, the saxophone, the church youth group where they did community service, walking around the neighborhoods picking up trash, the food bank, the SAT tutor that cost a fortune, the chess club, the math club—there hadn't been any indication, not even the remotest possibility, that her son would come to this end. She stared up at the ceiling at the little green stars he'd stuck on it when he was eleven, and brought her hands together and closed her eyes very tightly and prayed.

Where are you, God?

She swatted her tears angrily and rose and turned off his light and descended the grand staircase and put on her coat and her old boots and shuffled out into the cold, grappling for her cigarettes. The coat was a dark green wool; it had been her mother's, and by now it was pretty shabby, the satin lining a little torn, the pockets bulging with restaurant mints, how old was anyone's guess. Her mother was a chain-smoker. Magda had quit years ago, but on impulse, at a weak moment, had bought a pack of Marlboros, and now she was right back at it. In truth, she liked having an excuse to go outside. To stand out in the cold. She lit one now in defiance of her life and the wreck she had made of it.

Everyone on this street had too much money. The houses, the cars, the help, the fucking landscape guys with their mowers and snowplows. The practiced aloofness of the other women, wives with husbands like Julian who were never home. How they'd pull out of their garages in their beautiful cars, the snotty wave if they happened to see her, the icy greeting when they saw her in town.

Magda was from another world, where small pleasures brought joy—her mother's pierogis, the homemade wine their neighbors made, the crash of glasses coming together, the stories people told around the table, the noise of laughter, the simple gift of being alive. Her parents had moved to this country to live a free American life. But what did that even mean anymore?

They were all under surveillance, the whole world. She was probably being watched this very moment, through some satellite. Even her phone and computers were apparently available to some unseen voyeur. There were cameras in town, perched in discreet corners. There were cameras on every streetlamp. There were cameras in doorbells. It seemed to her that a highly sophisticated conspiracy was at work. It wasn't really about the consumer or convenience. That was the ultimate subversive trickery. They were selling you their most up-to-date newfangled gadgetry, and you bought it, you had to have it. But it wasn't for you.

They—whoever *they* were—were watching your every move.

Her mother used to say, in her heavy accent, There is no such thing as a free country, even here.

She had taught Magda to keep her feelings to herself. You don't tell them nothing, she instructed her one morning before school, ironing the pleats of her uniform. You keep your feelings in here—she tapped her heart—where they belong. She'd braid Magda's hair so tightly it hurt, and on the bus Magda always unraveled it, setting free her wild brown mane. She was an American girl! This was her country! She had her own ideas.

At the base of her neighbor's driveway, she dragged on her cigarette like it was the very thing keeping her alive. At this moment, she felt entirely contemptuous of the world. She didn't belong here; she never had.

She ground out the cigarette and, looking up at her neighbor's house, glimpsed a woman she'd spoken maybe two words to in the entire time they'd lived here taking a sip of wine in her kitchen. As if sensing Magda's intrusion, she went to her window, peered out a moment at the darkness, then pulled the shade, her concealment restored.

Part Four

Illumination

I don't think it's the job of art to entertain or offer reassurance. There are hard truths without easy answers. Maybe discomfort, in some way, can actually lead to illumination.

—Katy Grannan, *Aperture*

Theo

God was an indulgence, he decided. You couldn't prove that God existed; you couldn't prove He didn't exist either. You could talk yourself blue in the face and it wouldn't change the outcome. Alas, the burden of proof allowed you to assume that something in fact existed unless proven otherwise. There was evidence of absence, and yet there was also absence of evidence. You couldn't *see* God, so why assume He was *there?* And yet so many people did, and why was that? The professor gave other examples of things like ghosts and fairies, ephemeral entities.

His Philosophy of Religion class.

Mostly it was boring.

They walked together without talking. The sun on their backs. The sound of the wind in their ears. She had long black hair, small shoulders, tiny bones in her back. Her fingernails white as shells. When they kissed, her small mouth was like a sea creature, opening and opening.

Her name was True.

His first time. It was back in October, this Halloween party in one of the dorms. People were drinking tequila and doing coke and Ecstasy, and a bunch of people started talking about getting some heroin, and Carmine said there was a girl at the party who had some but she was bad news and don't get any ideas, and when they got introduced, they looked at each other with a kind of psychic recognition, like they'd known each other in another life, and she smiled and said, I think I know you.

She had some on her and was willing to turn them on, and it wouldn't even cost that much, and it was great and safe, and they'd have a lot of fun. She was wearing a costume, Snow White, which was pretty funny, like pretty ironic, because she wasn't, and he was sober enough at that point to think of it as a political statement, because suddenly everything that happened on campus was political, and you were either on one side or the other. That first time he saw her, he felt a jolt go through him, like a cosmic wind full of black stars, and he trusted her and he held out his arm and said, Let's do this, and she wound it tight with a band, and he felt the prick of the needle, and about two seconds into it, he puked into a garbage can, and people were laughing, and he lay back and gave in to it, and that's pretty much all that happened.

Somehow, he woke up the next morning in his own bed and reflected on the night and remembered doing the heroin and was amazed he'd done it and survived, and he felt all right. He thought maybe he was a little hungover, and he staggered into the dining hall for breakfast, and all that morning he felt this nagging preoccupation with finding the girl, because he knew she had more.

Carmine told him she was no good. You don't want to find her, he said.

Yes, I do.

She's dangerous, man. She's, like, a dealer. She crashed our party. You have to trust me on this.

But he drove Theo downtown to the bus station, and there she was, standing on the corner in the wind with her crystal-blue eyes. She sold them some dope, and they fixed in Carmine's old black gypsy car with the beaded curtain in the back window and the fake-velvet seats holey with cigarette burns. It had a sunroof that was stuck open, so it was always cold, but you could see the sky, and if it rained, the drops shot right down on you. They were sitting all three of them in the front seat, and she was in the middle, and she took his hand and held it a minute, and he felt like it was about to catch fire, like it was a burning torch held high in the air. A proclamation, he thought.

He didn't want to be afraid anymore. He'd grown up afraid of this and that. Dangerous people, germs, bad luck, deception. But Carmine wasn't afraid of anything. With Carmine, you saw life. You walked straight into it.

They walked the triangle of tracks in the train yard and slept in the retired train cars. You'd hear the blasting freighters all night long with their clanging bells. Sometimes they went down to the river and hung out under the bridge. There was a whole community of people down there existing along the shore of the Hudson. It was only a couple miles from campus, but it was this whole other reality. Some of them had made huts out of cardboard and corrugated plastic. Some lit kerosene lanterns, and from a distance you could see the flames flickering, and you came into it like into some magic land. Even in the dark you saw the hard lines on their faces, the pain that had marked them. It made Theo mad, and he felt something deep inside him, the desire to help, to make the world better somehow—but he knew he couldn't. How could he? What would he do? What could *he* do? They weren't looking for help, not from him or anyone else. They were just getting along, and that was all right.

They were nice to him. Even with nothing, you felt welcome. Unlike people in his other life, at school, or back home, these people had nothing more than the tiny world they'd pulled around them. They didn't have tables or chairs or couches or dishes or TVs. They didn't sleep in beds. They had their hands. They had their bodies, their feet. They had their brains. They had eyes, ears. And that was all.

Carmine walked around like a wizard in this long hobo coat, and he had all these crazy tricks up his sleeve. He was the sort of person who made you believe he was helping you, when all along he was just making things worse. You got deeper into the darkness with Carmine, and sometimes it was so black you couldn't see two steps ahead of you, you couldn't see your own hands.

He knew it was about love. He loved Carmine in a fucked-up sort of way. Just like he loved heroin. He knew this rim of life coiled him in deeper. It was his feet dipped in tar.

They hung out a lot at the bookstore, the word USED in red neon in the window. He and Carmine sidled in like gangsters looking for trouble, but all you saw were books and more books and the little old man at the register, hunched over the crossword puzzle with one of those short little pencils, and they got lost in the back rooms of the place, and Carmine showed him all the first editions, with their thick green and red bindings, that nobody ever looked at and were covered with dust.

He came across this old book of poems by Rilke—pronounced *Rilka,* Carmine corrected him—and they were *elegies,* which he knew had something to do with death, and he stuck the book in his back pocket like he already owned it and walked right out of the store, and nobody cared, nobody came running, and he felt like some angel had left the book for him, some angel had wanted him to find it, so he read it, and on one level it saved him from himself, it saved him from death, and on another it freed him in his own mind. At night in his dorm he read in bed by the light of his phone. He read the lines again and again and then again. He really liked this guy, Rilke. Life and death and sex and angels, and really, what else was there?

Oh and the night, the night, when the wind full of space
    wears out our faces...

It had come down to the simple fact that life was harder than anyone
had told him it would be. There was this pressure in the air, pressing
down on everyone. It was hard to get anything done. Nobody spoke
up in class, and if they did, it was some form of relatively applicable information deduced from a couple introductory paragraphs of the text.
Meaning that everyone was coasting. Just doing the bare minimum.
The professors had a hard time. And it was no different outside class.
Everybody staring into their phones all the time. Nobody wanted to
talk. You had your fake life online convincing people that you existed.
It was enough. People wanted to be left alone.

His hair had gotten longer. He'd stopped shaving, and now he had
this stubble that kind of looked like fresh dirt. Plus, he'd lost weight.
He'd look at himself in the mirror like a farsighted person and think,
Is that really me?

He'd missed a couple deadlines. His teachers sent him emails,
encouraging him to get the work in before such and such a date, when
they'd have to take drastic measures.

The nice thing about heroin, it stopped time. You folded into an in-
between, where you could hide for a couple hours. Like if you stopped
a movie and you were the main character, and all the people in the
audience instantly lost interest.

He'd started having all these health issues, like he was really fucking
sick, and the only thing that made him feel any better or let him
forget he was feeling so bad was doing more. And that became his life.
Doing more.

It didn't seriously occur to him to stop. Distantly, maybe, in the back
of his mind. Way, way back. It was kind of a preoccupation, like, this is
my life now. I have this condition and I have to deal with it. And that's
pretty much all he thought about.

For some reason he stopped going to class. At first it was just going to be the one time. He'd hang out with Carmine. Or Lucia would come to his room after lunch to blow him. But his professors only annoyed him. To be honest, they seemed insincere, like their minds were elsewhere. Most of the lectures were recorded, so you could easily catch up online. In theory this made sense, but he had yet to check that out.

One morning he woke up to Lucia shaking him and slapping his face and screaming in his ear. Jesus, Theo, I thought you were dead.

A couple of days later, his parents came up to rescue him, and he took off. He didn't want anything to do with either one of them. They weren't in the same reality anymore. He could never make them understand how good he felt on heroin and why it wasn't something he could give up right now. What did the talk show hosts call it—*self-medicating?*

Yeah, that's what he was doing.

That cold night, he walked all the way down to Hamilton Street, at least a five-mile walk from campus, and found her at a little table in the bus station café, and she took his freezing hands and put them inside her pockets and looked up at him, straight into his eyes, and said, You found me.

By then it was nearing the end of the semester. It was a week before Christmas. They were closing the dorms. He'd gotten a notice about missing too many classes and the possibility of academic probation next semester if he didn't fulfill the following tasks—they'd made a list.

You should go home, man, Carmine said.

Tomorrow, he told him. But they both knew he wouldn't.

They went to Carmine's. It was late, and the house was dark, but they had a tree in the living room with twinkly lights. They stood there, looking at it. Theo pictured his mother setting up their tree all by herself, and he felt bad. He wondered if she'd actually gone to the trouble to buy him a present and he hoped she hadn't. But he could picture the box wrapped up under the tree with his name on it. And what had he gotten her? Nothing.

At Carmine's, you saw crosses everywhere, over the doors, over the bed, even in the bathroom over the toilet. He said his parents were superstitious more than religious. They wanted protection. There were pictures of Jesus hanging next to family pictures, in the dining room, up the stairs, and one in Carmine's room over the desk where he'd done his homework his whole life. Nobody in Theo's house actually believed in God, but here was a family who had laid their trust in the Lord Jesus. Even when Carmine was snorting coke, you'd see his St. Christopher's medal dangling over the powder. When he was high, he talked non-stop. You couldn't shut him up. Theo didn't like to talk when he was high; he couldn't. That night, he lay on one of the twin beds while Carmine went on about this girl Melanie he'd started seeing and all her extraordinary qualities, her blond hair, her huge butt, so big, he said, it was like a big-assed sandwich you couldn't get your mouth around and you had to hold, like this—he demonstrated—with both of your hands, and eat a little at a time. Theo could hear the TV in Carmine's parents' room next door and sirens out in the night and the dogs in the neighborhood barking like they'd bite your head off every time some-one walked by, and he stared at that picture over Carmine's desk, the one of Jesus, the long hair, the eyes, the compassionate expression, the white robe, and thought how crazy it was that this person, this single individual, had had such an impact on so many people all around the world for, like, centuries. You couldn't make that shit up.

His mother once told him she'd given up on God. There are too many bad things, she said. But don't take my word for it. Make up your own mind.

Theo had. He believed in science, empirical evidence. Everything else was crap.

He knew it came down to perspective and where you grew up. He and Carmine were close, but they had essential philosophical differences. Theo came from another world, a world called money. His house was a lot nicer than Carmine's and they had all this high-end stuff. And unlike Carmine's father, who shouted and carried on when something bothered him, Julian never raised his voice—ever. Which was almost worse, scarier. Because you never knew what he was really thinking. Julian was a quiet, intense person, deliberate in everything he did. He wasn't a big talker, but he'd been on a debate team back in college and knew how to present an argument. You had to be sort of prepared to state your reasons for wanting something, because he could usually talk you out of it. Theo resented how his mother always seemed to need permission to do things, like even if it was just a trip to the city to walk around a museum, like she was Julian's employee, not his wife. He found it annoying.

When his mother went back to work, doing weddings on weekends, he and Julian were alone together more and mostly hung out and watched movies. Julian had a stellar film collection. He loved foreign movies. Fellini, Godard, especially Antonioni. You didn't just watch Antonioni, Julian liked to say. It wasn't only what was *in* the frame that mattered. It was about what was just out of view. How the actors moved *through* the frame: into the frame, and then out of it. You were always wondering what was beyond the frame, and then the camera unhurriedly glided over to show you. You *gazed* at the naked shoulders of beautiful women, the sloping hills of a remote island, the dark water of the ocean, or the long shadows of the trees.

On their movie nights, they would sit on opposite ends of the sofa with a bowl of popcorn between them. Julian slouched down on the pillows and crossed his legs like a woman in his Italian loafers. He was a skinny guy, with slippery black hair and dark, unrevealing eyes, and always a shadow on his face like he couldn't shave fast enough. One time they watched *A Man and a Woman,* this love story about a race-car driver and the gorgeous French woman he's in love with, and Julian would talk about how these movies had taught him a lot about how to sell things to people, because it wasn't really about the product when you came right down to it. Essentially you were selling this idea of a life, the possibility of having something better. That's what people needed, he said. They needed to believe there was more.

More, Julian said, the most significant noun of the twenty-first century.

Even when you had to sell a product like Motus, you were selling a lifestyle, he told Theo. So instead of focusing on the drug itself and what it did to you once you took it, he gave people the sense that the drug could greatly improve their lives, reinforced by the happy people in the ad doing happy things—a woman in the garden, a father playing catch with his son (something Julian had never thought to do with him), or a family sitting around a table having dinner, all this stuff happening in the background while some guy talked about the actual product and its possible horrific side effects, like vomiting and liver disease and kidney failure. The commercial convinced you that, by taking the drug, you could actually achieve happiness, not only because you could finally move your bowels but because it could help you feel in control of all these other aspects of your life. If Theo were going to shoot that commercial, he'd show some dipshit opioid addict staggering down some street, trying to find a toilet to sit on without anybody bothering him or seeing him, because he'd have to sit there for like a week, just praying something would come out.

Everybody said it was dangerous, but it didn't feel dangerous; it just felt nice. Like really *nice.* And he stopped worrying. And for a couple hours he could float along. At first he thought it made him smarter. Like he had all these fucking brilliant ideas shooting into his brain like meteors. Yeah. Like a meteor shower. But after a while, a month or so, say, he was tired of the ideas, tired of thinking, and you just wanted to lie back and *not* think, and let it take you.

He knew every time he used, it hurt Magda, but after a while, he thought only of himself, not of his angry, disappointed mother.

There were others like him out on the street. They'd walk together in a group. It was harder to be alone. You got scared, scared out of your mind. Because you knew every time you did this stuff, you could die.

That was the song always playing in your head.

You can feel it watching you.

Death.

Just kind of snickering.

It was like somebody telling a joke about you just out of earshot, and you can't hear the fucking punch line.

He wasn't going to go home for Christmas. He stopped calling his mother and taking her calls, and when he'd used up all the money in his bank account, he did something stupid, he sold his phone.

He was starting to feel a little lost. Like he was actually in real trouble. Like deep.

True was the only one who cared. She'd say things that made sense, and he'd feel better. He'd feel like this was just a phase he was going through. Like pretty soon he'd be done with it and his life would go back to normal.

She talked about her past. Her parents had split when she was little, and she hadn't seen her father since. Her mother was big and fat, like four hundred pounds. She lived upstate somewhere and owned a fried-dough truck. She does all the carnivals, she said.

I never had fried dough. Is it any good?

Yeah, it's good. The sugar comes off on your fingertips. We used to go around leaving our fingerprints everywhere.

They were sitting on a bench in a small park in the bright, cold sunshine, and she was rolling a cigarette with her delicate fingers.

I used to work for her on the weekends. It was so hot in that damned truck. The sweat just rolled off me.

Why'd you leave?

Her boyfriend moved in. Bobby. He was a short-order cook. He had this gold tooth. He was mean, but he made good pancakes. They'd be sitting around, drinking rum and Cokes while I was trying to do my homework. I was a good student. I got all As. This one night he came into my room.

She went quiet and lit the cigarette and blew the smoke out hard. Then she looked at him with her blue eyes. He put his hand over my mouth, she said.

That's horrible. I'm sorry that happened to you. Did you tell your mother?

She shook her head. What for? She wouldn't have believed me. I left in the morning. I was only fifteen. Didn't even finish high school.

What happened? Where did you go?

I came here. I hitchhiked. This nice woman picked me up. She helped me a lot. She knew about this place I could live and get my GED.

What about your mom? Did she try to find you?

No. She took a final drag of her cigarette and flicked it to the ground. I never want to see her again.

They walked with their signs under their arms. The thought of never seeing his mother again filled him with an unbearable despair. He couldn't let that happen, wouldn't.

True touched his arm. Hey, she said, and smiled. Sorry. I know that's a weird story.

Don't be sorry.

I'm trying to put it behind me.

Good. You should.

Just sometimes it makes me sad.

He looked at her and took her hand. You'll be all right.

Will I?

He nodded, but he wasn't sure. He didn't know how a person could recover from that. There were a lot of bad people out there. Too many. They got away with terrible things.

They crossed the street and headed toward the expressway ramp.

I used to walk on stilts, she said, balancing on the narrow curb like a tightrope walker, with her arms out.

Stilts?

This old clown gave 'em to me. I'd walk on 'em, all around the trailer park. I was like a giraffe walking around the place. You'd see all these pickups parked in zigzags. You could smell everyone's dinner cooking. You could see into everyone's life. You could see what people were doing.

What were they doing?

Not much.

She wrote her name with a Sharpie on his hand, T-R-U-E.

Then he took the Sharpie and wrote, L-O-V-E.

But it wasn't true love, not really. And they both knew it.

You're a good boy, Theo, she said, and kissed him.

Once, she washed his hair. In this gas station bathroom. She used a bar of dirty soap, pushing the suds down the drain. He liked the feel of her skinny hands on his scalp. Then she made him kneel under the hand dryer, smacking around his hair like she was mad at it.

You could get free coffee at the shelter, but you could stand there for only so long before they made you leave. They'd stand out in the cold for hours. It was hard; it could eat you alive.

> The hero prolongs himself, even his falling was only a
> pretext for being, his latest rebirth...

Those lines of Rilke's roamed around his brain, and he saw himself as a fallen hero.

It was kind of a sad story.

He just wanted to get high. That's pretty much all he thought about.

* * *

Sometimes the world was too much for him. Sometimes just the sun, how it pulsed and cried, or the buildings, the dark lines, the old warehouses along the river, or the layers of wind and clouds, so gray and low, waiting to release, anticipating grief. He liked to walk in the city. The streets ran on diagonals, they led to nowhere. He liked the black doorways, just a hint of light on the narrow stairs. You couldn't ever tell what was up there.

Rye

An hour or so outside Albany he called Constance. She sounded happy to hear from him. She was going home in a few days for the holiday, she reminded him.

Have a good time, he said. How's Simone?

She misses you. You should call her.

He hesitated; he didn't like his assistant telling him what to do. Tell her I called, he said, and hung up.

He made it to Albany before noontime and easily found the SUNY campus, which occupied six hundred–some acres in the middle of the city. He drove around its circumference, getting his bearings. The campus was desolate, and it occurred to him that it was closed for the break. Tinseled decorations shimmied on the streetlamps. He pulled over and opened his window and looked out at the gray sky. It was colder up here, and it was starting to snow.

He took out his phone and glanced at the photo Magda had posted on her Instagram page of Theo and the girl at the Chinese takeout, Kim's, it was called, and he googled directions. It was downtown some-where, on Broadway. He drove off campus and turned onto Western

Avenue. He meandered through narrow, haphazard streets; some were cobblestone, flanked with row houses and older brownstones. As he neared the river, there were abandoned warehouses, condemned buildings demarcated with large red Xs, boarded-up storefronts. Kim's was near the corner, adjacent to the elevated expressway and a few steps from a budget motel. He parked on the street and sat there for a few minutes, taking in the scenery. You could see the cars screaming by on the overpass. Under that was a wide stone tunnel through which he could see the river. But it was a waste of waterfront. There was nothing down here. Many of the surrounding buildings were very old, late seventeenth century, probably Dutch. He saw a guy standing at a traffic light at the expressway entrance ramp, holding up a cardboard sign. Not Theo.

Kim's didn't have any customers. It wasn't the easiest location. It occurred to Rye that he was hungry; he hadn't eaten anything since earlier that morning, when he'd sat across from Magda like a displaced person, determined to abandon the rest of his life, his wife, his daughter, his career, to return to their bed. This hunger he felt for her was destructive, because he knew he'd do whatever it took to get her back.

He decided to go inside and order something. A woman was standing behind the counter. Her long fingernails were painted green. The floor was dirty. He ordered lo mein. While he waited, he showed her the photograph of Theo and the girl and asked if she knew either one of them, and she nodded and said in a thick Cantonese accent, She around the corner.

Where?

Around. She gestured. Bus station.

She handed him his bag of food, and he paid and thanked her and left and got back into his truck and sat there, eating with chopsticks as the snow began to fall. When he was done, he drove around the block, passing two other kids with signs, their backpacks at their feet, and found the bus station. There were people standing out front, smoking, jumping up and down in the cold. Taxis waiting. He parked in the lot and went inside to have a look around. He used the restroom and washed his hands and walked to the rear of the building, where the gates to the buses stretched all along the corridor. On his way out, he passed the nearly empty café, where a woman with tattooed breasts was nursing her baby. He didn't see the girl anywhere.

He drove around for another hour or so, circling the area. It was starting to get dark and by now the snow was falling heavily. It was windy and very cold. He decided to check into the motel on the corner. He parked in the lot and got out and locked his door, then entered the small lobby. The motel clerk, a man wearing a turban, slid Rye's credit card back to him across the counter and glanced at him with curiosity. You are here on business?

You could say that. He put his card back in his wallet. Thank you.

For how long will you stay?

I don't know. Maybe two nights.

We are happy to have you, he said with a politeness only immigrants possessed, and, smiling, handed him the key. Your room is just down there, on the left.

The hall was long and narrow and smelled of ammonia and somebody's microwaved leftovers. He found his room and unlocked the door, reflecting on how, within just a few hours, his circumstances had profoundly changed. He stood there a moment, staring at the dubious carpet, the shiny orange drapes, the mud-brown bedspread. A long black stripe ran the length of the wall, drawn by an unwieldy suitcase. A portal of dislocation, he thought. Another kind of in-between.

So be it, he thought.

He turned on the small lamp on the nightstand and set his pack down on the desk. He took out his phone and glanced through the window. Cars were pulling over, idling with their wipers going, the snow collecting on their windshields. He heard a man's guttural preview of the spit he would expel on the asphalt. Two women who might have been hookers staggered across the lot, holding hands. There were people here, living their lives, doing what they do. He was the stranger. He tugged on the string and closed the drapes. Show's over, he thought. He turned the heat to full blast. He sat on the bed and considered calling Magda. But the more he thought about his plan— finding Theo, trying to talk him out of doing heroin—the more it felt like a bad idea.

He took out the photos she'd given to him. He flipped through them again and again, finding himself in the boy's face. He was nearby, he knew it; he could sense his presence. Just out there. Wandering the surrounding streets. He would find him. He would at least try.

He pulled off the bedspread and inspected the bed; it looked clean. Then he lay down, turned off the light, and closed his eyes.

His phone woke him. The room was dark save for the light from a streetlamp, slipping through the crack in the curtains.

How are you?

I'm in a motel. He switched on the lamp. It was ten p.m. He told her about his day, the Chinese takeout, the bus station, the kids on the street.

I can't stand this, she said. I can't do anything. I can't work. I can't eat.

I know.

Everything's different now. The whole world seems—

It's very hard, he said.

She complained about the political situation, the liars in Congress, the pervasive deception, all of the terrible things that were happening around the globe, how powerless she felt.

He heard people in the parking lot. He got up and drew the curtain aside and peered out.

It was still snowing. Cars passed by slowly, their lights blurred. He saw a man in a heavy coat, walking against the wind.

It's really snowing here, he told her.

Here, too, she said, and he tried to picture her in her suburban kitchen, the one she had shared with Julian Ladd; he couldn't. He resented her life, her bad decisions. Her inferiority. He thought of her now with an unsettling measure of contempt. She was not his lover, he decided. He would not allow it.

Rye, she said. Are you okay?

Yes. I'm fine.

You don't sound it.

Just tired.

Thank you for doing this.

Don't thank me yet.

He promised to have some news for her tomorrow, and they hung up.

He thought of his wife. That certified letter Magda had sent all those years ago. Was it possible that Simone had signed for it? Maybe she'd forgotten to tell him, he thought. It could have been an honest mistake. Somehow he doubted it.

He turned off the light and lay awake in the dark, staring at the shadow on the ceiling, shaped like an icepick, from the crack in the curtains, he surmised. As he lay there, his mind brought her back to him, the hotel room, the white sheets, their pillows tossed to the floor. How she had stood before him naked in the streetlight. Look at me, she'd demanded without speaking. *Look at me.*

He lifted his hands to his face, his arms, but her scent was gone.

He drifted off and woke to voices in the parking lot. It was seven a.m. He glanced through the parted curtains and saw a few kids standing in a huddle, a mix of colors, sizes, genders, some with signs, some with their hands pushed in their pockets—they were their own species, he concluded, a melancholy tribe. He opened the curtains to get a better look and that's when he saw the girl, standing off to the side, smoking a cigarette. He reached for his camera. She was beautiful, he noticed, even like this. She had unusual eyes. The sweatshirt hung on her thin frame, under a grease-spotted, rust-colored down vest zipped to her chin. There was no sign of Theo. He brought the camera up and framed the shot and took it.

He set his camera down guiltily. It had been a long time since he'd taken a picture of somebody without their knowing it. He did a lot of studio work these days. People would come. He'd study their faces closely. Their wrinkles, blemishes, birthmarks. They were like patients, he often thought, waiting for a diagnosis, the thing nobody else could see that was wrong with them.

He washed and dressed quickly, layering his clothing, pulling on wool socks. It was even colder today. Winter had come in earnest. He'd brought a few pairs of old trousers and one or two shirts. He never packed much when he traveled for work. This felt like work, but of course it wasn't. It was personal, and it was difficult for him, as most personal things were. He was a little frightened.

He was feeling a nagging desire to photograph the crumbling old buildings, the boarded-up storefronts, the faces he encountered on the street, the blight of ennui. He pulled on his old peacoat and grabbed his camera; he couldn't be without it.

There was a new person at the desk, a woman this time, wearing a headscarf, preoccupied with something on her computer screen. The cold air hit him hard. The clouds were low and dense. He pulled a black skullcap over his ears.

With the snow, the streets were empty. Two obese women who looked like twins ambled up the sidewalk, carrying bulky yellow ShopRite bags. In the distance, he could see the broken windows of a dilapidated factory. A hawk slowly circled the sky above.

He spotted the girl and her friends heading toward the expressway entrance ramp, their panhandling posts. They dispersed, holding up their signs. He sat on a metal barrier across the street, where he could watch her from a safe distance. Discreetly he took a couple photographs. After a while, a white van pulled up, and the girl got in. As it drew away from the curb, the driver, a man of maybe forty with matted blond hair that looked dyed, glanced at him. It was the kind of look that meant something. A face Rye wouldn't forget. He watched the van drive up the road, its back door dented, two stickers, an American flag and PROUD VETERAN, plastered on its bumper.

He waited around for Theo. He waited a good hour before giving up.

He found a coffee shop down the street and sat at the counter and ordered the breakfast special. The coffee was hot and strong. He discerned from the chatter around him that the place catered to state workers and legislators. He studied his phone, thinking of Simone. He knew he should call her; he couldn't. Even as he grappled with all the reasons he needed to be here, none of them were easily explained. He had come to find his son, but in truth he was looking for something else, himself.

Theo

This used to be forest, she told him.

She waved her arm across the horizon of smokestacks, the factories down near the port. Under all that cement is the land. My grandma used to live over there. They took her house down. Put up a truck stop. It's what killed her in the end. Losing that place. That land. She had the softest hands. She smelled like biscuits. She used to take care of me when I got sick. Nobody loved me like her.

They stood out on the ramp together. Their signs said HUNGRY, but they weren't, not for food. There were places all over the city where you could eat without so much as a dollar in your pocket. The shelter was pretty good or the soup kitchen at St. Peter's Church. Maybe he wasn't hungry, but the word described a longing he felt inside for something he couldn't really name. He only knew that he needed it very badly. And he might never find it.

Usually she did better than him. Maybe they felt sorry for her because she was a girl, all alone out there, skinny and with shoulders kind of hunched and a long braid tied off with a rubber band. They'd take one look at her face, which was an angel's face, and put their window down. People gave her things: change, lifesavers, chocolate bars, even a ball of wool once. She showed it to him, holding out her palm. She carried that tangle of wool around in her pocket like a bird's nest. They were the same age, but she'd lived too much. Inside, she said, where it mattered, she was already old.

They pooled their money. It was starting to get really cold out. He would hold her hands in his own, blowing on them to make them warm. A few nights they slept on the street, in the vestibule of the Asian Market, where they kept the fish tanks on the other side of the glass. If you leaned up against it, you could almost feel warm. He told her the dorms were closed and he couldn't go home, and she said she knew a place where he could stay.

There was an island down near the port, some kind of nature preserve right in the middle of the Hudson River. You crossed a bridge to get to it. You set your foot down on the land and understood what it was to be a stranger. She pulled him along, into the woods. Trees sprawled here and there. After a while, they came upon this ruined hotel, this decaying palace, surrounded by a high chain-link fence and NO TRESPASSING signs. Somebody had cut the fence with wire cutters and pulled it back on either side, and now it served as a kind of entrance. It was a beautiful old miserable place, paint rippling on the ceiling, falling off like moon craters to the bloodred carpet below, and when you were high enough, they almost looked like flowers. There was a big open room with a drained pool and one of those massive diving boards. People had scrawled graffiti all around the pool, and somebody had written END OF DAYS in black spray paint with a mean-looking smiley face in the O. All across the tiled floor you saw grass spiking up. You saw old chairs—lawn chairs with green-and-white straps and wooden chairs piled in the middle of the room like someone had planned to set fire to them. There were old phones with dials and squiggly cords, and there was a lot of wreckage, just broken stuff, like there'd been a war.

She had her own room, with a mattress on the floor. Old wallpaper peeling off. She kept it neat. She had this kind of altar to her lost boy, with his pictures taped up and a few of his Matchbox cars. In one photo, he had on a Rangers T-shirt. He was maybe three. That was right before, she said. Someone had taken him from her car in a Rite Aid parking lot. It wasn't even late at night, she said. She'd run in for a couple seconds to get a prescription, and when she came out, he was gone.

This is what it done to me, she cried, showing him her arms, her naked legs, the constellation of needle marks.

At night they'd lie there side-by-side. They were like people lost at sea, floating on a life raft under the black sky. Sometimes their hands would come together, their fingers entwining. Even in the dark you could see things. You could see the crazy shining branches on the ceiling. You saw mice jumbled in the corners, centipedes like the spine of a fish, and one time, a little bird flew from one side of the room to the other, and he thought it was death paying a visit. She was death, this girl. He had come to believe it. Death lying right there next to him, breathing the same air.

Out of nowhere, you'd hear the train whistle, and after a while, this light would come out of the dark, this white spotlight, followed by a chain of yellow windows moving through the night, and you could see the people reading the paper or just sitting there. And it was like they were in a whole other world, a whole different reality, and he and True and the others were far away and apart from everything they had known before.

She had this glow. Like she knew things. You saw it in her eyes. She was a city of shuttered windows. You got lost.

The world comes into your arms. It falls into you like so much wind.

When the weather wasn't good, they rode the trains. She knew one of the conductors. He let them ride for free. Theo suspected she'd done something to this guy, he didn't want to think what. He could only go so far in his thinking now. It was like a spell he was under. And she was part of it. They'd sit up against each other, watching the river and all its changes and the sleet frosting its surface, and they'd pull into one dreary town after another, and you'd see the people standing on the platform, waiting to get on, with their briefcases and bags and newspapers, and then they'd get going again, past old brick buildings crammed up one after another, and the river had no color, like a very old person's eyes. Sometimes they'd go into the bathroom to fool around. They'd cling to each other as the world flashed by with that sound in your ears and your eyes shut so tight you can see inside your head.

One morning he woke up and looked over at her and she didn't look right and he pulled off the blanket and she was, like, naked and gray and really, really skinny, and this cold feeling went through him, and he thought she might be dead. It was like he saw her for the first time, who she really was, this drugged-out girl, this whore. All marked up. Purple bruises up her legs. She was a broken person. And he felt sickened. He felt so very sick. He just wanted to go home. He wanted his mother. He thought how nice it would be, just sitting in the kitchen doing nothing but looking out the window, smelling the coffee brewing. Just that alone would be enough.

This is the last time, he said to her. Then I'm leaving.

That's good. You should.

He reached for her hand and held it, and it was so cold.

Let's just have one more night, she said.

One more. And then I'm gone.

She talked about her stolen kid. How she could be rough with him, impatient. That night in the drugstore, she was in a bad mood, feeling sorry for herself on account of she was only eighteen and had a three-year-old who she had to feed and look after and even though she loved him it wasn't fair how he'd come to her and it made her angry.

She took her time, flipping through some magazines. She said she deserved it, someone taking him. She was a bad mother. And now she was rotting from the inside. It was her punishment. God hated her.

She had no fear of death, she told him. She courted it.

You saw the real world out on the ramp. You saw the people in their cars. In those few seconds when they'd pull up, waiting for the light to change. Most of them wouldn't look at you. Or if they did, it was with disdain. It hurt a little, their judgment. Like you were garbage.

Take the lady in the white Mercedes. Behind the tinted glass she was like an alien insect-goddess, the dragonfly sunglasses, the fake-golden hair, the Rolex shaking on her wrist as she brought an apple to her lips and bit into it, baring her perfect white teeth. It was a long light, and he had about four minutes to make an impression, and he bowed a little, like her servant, and she finally looked at him, rolled down her window, and tossed out the core. Get a job, she said, and drove away.

That was always their answer: get a job. Not a realistic solution for someone in his situation. That's what they didn't get. It wasn't just about getting enough money for a fix. It wasn't about the fucking drugs. That was all of it and none of it. That was just the mechanics of the problem. Because you changed, you went through a chemical metamorphosis that turned you into another species. And you weren't really human anymore. You required certain things to survive, to satisfy the host. Pain was your compass. It's what got you up every day. And for a few precious hours, after you used, you were well again. But then it came back. And it wanted more. It drove you to it. It was all you thought about. It was your salvation.

What people didn't understand was that—

This one priest drove up and held out a twenty and told him to get some breakfast with it, and Theo nodded and said, Bless you, Father (for I have sinned), and left the ramp and walked in the direction of the diner, fully intending to get a plate of eggs, home fries, toast, but he ran into Carmine, who hooked him up in the parking lot behind the OTB. They sat there in the car a long while with the cold air coming in through the busted sunroof, and you could hear the sound of running horses and the men shouting at the screens.

At some point he understood that Carmine was driving, and it was a long drive, and when he finally opened his eyes, it was almost dark, and he was still in the car in the passenger seat but it was parked someplace in the woods and he was alone. He could smell somebody's cigarette, and he sat up and rubbed his eyes and saw Carmine talking to this dude Cyrus, who everybody said was, like, a psychopath, and who kind of oversaw the hotel and had people doing things for him in exchange for dope, and they looked over at him, and then Carmine was coming back to the car. He opened the door on his side and told him to get out, they had a job to do, so he got out, even though he didn't want to, even though he wasn't feeling right, and they went together over to Cyrus, who was standing there by his van, smoking, and you could hear the cars speeding past on the highway, and it was an unsettling kind of sound that made him distantly fear for his life. Cyrus opened the back of his van and pulled off a tarp, and that's when he saw her. She was naked, rolled up in a shower curtain, and you could see the long blond hair streaming out. He felt the puke coming up and had to lean over, and Carmine laughed like an outlaw, like he'd been there, done it, and Theo was just a baby, a kind of innocent, which he was, and then Cyrus handed them each a shovel and told them to start digging.

Who is she?

Just some stupid girl.

In the car on their way back, Carmine held the wheel so hard his knuckles went sharp. They were on the highway somewhere, and there weren't any other cars, and the streetlamps flashed intermittently like strobe lights, and it felt like they'd been transported to another planet, a strange, terribly quiet place, and even the dark trees along the road seemed monstrous. He looked at his hands and saw that they were dirty, the dirt caked under his nails, and there was dirt on the legs of his jeans, and he slid his hand into his pocket and pulled out a handful of dirt and watched it sifting through his fingers, and there was dirt inside his shoes, and he could taste the dirt, gritty and strange, inside his mouth.

He started seeing this man everywhere, this same individual. He was an older man with gray hair and unsettling blue eyes. A watcher, he thought. Sometimes he had a camera with him. He'd hold it up now and then. It was hard to tell what he was photographing. The old buildings. The shiny black windows. The fucking drug addicts loitering on the corner like zombies, skinny and hunched over and staggering.

He saw him over by the river a couple times in his sailor coat, a skullcap pulled low over his eyebrows, like he was trying to blend in or disappear, take your pick.

Sometimes he thought about his mother when he looked up into the trees.

Rye

Later that afternoon, when the sky suddenly filled with sunshine, he saw Theo. He was standing alone on the corner near the underpass, holding up the sign. Rye started toward him, walking briskly. His chest felt tight, his breathing shallow. His mouth was dry.

The boy turned as he approached. His eyes were hooded. His skin was gray, a cluster of pimples on his forehead under a sheen of sweat. What's up, man?

You got any smokes?

Theo dug around in his too-loose jeans that were belted with a length of rope and pulled out a bag of Drum and some papers and handed them over to Rye. Help yourself.

Thank you. Rye started rolling a cigarette. He was stalling, trying to figure out what to say. *You're my son,* he wanted to shout. He wanted to put his arms around him and pull him off the street. But obviously he couldn't do any of those things.

When he finished rolling the cigarette, he handed the bag of tobacco and the papers back to Theo, then lit the cigarette and tried not to cough. He hadn't smoked in ten whole years. The boy watched him closely.

I've seen you around, he said.

Rye tried to hide his surprise. Have you?

You're too old to be out here.

I know it. It's a long story.

The boy looked at him. You got any drugs?

No, I got nothing.

I'm out here all day. Nobody gives me anything. The cars just—

I got a little money.

Yeah?

You want to eat?

No, I can't. I'm waiting for someone.

All right, then take this. Rye shook a few bucks out of his pocket.

Theo took it.

You all right?

What?

Out here.

Yeah, man, I'm good.

You can do better than this, can't you?

The boy looked at him.

You look like somebody who could do better.

You don't know me.

No, but I see you. That's what I do. I see people.

The boy stared right at him.

You got a home somewhere?

Theo shrugged.

You should go.

I can't.

Why not?

I just can't.

Rye nodded.

It's just, everything's different now.

I can understand that.

I screwed up.

Yeah? Everybody does.

No. Not like this.

I know how that feels, Rye said. I've made mistakes in my life. You feel like you can't go home. You can't face those people.

Theo nodded.

But I can tell you. Based on my own experience. The people who love you want you back. They'd rather forgive you than lose you.

No. I can't go back.

You can, he said. It'll be different than you think.

What do you mean, *different?*

You've been out here for a while, he said. You're stronger than you were.

Theo met his eyes. He was about to say something when a white van crawled toward them along the curb. That's my ride.

Don't get in, Rye muttered. You don't have to.

Theo looked him hard in the eye. Fuck off, man, he said.

The driver of the van rolled down his window. He had long yellow hair curled back behind his ears. Rye could see the girl in the passenger seat. Get on in, the man said to the boy. Today's your lucky day. I got you a present.

Theo glanced at Rye without expression, then opened the back of the van and climbed in.

The driver looked him over, his eyes twinkling with menace. Then he spit onto the asphalt and pulled out.

Rye watched the van weaving through traffic until it turned the corner and was gone.

When he got back to the room, he called her. He was shaking. I found him, he told her. We spoke.

What do you mean *you spoke?*

We had our first conversation.

Well, how is he? How does he look?

Kind of strung out.

Oh, God.

Then this van came along and picked him up.

What? A van? She was becoming hysterical. You let him get away?

There was nothing I could—

You let him get away!

Magda. Please listen to me.

She was crying now.

He's a grown man. It has to be his choice.

All right, she said, her voice barely audible. All right.

You have to trust me. I'm out here for you.

For me?

For us, he said. For Theo.

I'm sorry. I'm just so worried. I'm out of my mind—

I know. I understand. It's a very difficult situation.

They didn't speak for a long moment. He could hear the faintest sound of her breathing.

I miss you, she said. So much. I can't even tell you. It's like a pain in my stomach.

I know, he said, and said it again. I know.

When they hung up, he called Simone. She answered immediately, her voice tentative, defensive. Where are you? You okay?

Yes. I'm fine. Now he was regretting the call. How to explain where he was, this peculiar odyssey? I'm working on something important, he said. That's all I can tell you. I might need a few more weeks.

She didn't say anything.

Simone?

I was starting to think you were dead, she said.

Simone

She'd never mastered his language. That was the trouble. When they were together, they spoke in a broken tongue, imprecise, vague. Her husband wasn't a person of words, she knew. He relied on pictures, images, to communicate how he saw and felt. But that wasn't good enough anymore, not for her, not for either one of them.

You should have an ear for the person you love.

The semester was coming to a close. When she wasn't at the college, she was alone. She had started to write her own poems. She'd sit at the table, drinking wine, writing by hand, the dogs sleeping at her feet.

She went to yoga, which helped. She'd lie there on her mat with her eyes closed, breathing in. Breathing out.

A stack of mail sat on the kitchen table. Rye got so much mail, especially this time of year, that they'd given his assistant the task of opening it all, but now that Constance was home for the holidays, it was up to Simone. She made herself a cup of tea and sat down and began, using a silver letter opener that had been her father-in-law's. The holiday cards, which celebrated Hanukkah, Christmas, and Kwanza, were addressed to both of them, *Mr. and Mrs. Rye Adler,* but they were mainly for him, from editors at the magazines, and some of the actors and celebrities he'd photographed over the years. Included in the pile were several bills. Rye always paid them; in truth, she'd never paid much attention to where their money was going. She knew it was the consequence of a privileged upbringing. She'd simply never had to think about it, there was always enough. But she did happen to notice that their Visa bill this month seemed rather high. Upon further inspection, she found a suspicious charge for a night at the Sherry-Netherland Hotel in the city, plus room-service charges, on the nineteenth of December. She sat back in her chair and tried to think. It seemed odd to her, and she feared they'd been hacked, but then it occurred to her that Rye had left on that morning. It was possible he'd stayed there himself. Still, it seemed unusual. It was more than he liked to spend. On the rare occasion when he needed to stay over in the city, he preferred a tiny boutique hotel in the village, where they knew him and gave him a discount. He'd sometimes have a beer in the bar before going up to bed. He never ordered room service. Never.

She tried his phone and wasn't surprised when he didn't pick up.

Trust, she thought. She supposed trust was an issue in any marriage. She lingered on that thought a bit longer than she would have liked.

It wouldn't hurt to have a look in his studio.

She plunged her feet into her Muck boots and put on her coat and tramped through the snow to the carriage house. It was very windy, and the branches glittered with ice. She thought of herself up here all alone in the cold and early dark. She hated winter.

She rarely entered Rye's studio. He never said as much, but it felt like sacred territory. She didn't necessarily like him going into her office either. But this was different. This felt necessary. She sat down at his desk and opened his laptop and checked his online calendar, but in truth Rye rarely wrote things down, let alone on his computer. He wasn't good at keeping track of dates. Often spurned friends and editors would call, irate when he'd forgotten a lunch, a drink. I keep everything up here, he told her, tapping his forehead. You want to know something, you're going to have to put me under and open me up.

He wasn't kidding. And opening up to her especially was something her husband rarely did. She didn't think it was deliberate; when his own memory failed him, he counted on Constance to keep track of things. And now Constance wasn't here and wouldn't be back till after New Year's.

Simone stared at the screen. She wasn't good at computers. She clicked on his Chrome history for the past month. There wasn't much that stood out. But then, scrolling down the list, she saw a familiar name. Magda Pasternak.

She sat there a minute just looking at it, her heart quickening.

He'd googled her on December 18, the day after he'd gotten back from Tokyo. It didn't mean anything, she told herself. Googling somebody wasn't against the law. She herself had googled people numerous times. Old boyfriends, the new professor, Caspar Ahmadi, his wife the oncologist. It wasn't unusual to google people you were interested in learning more about. But Magda wasn't people.

Had he stayed there, at the hotel—with her? Was it possible?

Had they been there together? Were they having an affair?

All those texts! Of course they were!

A familiar anger rushed back to her. She'd known it the day she'd met Magda, and she knew it now, still, after all these years.

She couldn't bear it. Magda—the fantasy of her—existed in the vague atmosphere of uncertainty that had remained between them like a curse.

Simone shook her head, annoyed with herself. What a fool she was! What did their marriage even mean?

Now that she thought about it, they spent more time apart than together. He'd go off on assignment doing God knows what, and she'd stay home, devoted as a house cat, waiting for the sound of his truck on the gravel.

She went back to the house, climbed the stairs, and got into bed. She was too angry to cry. She lay there, watching the treetops, hearing the wrangling chimes. Was he? she thought. With her? After all these years?

She switched on the TV and stared at it with vague interest. They were showing the melting ice cap. They were showing the fires in the Amazon. The images were frightening, but she couldn't quite process the fact that this was the beginning of the end. She didn't want to believe it. The earth had been ravaged. And yet—yet—there was so much beauty.

So much beauty, she thought, and wrote the words on a scrap of paper, entwining the letters with tiny leaves.

When she woke, the room was dark. She sat up, a little disoriented—and then remembered. The department holiday party was tonight, she had to go. Most of her colleagues would be there with their spouses. It was hard to go to these things alone, and she was getting tired of always having to explain Rye's absence. She thought of Caspar Ahmadi, the last time she saw him in the faculty dining room, how he'd insisted they sit together and had given her a copy of his book, signing it in perfectly legible script—unlike her husband's impatient scrawl. Rye's signature could defy detection, a refusal to claim the moment, perhaps, to recognize its importance in the scheme of things, leaving no discernible trace of his authentic self. At this very moment, that seemed significant to her.

She put on a skirt and blouse and a long black sweater and dabbed her lips with gloss. She chose the garnet earrings Rye had given to her on her last birthday and slid on her rings. Standing at the mirror, she wondered if people perceived her differently now that she was going gray. She could still see her old self in her reflection, the clever, seductive, impulsive, powerful Simone. You're still in there, she declared.

On the drive over to campus, she determined that she had no business feeling sorry for herself. Since childhood she'd lived a privileged life—private schools, country clubs, summer camp in the Berkshires. Her grandparents' home in Stockbridge. She'd met Rye her senior year at Barnard. They started off as friends. They had similar backgrounds, although her family was more progressive than his. They were both Jewish; his family was Conservative, hers Reform. Unlike some of the other boys she'd dated, Rye liked that she was as smart as him, smarter, he always said. By then she was nearly fluent in two languages. Rye admired her parents, who'd risen from nothing. He liked their brownstone in Park Slope, their famous art collection, which included works by Chagall, Soutine, and Munch. They were philanthropic, devoted to certain causes. He liked that Simone knew the city, people of influence. She knew how to dress, how to eat, how to write a thank-you note. She was unafraid at parties. They'd met that first time at Edmund's, a dark little bar on 110th Street where all the writers and artists went. She liked to sit alone at a table in the back with one of her poetry books—someone complex and riveting, like Yeats—and nurse a glass of whiskey. Rye and his friends, five or six of them, would stand at the bar, inevitably arguing some obscure photography topic. They had a certain tony nonchalance, with their sly, covert glances, flaunting their cameras like expensive jewelry. Rye stood out—those blue eyes, for starters. He had this aura about him, fearlessly open to life. He would talk to anyone. He was taller than the others and sort of loomed over the bar and wore these great vintage shirts from the forties. When he caught her staring, he walked right over.

I'm pretty sure I know you, he said.

That's so original.

No, I'm serious. I never forget a face.

Please don't tell me you're a writer.

Actually I'm a photographer.

Well, then, you're forgiven.

They looked at each other a moment.

Is it really true that you never forget a face?

Not one like yours.

She smiled. It was a good line.

I'm Denis Adler, he said, and reached for her hand. People call me Rye.

Like the whiskey?

It's a family name. What's yours?

Simone.

Simone. That's beautiful. His eyes took her in. It suits you.

She'd never thought of herself as beautiful. She was from a family of intellectuals where physical appearance was less important than the beauty of the mind, but she had what her mother called good features, a good profile, with her thick nearly black hair, her gray eyes, her wide mouth. She had a burning desire to write and dressed like the poets she loved, in black turtlenecks and jeans, heavy strands of amber beads, earrings from India that she bought on the street, pale pink lipstick. Her long hair twisted up in a leather clip.

They talked about their work, their dreams. She told him she was an English major, minoring in French. I wanted to be a poet, she said. But my parents talked me out of it.

That's too bad.

It's not lucrative enough to support my habits.

Most worthy things aren't.

I've been doing some translating. I'm kind of obsessed with Baudelaire at the moment. I guess maybe I'm too afraid to write my own poems.

You don't look like you're afraid of anything.

Of course I am. Certain things terrify me.

He looked at her with interest but didn't ask what they were. I've never met a poet, he said.

Well, there's a first for everything.

What's it like?

Quiet, she said. I do a lot of thinking.

And I can tell you're very good at it.

She always knew she would marry him. He had the qualities she was looking for. She didn't want someone hovering over her—she cherished her independence. They dated on and off. She was just beginning her PhD at Columbia when Rye moved to Philadelphia for the Brodsky Workshop. It was a time of growth for both of them, and they saw each other infrequently.

She knew about Magda. She knew the minute she met her. How he'd look at her as if his eyes were nibbling up her beauty as they roamed around her face.

It was the big show at the end of the year. She'd taken the train down from the city. He was living with Julian Ladd. Julian was a sort of nerd genius, strangely quiet, always watching them. To be fair, all the Brodsky people were a little odd. Photographers were their own special species, she often thought. When it came right down to it, they were unapologetic voyeurs. She remembered that night vividly—the gallery, the excitement in the room, a celebration of all that talent—and meeting Magda for the first time.

She was an unusual girl. Not the sort who had girlfriends. Tough. Competitive. Carnal. She had interesting looks, pale, Eastern Bloc, a sort of ravishing intelligence. Her ponderous gaze was difficult to interpret; Simone could tell she rarely shared her true feelings. She used her hands when she spoke, as if she hadn't quite mastered the language, when in fact she spoke perfect English with the trace of a Polish accent. She was a little taller than Simone, and strong, she had a certain grace, a certain presence. She drew glances as she crossed the room, the tight black jeans, the pendulous breasts under a black ILFORD T-shirt, the black boots. Her wrists shackled with bracelets. She was purposeful, direct. She claimed the space around her like the beloved statue in a small town.

This is my fiancée, Rye told her. This is Simone.

It was only because she detected Magda's attraction to him that Simone caught her reaction, like she'd been singed.

As she shook Simone's hand with her damp fingertips, she tilted her head and sized up her competitor, instantly determining that Simone was not a threat. She had a cold vibe, Simone thought. Painfully ambitious.

Rye toured her around the gallery. Simone could remember thinking how incredible all the photographs were, how distinctly each photographer saw the world. Magda's shots of the streets of her neighborhood, most of immigrant women and children, were at once edgy and poignant, very feminist, and Simone regretted her initial dislike of her. Magda did with housewives and teenage girls what Arbus had done with social outcasts.

She's the Helen Levitt of our class, Rye said. Simone wasn't sure if he meant it as a compliment—what she found out later about Rye was he didn't give compliments. He never let on what he really thought about someone's work. She once asked him why, and he said if he told people the truth, they'd never speak to him again. She quickly came to realize that when it came to photography, Rye Adler, with all his collegial modesty, was the most competitive person she'd ever known.

He took her hand and led her to the next series of prints. These are mine, he said.

There were early versions of the iconic images that would later make him famous, a waitress, a bank teller, a gravedigger, an EMT, a cop, shot in the rich, majestic colors of a Caravaggio painting, their faces, often lit from above, observed with a mesmerizing detachment that felt strangely intimate.

Oh, Rye. They're beautiful.

Do you really think so?

Truly. They're incredible.

The question is, do they make you feel something?

She studied the faces. I don't know if I'd necessarily notice some of these people on the street. But here, you really see them. You see their humanity, their dignity.

He smiled and seemed satisfied with her analysis. The face is a map, he said. It can tell you everything. You just have to know how to read it.

She thought about those words for a long time, years. She often wondered what he saw in her face—how he read her. He rarely looked at her anymore.

It was noisy in the gallery that night, and people were drinking up the cheap wine, and a few important-looking people started talking to Rye about his work. She drifted away, drawn to some photographs across the gallery in a clearly less desirable location, and she had them to herself. They were pictures of lonesome places, empty city lots, boarded-up buildings. They had a certain poetic stillness, she thought, as if the places were waiting for something, she couldn't say what. Just waiting.

Those are my roommate's, Rye said, coming up behind her. Don't try to psychoanalyze them. You won't get very far.

I sort of like them, she said. They convey a kind of existential despair.

You're reading too much into them.

I think they're interesting.

Trust me, they're not.

For the first time, she detected a rivalry between the two men. One she knew not to mention. Whenever she teased Rye about being competitive, he always supplied the same answer: He didn't compete with anyone but himself. Moreover, he didn't begrudge anyone's success. But deep down she knew he had savage instincts when it came to his profession, whereby he'd push himself harder than his colleagues to get better results. But in this particular case, she doubted that Julian had anything over Rye. They had, it seemed, very different interests, at least when it came to photography. So if it wasn't the work, what, then?

Okay, she said, I'll trust you.

But he had already forgotten their conversation and was staring at something across the crowded room. She followed his gaze and saw Julian standing with Magda, conversing intently, his hand perched on her arm, his face alight with a shy, nearly desperate desire that, when she looked back at Rye, matched his own.

All these years later, Magda was still the proverbial thorn in her side. Simone would never forgive Rye for taking that photograph of her in her mother's kitchen. How she'd studied it compulsively, comparing her body to Magda's, her breasts, which were considerably larger than Simone's and asserted a certain sexual heft.

She couldn't reveal her feelings to him. She didn't want to sound like a jealous wife. That was beneath her. And yet she was. She was seething with jealousy.

Five years into their marriage, when Rye was offered his first major exhibition, that photograph was the first one you saw when you entered the gallery. She'd asked him not to show it. You know how I feel about her, she'd admitted. Rye was indignant. The photograph was nothing more than an academic exercise, and its subject meant nothing to him. Nothing, he'd repeated with emphasis. But even then she knew.

Because Magda had meant something. And still did.

They'd argued. Simone refused to go to the opening.

This is my work, Simone. I can't be worried about hurting your feelings every time I take a shot of a naked girl. It's my *work*, he insisted. It has nothing to do with us!

It wasn't true. She realized that now. It had everything to do with them.

Now that she thought of it, that shot of Magda had been personal. It hurt her feelings. She envied the rapt attention he'd given to her in those few hours—it seemed more potent somehow than her own time with him. And right or wrong, she'd never forgiven him.

In truth, from the very beginning, things hadn't really been right, even though everything had appeared to be perfect—their wedding that summer on a flower farm up in Chatham, gerbera daisies big as pinwheels on all the white tablecloths, lanterns in the grass; they'd danced barefoot to the band as the dark blue sky filled with stars. But even then—even that night—he seemed distracted. Like in his mind he was somewhere else—with her.

He left a few days later, excited about his first real job. She'd gone back to the city, to their new place on Leroy Street. Rye was traversing the Horn of Africa when a certified letter was delivered to the apartment. My husband is out of the country, she told the letter carrier. I'm his wife.

That'll do, he said, and handed her the pen.

It was an ecru envelope, expensive stationery. The return address bore the initials M.P. and a PO box in Port Richmond, PA. Simone carried it to the kitchen table. She brought it to her nostrils, imagining, perhaps, the scent of some exotic perfume, but the paper was odorless. She instinctively knew, as all women understand such things, that its contents had not been intended for her eyes and that there were laws and protections in place to prevent people from opening mail that did not belong to them. Most people, anyway.

Not wives. Wives were immune from the law.

The eggnog was spiked, and she drank too much of it. Caspar offered to drive her home. She told him no, she would sleep on the couch in her office. Well, let me at least walk you there, he insisted, taking her arm, and they set out across the cold, wet campus, talking sporadically about the situation of poetry, how so few people were reading it these days, and although he knew it shouldn't matter—it wasn't why he was writing, it wasn't the thing driving him—it somehow did matter, it was a commentary on the times, and he sometimes wondered why he continued, who he thought he was, putting these words down on the page when nobody really cared, he should have done something really useful and become a doctor like his wife, and she argued that people did care, and his poems mattered to them, and his words ran like water through their brains as they slept, like water over sand, over the shells and stones, and they thought about his poems the next day, even if they were doing something mundane, like shopping at the supermarket, his words were still in their head, and perhaps they even influenced how they thought and saw the world. That's when he took her hand. The building was dark and silent. Inside her office, he turned on the small lamp on her desk, and a pleasing orange glow filled the room. The big square window was very black and put her in mind of death, and she told him so. He sat with her a moment on the brown couch, and she could smell his lovely aftershave, and their hands touched accidentally on the cushion, and then she did something she would regret in the morning: she kissed him. He handled it well—she imagined women were always throwing themselves at him—and said to her, gently, that as much as he admired her and indeed felt attracted, it would never occur to him to betray his wife. This alone was humiliating, for she had indulged in the probability of his desire and wrongly assumed that he would be willing to set aside his morals for the chance to—

Caspar, she said, utterly embarrassed. Forgive me. It's just I've—

He favored her with compassion. No need to explain. And I am flattered.

She smiled. Thank you. And this is why you're such a fine writer. You have empathy even for me, and I deserve none of it.

Oh, that's not true, Simone. I see you as a very independent woman. But you are alone a lot, are you not? With your husband traveling so much. You have every right to be lonely.

He watched her with care and said, finally, I will pray for you. That you will come into some new and profound awareness.

She sat there, unmoving, with her hands clasped in her lap, projecting the timid grace of a condemned woman.

He rose. Good night, Simone.

Good night.

Her cheeks were very hot, her heart pumping, pumping the fresh new blood of longing.

It was dawn when she woke on the couch and slipped out of the building in her torn stockings and stupidly high heels and hurried across campus to her car. Even though nothing had happened, she felt tawdry and cheap. Luckily no one saw her. The dogs were waiting for her when she got home, and she fed them and exchanged her shoes, which had given her a blister, for her cold boots and pulled on one of Rye's old coats that smelled like him and filled her with such a deep, lonesome hunger, and they went out into the field under the falling snow and slowly climbed the great hill, the dogs sensing, in the way dogs do, that they shouldn't run off and leave her, that she needed them there, right by her side.

Rye

The girl was standing on the curb with her sign. The light was red. He was waiting behind two other cars, too far away to speak to her, and when the light finally changed, he rolled up to her and put his window down. Excuse me, he said, and the car behind him started honking.

Unperturbed, the girl looked at him, slouching, smoking.

I'll pay you for your time. I just want to talk.

You a cop?

No, I'm not a cop.

The car behind him swerved around him, blaring its horn, the driver cursing out his window.

How much?

You tell me. Let me buy you breakfast, and we can figure it out. What do you say? Aren't you hungry?

I guess.

Get on in.

Unhurriedly, she walked around the front of his truck and opened the door and climbed up onto the seat. She held her sign on her lap, her fingers curled tightly around the cardboard.

I'm Rye Adler. I'm not from around here. And I'm hungry. You know a good place we can get some breakfast?

Go up there and take a right, she said.

It was a diner on Central Avenue, across from the Golden Cue, a pool hall. Don't see many of those anymore, he said.

Do you play?

Back in the day, he said.

They took a booth by the window. Order whatever you want, he said.

She stared at the menu.

A waitress came over to take their order. I'll have the poached eggs, he told her, with whole wheat toast and home fries.

You can get bacon for an extra dollar.

All right.

You, ma'am?

Can I please have the special with the eggs and pancakes?

Of course you can. I'll be right back with your coffee.

Up close she was very pale, her eyes like crushed glass. They were rimmed in black pencil, her lashes thick with mascara. What's your name?

Enid's my given name, she said.

That's an old name, isn't it?

Yes, sir. It was my grandma's. But most people call me True.

Why's that?

She shrugged. It just sort of stuck.

Where you from?

From right here. We moved upstate when I was thirteen. I came back five years ago.

She looked at him warily, and he could see in that moment the troubled history she'd left behind. It's a big state, isn't it?

Yes, sir.

Well, I'm a photographer. It's what I do.

The girl gazed at him thoughtfully. What kinds of pictures do you take?

All kinds. I'd like to take yours if you'll let me.

She frowned. Why would you want to do that?

Because you're beautiful, he said.

She allowed herself to smile. I used to be prettier, she said.

The waitress brought over the coffee. They watched her pour it into their cups. Your food'll be right out.

Thank you, he said.

He poured cream into his coffee. She drank hers black and added three sugars. Her fingers shook a little, and some of the sugar sprinkled onto the table. Using the wrapper, she swept it into a little pile, her fingernails grimy with dirt.

She glanced out a moment at the street. It was the morning rush hour, and you could see the cars reflected in the dark windows of the pool hall. The shades were pulled low now. It looked like an Edward Hopper painting.

She'd been in there one time, she told him, but they made her leave. Sometimes, when it wasn't too cold, she'd stand at the window, big as a movie screen, watching the pool hustlers. She liked that sound when the balls hit. It was the sound of a yes.

The waitress brought over the food and set it carefully on the table. The girl sat there, looking at it. There were three pancakes stacked up and two fried eggs and bacon. The waitress set down two small plates of buttered toast. That should do it, she said.

Thank you, ma'am, the girl said.

You're welcome, hon.

Carefully, she took her napkin and set it on her lap. Then she doused her pancakes with syrup. She picked up her silverware and carefully cut a pancake into pieces, then forked a bite into her mouth. It's good, she said.

Mine too, he said.

They ate. He pushed his toast into his eggs and scooped them into his mouth. When his plate was clean, he sat back and watched her eat.

She ate slowly, like she was savoring every bite. She had good manners; he could tell someone had raised her right. I wasn't always like this, she told him.

You got family around here?

My mother. She's up near Seneca Lake. But we're— She shook her head. We're not on speaking terms.

You got a father?

Gone. Left when I was little. Savore was his name. He sold things out of his suitcase. I can remember this old brown case sitting there in the hall. One time he gave me a bar of soap and told me it was lavender. I used to keep it under my pillow. He said it would make me sleepy.

Did it?

What?

Make you sleepy?

She smiled. I don't remember. Maybe.

Can I ask your age?

Twenty.

That's not very old.

I've lived a hundred years, she told him.

I believe you have, he said.

She smiled a little. I can't stay here too long.

We can go whenever you say.

The waitress came around and refilled their coffee cups. I'll be right back with your check.

This is really good, the girl told her.

I'm glad you're enjoying it, hon.

The girl sat back. Well, I'm full.

Can I ask you something?

Sure.

How much you make out there in a day?

On the ramp? Sometimes fifteen dollars.

I'm looking for somebody, he said. He's been out on that ramp.

She sat up a little taller and pushed her hair back over her ears. Who is it?

He took out his phone and showed her the photo of her and Theo.

She blinked, surprised. When did you take that?

I didn't. Somebody else did.

Her eyes glittered, and she crossed her arms over her chest.

I know it must be weird to see yourself on a stranger's phone, he said.

Yeah, it is. She looked at him hard. I have no idea where he is.

But they both knew this wasn't true.

Look, I really need your help. He took out his wallet and started counting out twenties. You just tell me when to stop.

She watched him. She put her hand on his. That'll do, she said, and took his money.

The waitress came over with the check. You folks need anything else?

No, ma'am. Thank you.

I'm going to use the restroom, the girl said.

I'll be right outside. Take your time.

He paid the check and laid a tip on the table, then went out to the truck. It was cold, and flurries twirled down like confetti. He started the engine and sat there waiting. He was starting to think she'd given him the slip when he saw her coming out.

Sorry, she said, climbing into the truck. She smelled like roses. She held her hand up to his nose. Nice, right. They have a very clean bathroom.

Glad to hear it.

Thank you for the meal.

No problem at all.

You want one? Her palm was full of wrapped candy suckers.

No, thank you.

She unwrapped one and put it in her mouth. I'm sick, she said. I've got to get back to my room.

I'll take you there.

She directed him through the city. They turned down Ontario Street. She pointed to a large yellow house with a front porch. I used to live there with my little boy.

That's a big old elephant, isn't it?

It was nice, she said. It's all apartments. We were on the top floor.

Why'd you move out?

Money, she said.

I didn't know you had a son.

Not anymore. She opened her window a little and put her face up to the wind. It sure is cold out. The snow makes everything pretty.

Yes, it sure does.

They drove in silence, and he told her he'd seen Theo getting into a white van.

Cyrus, she said. We work for him. He's the one made me go to that party over at the university. I didn't want to. But he said it was good for business. He said he'd hurt me if I didn't.

Has he hurt you before?

She nodded her head quickly, like whatever he'd done was too awful to say out loud.

Is he a veteran? I saw a sticker on his van.

She shook his head. He bought that van used. That was somebody else. He said when the cops see it, they don't bother him.

Is that so.

He said he could track me to the ends of the earth if he wanted to.

Do you believe that?

She nodded. He's a bad person. But I can't seem to get away from him.

He knows how to keep you close.

Uh-huh. I know it.

Maybe one day you'll just walk away.

She glanced over at him.

One day, he said. When you're ready.

They were downtown near the river. You could see the factories in the distance, the large blue-and-white oil drums, and the long freight trains waiting on the tracks.

Sometimes I feel so small, she said. I'm just a speck of dirt.

That's not the girl I see, he told her.

She showed him where to turn, and they entered a desolate parking lot alongside the river. It was an old carnival site, a mile of pocked asphalt. The rides were rusted and broken. Like some garish art installation, he thought. You could see the sun glinting off the Ferris wheel, the metal seats rocking in the wind. She showed him where to park, and they got out.

Lock your truck, she said.

He followed her. They came to an old footbridge. There was a rope blocking its entrance and a sign swinging in the wind: NATURE PRESERVE CLOSED.

Come on, she said. It's just over this bridge.

Sure is high, he said. He leaned over the railing and looked down into the water. The water was black. He had the sudden memory of crossing a bridge as a boy, holding his father's hand. That sense of displacement he'd felt when he saw the rushing water beneath his feet.

At the end of it they stepped onto the land, an island of wilderness. I like it here, under the trees, she said. It's where I belong.

They started down a trail. She pointed out the signs to the nature preserve, but it appeared to be nothing more than trails through the woods. As they walked, you could hear the ancient trees bending, the cries of the crows. And you could hear the river.

That sound, she said. It's like the inside of a dream.

They came to a high chain-link fence scrambled in vines of twisted overgrowth. NO TRESPASSING signs stuck in the snow like markers at an accident site. Someone had cut an opening in the fence. They stepped through it, and there it was, the ruined fortress.

What is this place?

Used to be a hotel back in the day. Like a fancy resort. It's been closed since the seventies. There's other people here like me. Sleepwalkers, she said. Shadow people. Tweakers.

What about Theo?

He'll be here, she said with confidence. Later, when it gets dark.

She took his hand and looked at him with a sort of hope and pushed aside the bramble, and they stepped into what was once the lobby of this grand hotel. Under the dirt and scattered trash were the original marble tiles, and the reception desk was mahogany with a thick marble top. A grand oil painting hung over the fireplace—it might have been a Thomas Cole—and there were a couple chairs that had been slashed with a knife, the stuffing spilling out.

Up here, she said.

The stairs were mahogany too, with a red runner that continued down the long hallway lined with doors. True had claimed a room, with a bare mattress on the wood floor in the middle of it. In here, she said. Only there's no toilet, so.

So, I go outside if nature calls.

Yes, sir.

Sunlight streamed in through the window, motes of dust. You could see the scars of time on the old plaster walls. He took out his camera and started shooting: the broken windows, the stained mattress, an altar of sorts she'd made out of cardboard for her little boy with flowers and rainbows drawn on it. There were a few pictures of the child, a three-year-old in a Rangers T-shirt. That's my son, she said. Bodie.

What happened to him?

She sat there, staring into her hands.

Was he sick?

She shook her head. Somebody—

Somebody what?

T-T-Took him, she stuttered.

Took him?

She nodded.

You mean, like, stole him?

She dropped her head. I need to—

Go ahead. Do what you need to do.

I'm an—

I know what you are, he said softly.

She had a fresh syringe from the needle exchange. She said she didn't want to fix in front of him. She went into the bathroom and closed the door.

He waited. He felt somehow at a loss.

She came out and shuffled toward the mattress, her face like a blur.

Let me just lie down here a minute, she said.

Go ahead.

She dropped down to her knees. Somebody…took…took him, she mumbled, falling into darkness, her waiting grave.

Theo

He woke sick in a bus shelter. He was alone.

It was very dark, and he was scared. He was cold. He was shaking.

He was near the end. He knew it.

He didn't want to, but he knew he would.

He had lost himself, his soul. It had climbed out of him when he was sleeping and now he was soulless.

He pulled himself to his feet and started walking. He could feel the wake of passing cars, the road trembling beneath his feet. The streetlights with their bright, round faces. He walked for a long time.

Carmine's mother answered the door. She was wearing black. She had a cold look on her face, and she didn't invite him in. There were other people inside, some speaking Italian, and he thought he heard someone crying.

Is Carmine—

No, he's not here, Theo, she said.

He couldn't look at her.

We found him this morning. He's gone.

Gone?

Dead.

His head started to pound. I'm—

Please, she said. Don't come here no more.

Theo shook his head; he couldn't seem to breathe. Tears rolled down his cheeks. Carmine's father appeared behind her. Go home, Theo, he said. Go home and get some help.

He closed the door and turned off the light.

Theo stood there in the dark. He could hear the dogs on the street, barking like crazy, and it was the sound of his own anguish, and he started walking, and they kept on barking and didn't stop even when he got to the end of the long street and turned onto the main road.

Rye

He waited there in the girl's room for Theo to show up and finally fell asleep. When he woke on the wood floor, it was just getting light. His back hurt and he was very stiff. He felt tired, intensely drained. He wanted nothing more than to leave this place.

He thought distantly of Magda, her breath on his neck.

A little desperately he felt his hunger for her.

Outside, the sky was white. He glanced at his watch. It was almost seven.

He looked over at the mattress. She was sleeping, curled up on her side, and in that moment he could see the child in her. He found his camera, a little amazed no one had stolen it, and rolled onto his knees like a man praying and got to his feet. He framed his shot and took the picture. She didn't move.

He looped his camera around his shoulder. He had to piss. He staggered out into the hall and down the stairs. He passed the open door of another room, a man asleep on the floor, the torn shade banging, banging.

He stepped outside and relieved himself under the wild trees. The cold air revived him. He could hear a passing train and tried to orient himself. He made his way around the outside of the place, stepping into the footsteps of strangers. He didn't see anyone.

Once, as a boy, he'd stayed in a hotel like this. It was winter vacation. His parents had taken him to the Catskills. He remembered the food: iceberg lettuce served in fancy iced bowls, herring, jellied pike, shrimp cocktail, consommé. For dessert, Baked Alaska and Cherries jubilee, seven-layer cake. Food nobody served now. There was skiing and sledding and skating, great, crackling bonfires, sing-alongs. They dressed for dinner; he wore his bar mitzvah suit. He sat at the table, watching his parents dance to the orchestra. After dinner, they saw a show—it was *Carousel,* he recalled—in the small, rustic theater. It was a place just like this, an iconic resort now in ruins. He knew there were others. When you traveled in Europe and Greece and the Middle East, you saw ruins of stone castles, churches. These were American ruins. They represented a way of life that had lost its relevance.

He wandered the rooms of the first floor. He'd never seen such extravagant decay, walls swarming with graffiti, hallways obstructed with trash. Sleeping drifters curled up in the corners. It was like the set of a horror movie, he thought. Only this was real.

He came to a large solarium with an empty pool, its cement bottom covered in more graffiti. Declarations of war and freedom, solidarity built on scandal, propaganda. There were few original thoughts left, he realized.

Across the empty pool he saw a boy sitting alone, hunched over on a metal folding chair. Watching him, he felt a kind of hopelessness. It slowly occurred to him that it was Theo.

Hearing his approach, the boy stirred and sat up. You've been following me, he said. He gave him a questioning frown. What do you want?

Nothing. True is a friend.

She doesn't have any friends.

Theo took out his bag of tobacco and rolled a cigarette and licked its edge, then put it between his lips and lit it. He surveyed Rye from top to bottom. You're still here, he said.

Yup.

You got any heroin?

He shook his head.

Didn't think so. You do her?

True? No.

Everybody does, he said. Eventually. She gives in easy.

She's a good person, Rye said, and he believed she was.

Theo snorted. Yeah, she is. She's also a fucking dope fiend. Sit down, man, you're making me nervous. I thought you were a cop.

Nope. Not a cop. Rye looked around for another folding chair and pulled one over and sat down.

Then what are you doing here, man?

Do you really want to know?

Theo stared at him uneasily.

Rye met his eyes. Looking for you, he said.

What? He'd heard him.

That's right.

What for?

Because you're important to me.

Oh, man—

Theo started to stand.

I don't mean you any harm, Rye calmly explained. My name is Rye Adler. I'm your father.

Theo stared at him. He sat back down. He blinked.

For a very brief period of time I was in love with your mother. And you were a product of that love. I didn't know about you. I was already far away from her. I was out of the country, watching a beautiful place be destroyed. Just like I'm watching you now. Watching you destroy yourself.

The boy gave him a cold look.

I didn't know about her. I didn't know she was carrying you. We'd had something powerful together, and it was great, but we were young and had things to do. We went our separate ways. And I can't say, even if I did know about you, that I would have changed anything. That's the honest truth. Money, maybe. I would have sent her money. It wasn't fair to her. And I regret that. I regret it deeply. But sometimes you can make a mistake and it has an effect on others, and you don't realize it at the time because you're too absorbed in your own life, your own troubles, and your own victories, those too. Those are even more dangerous.

What do you mean?

Success can be isolating. People tend to back away. They think you're too good for them. So they leave you alone.

The boy looked at him without judgment.

This, he said. This life here. Is it what you want?

Yeah, Theo said. It's what I want.

Okay.

Okay what?

Rye shook his head like he didn't care. I didn't come here to tell you how to live your life.

Oh. Well, that's a relief. He took a final drag, then dropped the cigarette on the floor and ground it out with his sneaker. I get it. I see what's going on here. It's her, right? Magda.

Rye waited.

She sent you in here.

What if she did?

Theo shrugged. I don't know. She told me about you. You're the photographer.

That's right.

And you came all this way to take my picture. Well. Isn't that something? Go ahead. Go on and take it.

Not interested.

No?

Not like this.

Why not? This is the real me. It's what you want, isn't it? The truth? That's what you're after, according to my mother. The truth will set you free and all that bullshit.

She's right, it will. I've come to that conclusion.

Go ahead and take it. I want you to.

They looked at each other. Rye took off his lens cap and held up the camera. Smile, he said.

And Theo did. An unexpected and genuine smile.

Thanks, Rye said.

Feel better?

Yes, actually, I do. It's good to have a picture of my son.

Theo shook his head. Who are you, man?

Good question. I've been trying to figure that out. It occurred to me over these past few days that I've been sort of hiding in my life, you know. For, like, a really long time. And years have passed. But you can't do that out here, can you? You can't hide.

Theo thought for a minute. No, I guess you can't.

I realized that nobody really knows me. My wife—

What about my mother?

Rye looked down at his own hands. He closed his eyes. I'm not sure.

Do you still love her?

Very much, he said.

They sat there a minute without talking. The windows went bright with the winter sun.

Look, give me your hand.

What for?

I just want to hold it, I guess. Is that okay?

Theo looked at him with suspicion and seemed to decide it was all right. He offered his hand. It wasn't really a boy's hand. It was cold and rough and dirty.

You're cold.

Always. He looked Rye right in the eye. Didn't she tell you? I'm already dead. This is just a dream. You can wake up and leave anytime you want.

Why are you so scared?

The boy pulled his hand away as if he'd touched a flame. I'm not.

Oh, you're pretty fucking terrified.

Theo stared at him, his eyes raw, determined. What the fuck do you care?

Rye said nothing.

You think you can just come in here, just step into this shit?

That's right, Rye said. That's exactly what I think.

You're wasting your time.

Good to know.

I know what you want, and you're not getting it.

Tell me what I want.

Theo stared at his hands. I can't be that. I can't be that person. Not for you.

Okay, Rye said gently.

You don't deserve me.

No, I don't. You're right. But it's not a good reason not to stop.

What do you think, I'm stupid?

No, I know you're not.

I tried to stop. A couple times. I couldn't take it. There's this voice in your head, see. It drives you fucking crazy. It's like you're not even in control.

That sounds really hard.

Yeah. It is.

But there are worse things. Tell me this. I'm just trying to understand. Did something bad happen to you?

What?

Were you, like, abused or something? Or bullied? Something with a girlfriend? Did you, like, fail a class?

Theo shook his head. Nope.

What about your mother—did she hurt you somehow?

No. Never.

What about Julian?

You mean my stand-in dad?

I mean your father. Is he a good father?

Better than you.

Rye nodded. All right. Good. I feel like we're getting somewhere.

Theo snorted a laugh. Yeah, we're getting somewhere, all right. But to answer your question, there wasn't any reason I can think of. Nothing I can put into words, anyway. No big bones in my closet. You do it once, twice. It rolls up on you. The only reason you do it is because it feels good. In fact—

Theo started to roll up his sleeve.

Please don't, Theo.

Give me one good reason.

Rye sifted through a hundred answers in his mind. Because I'm here, he said. It came out sounding lame. Because I'm here with you.

But Theo was already engaged in the procedure, tapping powder into a spoon. You're too late, man, he said. You're too fucking late.

Rye rose to his feet. All right. Then what should I tell her?

The boy flicked his lighter and held it under the spoon. Tell her whatever you want. I don't really give a shit.

I don't believe that.

That's your choice, man. You want to believe I'm better than this. Right?

I know you are.

Well, you would be wrong.

He drew the murky liquid up into the needle. It looked like burnt butter. He glanced up at Rye before shooting it into his arm. This one's for you, Dad.

Rye watched the drug hit him, its effect languorous, torpid. He slumped down in the chair and closed his eyes, his arms crossed over his chest. He tilted his head just enough to crack open an eye and focus on him. He stared at Rye like that, like the one-eyed head of a squid, dumb, reeling.

He couldn't look. He rose to his feet. He wanted to leave. He turned toward the enormous room. He saw people lying against the walls, each in their own world. They were like travelers, victims of unforeseen delays, waiting to get somewhere.

Theo was breathing funny. His lips looked blue.

Theo? You don't look so good.

The boy said nothing.

Rye stood there, watching him closely. Theo? Theo, can you walk?

He slowly shook his head. Another minute passed before he fell to the floor.

Hey, he called to the room. Hey, I need some help!

Nothing. Not a sound.

Hey! Rye shouted. Anyone!

One of the skateboarders ambled over. He ain't gonna make it, man. Seen it a hundred times.

He will. Come on—grab his legs. I got a truck out there.

I can't, man. Wish I could.

Without giving it a thought, Rye punched the guy in the face. The guy cowered and winced. Hey! That wasn't—

Get the fuck out of here.

True appeared in the dark hallway. She hesitated like she was frightened, then ran over. She found a small plastic bag on the floor with a red flag on it, and her expression went dark.

This is…it's cut with Fentanyl— She shook her head helplessly.

Come on and help me. He gripped the boy under his arms, and the girl grappled with his legs. He was deadweight. Rye ended up dragging him most of the way. His head lolled from side to side. They were out in the cold, now, fighting the onslaught of branches. She dropped his feet and sank to her knees. I can't, she cried.

It's not that far, Rye said. Get up.

This is my fault. I can't—

But he grabbed her arm and pulled her up, light as paper. I'm tired of that word, stop using it.

Tears came to her eyes. She wouldn't look at him.

It's all right. Now get his feet. Come on, now. Help me.

She helped him to the bridge, up the steps, and then a power he'd never known came over him, and he hoisted the boy over his shoulder and ran with him in his arms. The truck was a hundred feet away. He could make it, he knew. And he did.

Get my keys, he said, and she groped inside his coat pocket. Open the door.

She did, and he set Theo on the passenger seat.

Get in, he said.

No. She backed away.

He looked at her a long moment.

I loved him, you know.

Did you?

Then he got into the truck and pulled out of there.

He drove with one hand and groped with the other to feel the boy's pulse. He couldn't find one.

He glanced at his face. He looked gone.

He followed the blue H signs. The hospital wasn't far, just a few miles. He pulled into Emergency and parked at the curb and got out, shouting like a crazy man. They came out with a gurney and pulled the boy out of the truck and laid him on it and rolled him inside.

Rye stood there.

A nurse came up to him. She wanted to know who he was.

I'm his father was all he said.

Theo

Theo awakened in a hospital bed, wearing one of those gowns and hooked up to an IV. He looked around, getting his bearings. He felt dead.

Fuck, he thought.

Adler was sleeping in a chair. Theo watched him. It was hard to get used to the idea that he was connected to this stranger. This stranger who had saved his life, he thought. Not that he wanted to be saved. It had been a stupid thing to do, shooting the heroin in front of him. He hadn't really needed to at that moment. It was just to show off. It was just to say *fuck off*. Adler was older than Julian by a couple years. Worn down. He looked like somebody who had walked through a strong wind. He watched the rise and fall of his chest. His gray hair was greasy. His hands as they lay in his lap were square and still. He had on an old gray sweater, unraveling along the hem.

He suddenly thought of True.

It was a good time to leave. He thought: I'll just pull this thing out of my arm and walk the fuck out of here. But then some guy in scrubs came in with a tray of food, and Adler woke up.

Hey, he said.

Hey.

You okay?

No.

Give it some time.

You should've left me alone.

I'm glad I didn't. Are you hungry?

No.

Have a little tea, maybe?

He hadn't eaten in what seemed like days, but he couldn't imagine eating now. I don't want anything, he said.

He wasn't thinking clearly. He only knew how he felt, like his insides were on fire. He yanked out the IV and his arm started bleeding. He wiped it away angrily and tried to stand. He was fine.

So, what now? Find the girl?

We're in love.

Are you?

What would you know about it—you fucked my mother over.

Maybe. But we're not talking about me here.

Fuck you. Go fuck yourself, Adler.

He found his clothes on the chair. They were dirty compared to the hospital gown. He put them on anyway. His father watched him.

Later, he said. And walked out.

He was like a criminal fleeing a crime scene, he thought. And it was an awfully long corridor. He was thinking, any minute somebody would come up and grab him and drag him back to the room and, like, put him in a straitjacket or something. But nobody did.

He had to wait for the elevator. It was really slow. He felt stupid standing there, his whole stupid life crashing down on him. Finally he heard the ding of the elevator, and the doors opened.

And there she was. Mom, he said.

It looked like she'd been crying a lot. He thought she was going to be mad, but she stepped out of the elevator and opened her arms. He let her hug him, and he found himself melting in her embrace like a little kid, and he started to cry, and he cried a lot, and it was all he wanted to do.

They went back to the room and he got back on the bed and his mother sat next to him and Adler was in the same chair as before and his mother took a sip of water and her hands were shaking and Adler reached out and took her hand and looked at her and it seemed like they had this silent language where neither of them had to speak and they were like communicating with their eyes and they just knew, you know, they just knew.

A nurse came in and showed her how to use Narcan, and his mother watched the woman's slim brown hands as she explained the steps. Then the nurse looked at Theo. Are you planning to go to rehab?

He glanced at his mother.

I called around, his mother said. They can't take him for three weeks.

The nurse nodded; she wasn't surprised.

We're going to do this on our own, his mother said.

The nurse looked at Theo. You okay with that?

He nodded.

Do you want Suboxone?

No, ma'am. No I don't.

Are you sure?

I'm gonna do this cold.

I believe that, the nurse said, and left.

After a while, the nurse came back in and checked his vitals and said he could go. By now it was dark and pretty late, although he couldn't say what time it was, and Adler helped them out to the parking lot to his mother's SUV. He handed her an old iron skeleton key and she held it in her hand and looked at him and wrapped her fingers around it. It's the only one I have, he said.

His mother nodded.

I'll be out there as soon as I can. I need to stop and get gas and check my tires.

Thank you, Rye, she said. Thank you for this. I'll never—

It's all right.

He wasn't the type who liked to be thanked, Theo thought.

Theo climbed into the passenger seat and Adler came around to his side and stood there a minute and put his hand on the top of his head, and it was warm and heavy, and he slid his hair back off his forehead. You all right, Theo?

He wasn't all right, of course he wasn't, but he nodded, and Adler looked at him and nodded back, and that was all. Then he shut the door and walked around to his mother, and she was looking up at him, and you could see the thing they had between them, the love. He did the same thing to her, smoothed the hair back from her face, curling it behind her ears like she was a little girl, and then he kissed her.

As his mother pulled out, Theo watched his father in his visor mirror standing there under the streetlamp with his hand in the air. He kept watching till he couldn't see him anymore.

It was quiet on the road, and they didn't speak, and it was dark, and he was really scared. After a while he fell asleep, but then he woke up, feeling sick again. He'd broken a sweat and now he was shivering, and he started machinating a way to find somebody to make a drop for him at a rest stop along the highway, and his mind kept on churning like that for a long while. She looked over at him and saw that he was shaking, and she covered him with a blanket.

Hold on, now, she said. You've got this. We know what's coming. I'm right here. I'm right here, okay, Theo?

He nodded. He felt really nauseous. She had a bucket there in case. She was prepared. She had done her homework. She'd bought some candy bars to help him deal with the cravings, but he didn't feel like eating anything now, and he was regretting not taking the prescription, but he'd heard about Suboxone, that it was like this whole other thing, and instead of the dealers making money, it was the drug companies, which kind of sucked, and he didn't want to be a part of that.

He knew he had to do this cold, if only he could.

But on the other side of his brain, he was still playing out his plan for getting more. It was still right there, that word, like a blinking cursor on a computer screen: MORE, MORE, MORE. Maybe if they stopped and she went in to use the bathroom, he could text somebody on her phone. He needed to pay attention; he needed to be vigilant.

You've got this, Theo, his mother said.

I'm gonna need to—

I'll keep my eye out, she said, even though he knew she had no intention of stopping. Try to relax now. You've been through a lot. We've got a long drive ahead.

She turned onto the interstate, and they didn't talk for a while, and she was alert and making her own plans, and finally she said, Look, Theo, I need to tell you this. I need you to listen. This thing. This thing is about trust. I need to trust you. And I need you to trust me.

I do, he said, but he wasn't sure. Maybe he'd never really trusted her. Sometimes she said one thing and did another, made a plan then thought about it and changed her mind. When he was little, it drove him crazy. And sometimes she lied. She'd say she was fine, happy, when he knew she wasn't. She always told him she loved Julian, always making excuses for his failures, but he knew she didn't.

But even more important, Theo, she went on. Even more important: you need to trust yourself. That's the only way this is going to work. You need to trust that you can do this. I know you don't feel that way right now. I know you're doubting everything. That's okay. That's part of it. Doubt isn't a bad thing. It keeps us safe sometimes. It guides us. But not now. Not here. Right now, doubt is your enemy. You have to fight it. With everything you've got.

I'll try.

That's not good enough, Theo. I can hear it. I can hear your doubt. It's still controlling you. You have to commit to this. You have to massacre it. You have to commit to it harder than anything you've ever tried to do in the past. This is like the fucking Olympics, okay? It's like a marathon. And you have to finish. You have no choice.

I know.

You have to finish, she repeated.

I'll try, Mom.

Still, that wasn't good enough. She was wide awake. Like sleep was no longer necessary. Like her determination was the only thing she needed now. She was like one of those people who could lift a car with their own hands if it meant saving a life.

I can't hold you here, she said. I can't make you do anything you don't want to. I can't make you stop. I can't do this for you. I can't. She was crying now. This is one fucking thing I can't do for you. I'll pull over if that's what you want. And you can go back to where you were. And we can say goodbye. You just let me—

No, I don't want that, he said.

Okay. Good. Good. I'm glad.

They looked through the windshield at the long, dark highway. They hadn't passed even one rest stop. He was starting to see the strain on her face. You look really worried, he said.

Of course I'm worried. And I'm scared for you. I'm scared out of my mind. Because I know how hard this is. I know, and I'm really scared.

I'm scared too.

She glanced over at him and nodded. But I figure if we're both scared, we can protect each other. We can help each other, you know. I'm talking a lot.

It's okay. I like it. It distracts me.

I do know this, she said. I know it's going to get easier. Maybe not the first week. But after that, it'll start to. Time is our friend in this case, you know. I promise, Theo. I promise, okay?

He slept for a while, at least a couple hours, and when she woke him, they were there. The sky just getting light, and he could see the ocean all around them, and it calmed him down, and he felt like he was away from everything, from his old life, and this was all new and fresh and good. She pulled up the dirt driveway and parked, and they sat there a minute, just looking around. It was an old house, like a sea captain's house, and there was nothing around but the ocean, not even any trees. Just the wind and the ocean. And the ocean was black.

He felt like crying, he couldn't help it.

What is it?

I don't deserve this. I don't deserve to be here. You should have dumped me in some rehab.

If I'd done that, you'd never stop. I'm not going to ignore you. I'm not letting someone else do this. You are *my* son. You are my fucking problem.

He nodded that he understood.

I've got you, Theo. I'm your protector. So let me do that for you, all right? Please, just let me.

He cried some more. He couldn't explain it, but he was afraid. Like, what if he couldn't do it?

Look at me, Theo. Do you see me? Do you see the mother bear in me? Look at me! Look how strong I am. Look how fierce. Look at my hands. My claws. Do you know I would kill for you? That's how much you matter to me. Because your survival is my own. Do you understand?

Yes, he said.

Listen to me. Let's try not to question anything—this. Let's just try to be here in this amazing place. This is a gift from your father; let's use it. Let's not doubt it. I'm so tired of doubting, aren't you? I don't want to be this person anymore.

Me neither, he said.

She stared out through the windshield a minute, into the nothing that was out there, then put her hand on the door and grabbed her bag.

They got out, and he felt his feet on the earth, and his bones ached like he was a hundred years old. The wind circled around them like a stray dog.

They walked up the brown lawn and stepped onto the old porch, and again he looked out at the ocean, and it was still nearly black, but now there was a glimmer of light in the middle of it like the stroke of a white paintbrush. The wind smashed up against them, and he felt like it was angry, and he was angry too, and he wanted it to keep blowing and howling and he hoped it would.

His mother unlocked the door with the iron skeleton key and pushed it open, and they peered inside, at the furniture covered with white sheets, the old grandfather clock, and she was shaking a little, and he could tell she was scared. Are you ready?

Yeah, he said. Let's do this.

Part Five

The Aperture

I have roamed distant corridors of the planet where nature's wonders never end; where, in some place or another, humanity reveres or defiles them. Tyrants, dictators, dethroned kings, beggars, queens, harlots, priests, the uplifting and the despoilers—all stared into my camera with eyes that were unveiled. The camera revealed them as they were—human beings imprisoned inside themselves.

—Gordon Parks, *Half Past Autumn*

Rye

He had saved Theo's life, that's what they told him, and he sat there in the waiting room with his heart pumping, jacked up on adrenaline. He had no idea what to do with his hands. He felt a little light-headed, and his muscles ached, and when he thought of the incident now, carrying Theo in his arms, driving like mad to the hospital, he could hardly believe it had happened. In those moments, he had been in another place, an ethereal warp of time.

Much later, a few hours after Magda arrived and they had sat together, side-by-side, in the plastic chairs, holding hands, the nurse came in and told Theo he could go. There's nothing more we can do, the nurse told Theo. The rest is up to you.

They were the hollow words out of some TV movie. While maybe it was true, for whatever happened to Theo next would be the result of his own inclination, it seemed an empty, naive proposal. Take care, he had said uselessly to Magda. Be safe.

Outside in the parking lot, he stood in the darkness, watching her pull onto the road, his hand raised in the cold air until she had turned out of sight. When he had called her all those hours ago to tell her about Theo, she was unable to speak for several long minutes. She stammered, gulping through her tears, trying to get the words out. It's how fear disables you, he knew, when even the smallest gestures seem impossible. When you are stranded in the midst of the wreck that is your life.

That's when he told her outright that he loved her.

He glanced at his watch. It was two in the morning. He was enervated, now, after the ordeal. But it had all been worth the effort. Theo had a ways to go, but at least he had that chance now. Yes, he told himself, he had that chance.

Where had he parked? He spotted his truck deep in the lot. When he got there, he found a piece of paper stuck in the door. It was a note with only two words. *Forgive me.*

It was from True, he knew, and he carefully folded her note and pushed it under his visor.

If only he could tell her he already had.

It was very cold out, and he couldn't wait to get out to Montauk, to be alone with her and the boy in the house. Since his mother's death, he rarely went out there anymore, and his sister, Ava, seldom came from Chicago. He would make a fire, and they'd have something to eat. They'd feast. But that only made him think of Simone's cooking, and he ached for her now too, and for his home. Even with his feelings for Magda, he'd always loved his wife. He loved her still.

The lot was quiet, desolate. A greenish light shimmered on the tops of the cars. He started the engine and turned the heat to full blast. He was about to back out when he heard someone knocking on his window. Alarmed, he turned. There was a man standing there. It was someone he recognized.

He rolled his window down.

Did I scare you?

Julian, he heard himself say.

Hello, Rye. I was hoping we could talk. Can I get in a minute?

It's pretty late.

Won't take long.

All right, he managed. Sure.

He sat there, trying to think, while Ladd climbed into the passenger seat of his truck. It wasn't until he was sitting there in his heavy cashmere overcoat with his seatbelt around him that Rye realized he'd possibly made a mistake, that, under the circumstances, having Ladd in such close proximity wasn't a good idea, and now he was noticing the black leather gloves and the icy rigidity of his movements, how he was staring straight ahead as if he couldn't bear the sight of him.

I guess I should thank you, he said. For taking such good care of my son.

Rye nodded. It was nothing.

We didn't know what else to do.

Sorry?

About Theo.

It's a difficult problem, Rye said uncertainly.

She was desperate. That's why she called you. He glanced over at Rye. Don't think for a minute it was anything else. That business at the hotel, for instance. That was all part of her perfect little plan. My wife can be very determined when it comes to getting what she wants. She'll do whatever it takes. He shook his head and smiled. Oh, the things she'll do. She can be a very bad girl.

That's when he saw the gun.

Julian, listen—

The truth is, he continued in a dull, monotonous tone. Marriage. It's a bit of a drag, isn't it? They don't call it an institution for nothing. And I admit it makes me a little crazy. Years go by and you do all the right things, the house, the cars, the schools, until one day it finally sinks in that the person you're lying next to night after night is a total and complete fucking stranger.

What is it you want, Julian? How can I help?

Oh, I think we've had just about enough of your help.

Voices were approaching. A couple were getting into the car parked next to him.

He jammed the gun into Rye's side. One fucking word and I fire it.

They waited in the thick quiet while the people backed out and drove away.

Julian, look—

Drive, he said.

Rye pulled out of the lot. His hands were slippery. He searched for somebody, anybody, but the streets were deserted. Even the gas station where he'd planned on getting gas was closed. They drove for a while along the river. They came to the parking lot of the fairground, the dead rides swaying in the wind.

Pull over there.

He did and parked. He realized he was sweating. He could feel the warm dampness all up his back.

Julian held up the gun. Take off your wedding band.

What?

You don't deserve to wear it. Go on.

Rye twisted the ring off his finger and dropped it into the cup holder.

That's better. Now get out.

Julian—

Shut your mouth.

They walked in the cold. His feet hurt. Everything hurt. He was terrified.

Get up on that bridge.

Rye climbed the steps up to the bridge. There weren't any lights and it was very dark.

Move.

They started across. Julian was behind him, holding up the gun. Rye was thinking he could take him. Knock him over. But he needed to gather his strength. He needed to find his courage. Julian, he said, turning around, walking backward. What are you thinking?

Julian didn't answer. He raised the gun a little higher.

Look, please, let's talk this through.

Get over there.

Whatever it is, I'm sure we can—

This is the end, Rye.

What? What are you saying?

You see, I can't—

Can't what?

She doesn't love you. I'm the one—

I know that, Julian.

Don't think for a fucking minute she ever did.

I never thought—

I didn't even care he wasn't mine. I think maybe I always knew. I tried, you know, with Theo. I tried really hard. He shook his head. But my own kid wouldn't be this stupid.

There was no decent comeback for that, Rye decided.

Julian shook his head and muttered a laugh. You never wanted to see me.

What do you mean?

My work. You never wanted to believe I was as good as you. But I was just as good as you, Rye. And you couldn't stand it. I had real talent. And you just crushed it. You crushed it.

He held the gun out in front of him with both hands.

Julian. Please!

I tried to forgive you. I tried. But I just can't.

Julian! This is madness! Rye held up his hand like a shield.

And Julian put a bullet through it.

The pain was astonishing.

Rye curled in on himself and staggered, hurling his weight into Julian, and Julian went down, and the gun skidded across the snow.

Julian took control and climbed onto Rye's hips, pinning down his arms with his knees, and he held Rye around the neck with both of his hands, squeezing, and Rye knew he had to move, and he somehow freed his good arm and pushed his fingers into Julian's eye and Julian let go, cursing, and he was able to roll to his side, and he could hear Ladd moaning, my eye, my fucking eye, and Rye lay there, gasping for air, and for a moment he thought they were done, that they'd fought, and all those years of rage Julian had been holding on to were suddenly gone.

But then he saw. Julian was on his feet, coming toward him, his shoes, the wide black legs of his trousers, the flash of an argyle sock, and the force of his leg like a mallet as he kicked him again and again.

Rye couldn't breathe. Like he'd forgotten how. And he knew in that moment that this was going to end soon, and that one of them was going to die.

He rolled over and got to his knees, and then he was up, and again he hurled himself into Julian, and they fought, tearing at each other, and Julian again took control, twisting Rye's blood-soaked arm up behind his back, pushing him against the metal railing, where he could see the water churning below, and in that instant, he lost all faith in himself and knew, without any doubt, it was where he was going.

Once, he'd seen a man fall off one of his father's bridges, a forty-five-foot drop. They'd been installing concrete forms. People said he'd survived because of the position of his body when he'd sustained the impact.

This scrap of memory pushed into his head as he turned through the darkness like a breech infant, kicking his legs together, feetfirst, his arms flat at his side like one of those circus performers about to fly out of a cannon—this all within seconds, with no time to pray, and the black river broke open into a hundred pieces, and cradled him in its frigid womb.

Magda

She wakes on the couch and takes in the room, glances at her watch. It is nearly nine a.m. and there's no sign of Rye. Groggily, she looks around. A little weary, stiff from the long drive, she pulls herself up and looks out the window, but Rye's truck is not out there. She sees the ocean. The opening sky. Maybe he decided not to come after all, she thinks, regretting now what she'd done with her phone. At one point on the drive, after Theo had fallen asleep, she'd opened her window and tossed it out onto the Hutchinson Parkway. She doesn't want Julian finding her, that's the last thing she and Theo need. It occurs to her now that, for all of the years they've been married, she's felt like another one of his possessions. Like he owns her. Not anymore. Never again. A rush of cold air circles her feet. This is what it is to be free, she thinks. This—here. Right now.

She climbs the stairs to check on Theo. It's a smaller room down the hall, the room he'd chosen. He lifts his head a moment and tells her he just wants to sleep. She nods and backs out silently and closes the door. Downstairs, she stands in the empty living room, looking out at the ocean. The house is almost exactly as she remembers it all these years later. The furniture covered with sheets. The old clock, no longer ticking.

This place, she thinks, is like a time warp. She finds a rotary phone in the kitchen and dials Rye's cell phone, but it just rings and rings. It concerns her a little, and confuses her, but she is unwilling to take it personally. By now she is used to being disappointed by him. But still, it hurts. Maybe there's a good reason for it, she decides. Maybe his truck broke down, something like that. Or maybe he thinks she needs the time alone with Theo.

Maybe he is regretting what happened between them.

She can only assume he has gone home to his wife.

Vaguely, she considers calling their house, hoping he'll pick up. But what if he doesn't? What if it's Simone who answers?

It doesn't matter now. She has more important things to worry about. Now all that matters is this gift he has given them, this place, this quiet, this peace. This time to heal. Not just for Theo, for both of them.

The days pass. One and then another. She tries Rye again and again, but there's still no answer and finally she gives up, a little angry, a little hurt. He could have tried to reach her on the landline. It's not like he doesn't know the number.

Slowly it becomes clear to her that this battle with Theo is theirs alone.

Together they will fight this beast of addiction. If it's the last thing she does.

He cries a lot. It's very difficult. He seems really down. Confused. He stares into space. He hardly looks at her. He hardly eats. He's very thin. He'll eat ice cream, that's about it. Coffee, his favorite flavor. She knows it's hard for him. She respects the struggle, but it breaks her heart as she watches it unfold. It's difficult to see. She is a mother, and he is her child. This is a glitch, an aberration. She couldn't have predicted it. She hopes he can survive it. Right now, she isn't sure. Time will tell, she supposes. Time is the thing.

His physical symptoms are manageable, like those of a bad flu, and with every day he gets a little better, a little stronger. It certainly isn't the horror of withdrawal she's read about in countless articles. It angers her, and she resents the media, and others, for claiming the physical trial of quitting is worse than it is, for making it seem impossible. She resents the clinics that exploit the families, taking their money and promising nothing. She resents the term *recover*. She resents the term *clean*. Because in life, if you are living it fully, you are always a little dirty. You carry inside you the child you once were, unafraid of the wet grass, the murky puddles of rainwater, the mud that stained your jeans.

The book on addiction is her bible. She reads it once, twice. Again. Trusts it.

She gives Theo a new journal, bound in cloth.

He runs his fingertips along its edge. Takes it upstairs.

Later, she finds him in bed. Curled in on himself. The pages of the journal are empty. He is not ready to write, she realizes. Can't.

He finds a book on the shelf, thick with dust. *The Brothers Karamazov*. He says he's reading it. He says it's good. He's been there on the couch, reading all day. But when he gets up to use the bathroom, laying the book open at his place, she sees he's still on the first page.

Julian

He was leaving his office when his cell phone rang. It was his wife. Crying into the phone, she explained what had happened to Theo. I wanted you to know, she said. You're still his father.

But this only annoyed him. In light of the fact that she'd told her lawyer she wanted nothing more to do with him, he found her blatant generosity patronizing.

He's in there now. They're saying he's going to be all right.

That's good news, he said.

He asked her where the hospital was, and she sighed irritably. I'd rather not say.

After the incident in the kitchen, where she claimed he'd lost control of himself, she'd gone to the trouble of filing a restraining order. He didn't think it was fair; the law favored the women. Maybe hitting her like that had been wrong, but he hadn't seen her complaining about the other stuff they'd done, when he'd had her on the floor.

Have you had a chance to look over that paperwork from my lawyer?

Under the circumstances the question felt like an insult.

There's a deadline, I think, she pressed.

Is there? I hadn't noticed.

That shut her up.

Well, Magda, he said in the tolerant voice he used with his new assistant. You take care.

She wasn't terribly smart when it came to these things. Long ago, and unbeknownst to her, he'd installed tracking software on her iPhone. At the moment, the little red throbbing circle on Google Maps was in the city of Albany, in the vicinity of Memorial Hospital.

He decided to go up there. Like she said, he was still Theo's father. He didn't want the boy to think he didn't care.

It took him a little over two hours, and he drove in complete silence with steadfast concentration. As it grew dark on the nearly empty highway, he thought of the Robert Frank photograph of a road somewhere in New Mexico, the conniving loneliness of it. It was a truly revealing photograph, he thought. For it represented the pull a man could feel when he is nearing the end of something, that inevitable vanishing point, where nothing lives.

He parked in the lot near the Emergency Department entrance. Maybe he had talked himself into a deluded fantasy that when she saw him, her love would come back. When she realized he'd made the effort to be part of this—what did they call it, *intervention?*—surely, she'd want him to come home, and they could go back to being a family again just like before.

But only seconds later, he saw them coming out, her arm looped in Theo's. They stepped under the bright fluorescent lights like actors on a stage.

That's when he saw Adler.

And all at once, he felt so very betrayed.

With growing agitation, he watched his adversary as he escorted his wife and son to the Range Rover he'd busted his ass to buy her. Adler was talking to Theo, the boy staring into his eyes with a glittery devotion that made him want to puke. Adler walked back over to Magda and took her into his arms and kissed her, lingering there with his tongue in her mouth as the seconds turned.

Julian swallowed. His heart burned. He played that kiss over and over in his mind even after his wife and son had pulled out of the lot, heading back into the life that no longer included him.

If there was any satisfaction, it was the look on Adler's face when Julian pounded on the window of his truck. It was the look of a guilty man. A man who knows what's coming.

There is a sound a body makes as it flies through the air, a sort of pleasant whistling, and then there's the inevitable crash when it hits the water's surface, like cement, he'd read—that's what they compared it to.

Up on that bridge, he'd felt a perilous elation—unlike the transformative effects of the alcohol or drugs he'd done in the past, this was permanently life changing.

It was an exclusive sensation, one, he knew, that few people would ever experience.

He could find no word to describe it.

He breathed the cold air into his lungs and felt his whole body renewed.

It was beginning to sleet. On his hands and knees, he groped around in the snow for his gun and tossed it over the railing into the river. He peered into the black water. There was no sign of Rye Adler.

Rye Adler was gone.

Like a pair of unseen hands, the wind shoved him to and fro as he opened his fly and urinated over the edge.

He crossed the fairground lot, where Rye's truck sat alone. He stood there a minute just looking at it, the streetlamp shining dully on its roof.

It was a long walk back to the hospital parking lot, several miles. He didn't mind it. He wanted to walk, to clear his head. He shuffled along. He was like a creature transformed, sniffing, limping a little across the ice and snow, and as he hurried along, it dawned on him that what he'd done could not be reversed. He'd committed a murderous act and he couldn't take it back. He alone had changed the course of destiny for both of them.

There was no greater power than that, he thought.

A storm was moving in from the north. He turned into the wind as he walked along the roadside, the sleet pricking his face. It took him over an hour to get back to his car, and once he'd settled in behind the wheel, he felt nothing but gratitude. He was tempted to pray.

He sat there for a long while. He found he couldn't move.

He retraced the route to the interstate and, about thirty miles out of Albany, picked up the Taconic. The road was deserted, nothing but black fields, distant farms. He drove cautiously with his wipers on, the road slick with ice.

For the entire ride, he contemplated what might occur if they found Adler. With this weather it could take time. At some point, he gathered, the body would wash up somewhere. It was unlikely they would connect Julian to the incident. He'd been wearing his gloves, he was still wearing them, and nobody knew how he'd felt about Rye. Nobody.

Maybe he believed they'd be there. Sitting at the kitchen table, drinking tea. Maybe they would welcome him home. Maybe she would look at him the way she did sometimes, when he could see her love. When he could tell she wanted him.

But the house on Farrington Avenue was dark.

Still, he pulled into the garage and went in. He walked from room to room, up the stairs and back down again, calling out their names. Then he sat down at the kitchen table and wept.

Magda

Routine, she has learned, is the essence of recovery. She has established a schedule. Running is their lifeline. It is the thing that matters most.

At first he didn't want to. Said it was too hard, he couldn't breathe. His chest burned. His ankles hurt. His mouth was so dry he couldn't swallow. *Let's go* was her answer, and they set out along the shore, their sneakers sinking in the wet sand. The wind against them. Stop thinking, she would say. I can feel you thinking. This isn't about thinking. This is about moving.

After a week it's easier, and he doesn't bother to complain, only rises from his bed, throws on his clothes, and reaches for his shoes.

There is no finish line, she tells him. There is no before and no after. The past is dust. Let it go. They take the sand into their hands and toss it into the sea.

The running changes him. Recycles him. Allows him to be better. It changes her too. She is stronger. More focused. Surprised by her courage.

Once more, and perhaps for the last time, she tries to reach Rye. How can it be that she hasn't heard from him? If she weren't so worried, she'd be insulted. Slightly desperately she dials 411, amazed that the old-fashioned service actually still exists, only to discover that his number—his and Simone's—is unlisted. She entertains driving out to his farm. She has imagined it many times, knocking on their door, coming face-to-face with Simone, a woman who has always despised her, who wields her superiority like a weapon. That time they met, under the guise of friendliness, Simone had inquired, Port Richmond, isn't it? We went there once, for pierogis. In other words: *I know where you come from. You're nothing.*

Once, after a fight with Julian, she'd packed up the car and taken Theo and driven all the way up there. Theo was maybe eight or nine, contentedly playing with Legos in the back seat. When she turned down their dirt road and saw their big house up on the hill in the distance, she couldn't do it. Couldn't go through with it. Perhaps she had too much pride. She pulled over and cried. What's the matter, Mommy?

I made a mistake.

Theo climbed over the seat and put his little arm around her. Don't cry, Mommy. Let's go home now.

She nodded and wiped her tears. Yes, let's go home.

Somewhere along the highway, they stopped at a McDonald's, and she bought him a Happy Meal and a Coke. And he was happy. And his happiness was hers; it was all that mattered.

She finds Theo on the beach, standing on the shore after his run. He has taken to wearing an old Columbia sweatshirt he found in Rye's drawer. From the back he looks tall and strong, a young man who can handle himself, but when he turns, she sees his fury. Hey, she says.

Hey.

You okay?

He only nods.

What is it?

I'm scared.

Tell me.

I don't think I can go back.

Back where?

To school.

No?

He shakes his head. Not there.

You can transfer.

He nods. Maybe.

There's no rush. You have time, Theo.

Only now he looks at her with uncertainty. Do I?

Of course you do.

What will I do? What if I don't, like, become something? What if I'm just—

Just you?

He nods.

That's more than enough.

He doesn't say anything, and she can tell he's not convinced. The water comes up to his sneakers. There is nothing to see but the ocean, the dark water, the endless white sky.

Listen, she says. When I was your age, I used to worry. I didn't know what I was supposed to do. I always used to think that if only I could do something really great, like really outstanding, my life would finally have purpose, and it would make me who I was. Like, for example, if I took an amazing photograph, one that really, you know, said something, and people realized how good I was, and I got a show, and the papers wrote about me, then, and only then, my life would matter. And I worried about it. Not mattering. Just like you're worrying now. There's this expectation, you know. To make something of your life. Like when someone comes up to you and asks you what you do, and they're not so impressed by your answer. You can just sort of see them judging you.

But when you break it down, that judgment is more about you, how *you* see yourself, what you expect of yourself. People think they're superior, they have more, they know more, but in the end, everyone has the same basic fears. I look back at when you were a baby and I was raising you and waiting for my life to start, and what I understand now is it already had. And you changed me. You taught me things. You taught me so much.

I did?

She nods. Listen to me, Theo. Take your time. This thing you're going through? It's important. It's necessary. It's yours.

Every day you know yourself a little better. You're turning the lens, clarifying your focus. The days come and go. There's no stopping them. This moment right now is already lost forever. You eat your bread, drink your coffee. You sleep, you wake. You notice the trees. You think about something—a story, a person you love. You think about the weather. The sunlight. The smell of this water. You get hurt, you get sick, and you realize how vulnerable you actually are.

This is what we have, Theo. We are nothing so special, really. Maybe we're here only to be loved, to give love. She shrugs. Maybe that's all.

They walk together up the beach. Up, and then back, and then up again. The sand is cold; the wind comes in gusts. It meddles with them, stirring up the sand, which prickles their faces. No matter, they walk right through it. They walk for miles. The sun is very weak. The wind blows too hard, they can't even talk. They don't need to; it's better they don't. They walk along, the wind blasting in their ears. The next morning, they find a pile of old bikes in the shed. They work together to fill the tires, fix their greasy chains. When they are finished, he tells her he wants to go on his own. She nods. What can she do? She has to let him.

She has to trust him.

Are you sure?

Yeah. I'll be fine.

But it's not easy waiting for his return. Not easy. She reminds herself that he knows the landline number. She made sure he memorized it; he can call her from somewhere if he needs her. At least there is that. There is no computer in this house. No emails. She cannot be found on Instagram or Facebook. These things, too, are addictions of a sort, dependent on use. It's a relief to be living without them. To be unfindable; anonymous. To figure out who she really is, without all that online canvassing.

I am trying to get lost again, Lange had said. More than ever, Magda is too.

To distract herself, she cleans the house. Folds the laundry. Makes bread, mixing, kneading. She can feel the strain in her arm muscles. With Theo out, she is tempted by an old yearning to drink, and searches every last cabinet. Nothing. Not a single drop in the house. Good, she thinks. But now it is getting dark.

She charges up the stairs to his room. Turns down the sheets, yanks the blanket. She doesn't even know what she's looking for! There is nothing. Nothing. What a fool she is! She surrenders, drops to her knees, beats the floor with her fists; she is too angry to pray.

She walks down to the beach. Confronts the ocean.

Somehow she will have to survive this, whatever the outcome.

She can't expect it to be easy, that he will miraculously overcome his addiction.

He will fail, she decides.

And they will start again.

She tries to remember the problems she caused her mother as a young woman. Her mother always seemed to be complaining, she was too stupid, or too careless, or too lazy, or too indifferent. She should be working harder. She should be working her fingers to the bone! Her mother was never satisfied. It was the family credo: you are never enough.

She had tried not to be that with Theo. But now she wonders, maybe if she'd expected more of him, this wouldn't have happened.

Again, she thinks of her mother, and understands, as if for the first time, that, even with all their arguing, everything she'd done in her life had been for Magda.

Mom!

She turns. Had she heard him?

There he is. Standing there with the bike. His hair blowing like crazy.

Mom, he shouts loudly into the wind. Mom!

Hey! She waves. She wants to cry. She bawls inside like a baby but doesn't show it. Theo! she calls.

He leans the bike against the wooden gate and comes down the rickety staircase, and when he gets close, all she wants to do is hug him. She wants to take him in her arms and hold him forever. But she doesn't. Can't. He doesn't have to know how hard it was for her. He doesn't have to know she doesn't trust him. She looks at him closely. His eyes. You okay?

Yeah.

That was a long ride.

Yeah. It felt good. Look at me. I'm really sweaty.

How far did you go?

Miles, he says. I just kept riding.

She nods, her stomach in knots.

You were worried, right?

Yes, I was. Sorry. I'm trying really hard not to be, you know, like a mom. I don't want you to feel—

I don't. I'm sorry I worried you.

Are you okay?

Do you mean did I buy some?

Did you?

No. And then he smiles.

I'm really glad you didn't, she says.

He nods. I wanted to.

I know.

It's really fucking hard.

I know it is. I'm proud of you.

He nods. She looks at him closely and he looks right back.

Getting cold out here. Should we go in?

Yeah, it's freezing.

Let's go. I made bread.

Together, they walk up to the house, the lamp shining in the window, the golden light spilling out.

Theo

When he saw the bikes just sitting there, he thought: today. Pumping the tires, he thought: in a couple of hours I'll be high.

He had a little money. He pushed the bills into his pocket and went down to the kitchen and told her he was going and slipped into the garage and got on the bike and set out. He decided he would pull over in town and find somebody who knew someone, but it was an old bike and a little rusty and hard to pedal, and he broke a sweat pretty quick, and he rode down the long dirt road to the paved one, then alongside the beach, and the plan started to fade.

It was overcast and cold, and, like, two in the afternoon, and the sky was like steel and the light was very bright, and there were a few people here and there, not many, but he knew if he rode into town, maybe not the first town but the second one, that he'd eventually be able to find some. It was never that far away. There was always somebody. Usually somebody had some. Or knew somebody who did. But he rode without stopping on the two-lane road all the way to Amagansett, and the harder he pedaled, the less he thought about heroin and the more he thought about the sky and the wind and the ocean and the grass, and he felt loose and happy, and he kept on riding, and then he realized a couple hours had passed, and he thought of his mother, and he knew she'd be worrying, and he turned around and started back, and started thinking about it all over again, his body telling him to want it, to long for it, to even pray for it, and he decided to stop once he got to Montauk and just buy some already and shoot it and get it over with, and there were some stragglers hanging around the old Memory Hotel, and he stopped there and they looked at him, waiting for him to say something, but he didn't ask, he just said, hey, how's it going, and they said it's all good, and he pushed down on the pedals and got going again.

He thought about it, but he didn't. He didn't. No. He didn't.

He had been reviewing the past couple months and everything that had happened and how he'd screwed up at school and how his best friend had died. He thought a lot about Carmine and decided that Carmine was still wearing his hobo coat up in heaven, dragging the stars across the sky with its ragged hem. If Carmine were alive now and knew Theo was here, he'd probably make fun of the fact that he was such a spoiled rich kid, escaping to this beach house in the Hamptons. Not many people had that opportunity; he knew that. It was a lot harder if you didn't have money or resources. Like if you ended up at some crappy rehab. It was hard all around, and he was lucky to have his mom. He loved her so much right now it almost hurt. He could see who she was, her strength. He had begun to trust her again, and trust was hard for him.

He thought about his time on the streets, the things he had witnessed, the people he'd met and exchanged stories with, standing around drinking coffee or having a smoke with, or the people he'd shot dope with. Everybody wanted to kick, to become something, to be smarter— they all did, but they just couldn't. At that point in time they couldn't. Because it was easy to fall into another life, one that wasn't yours, and to be stuck there, in that body, to *be* that stranger, for a good long while.

It was a disease; he understood that now. And it could happen to anyone. And it had happened to him. But he was getting better. He was a lot better already. And he didn't regret it. Because he had come to understand the darkness inside him. That same darkness in everyone that surfaces every so often when you forget who you are.

Rye

At first he is very cold. He is too hurt, too afraid, to move. Distantly, he hears the voices of children. The light comes and goes and comes again. He can hear the river, and there is the black smell of the earth and the foul stillness of the water. He knows this river. He knows it is winter, and the cold air funnels through his clothes. He shivers.

Inside his head, all the doors are opening and shutting, opening and shutting.

Magda, he shouts to the white sky.

Sunlight. The singing of birds. He wants to open his eyes, but even that is too much. He is too broken to move. He decides the birds are talking about him, attempting to discern if he is alive or dead. Maybe he is dead. Maybe this is death.

He had fallen. He remembers falling.

He remembers now the roar of water in his ears, the darkness as he swam up to the surface, his chest squeezing for air. The water was very cold. He could see the shore. He couldn't feel his legs.

He swam. His arms had burned with the effort. His hand ached. There was something wrong with it. But he swam anyway. He didn't stop swimming till he was there at the shore. Then he had crawled like an alligator onto the dirt, using his elbows to pull himself along. He can remember the wind sweeping over him and the darkness and the cold night air and how he shivered and how it shook him alive.

Later, voices. Children. Their voices bend around the trees, rising, falling. Then suddenly it is quiet. When he wakes again, he senses them near. Their heat. The heat of the living. Standing over him now, swaying like young trees. They crouch at his side. So near he can feel their warm breath on his face as they argue about his condition, what to do with him.

Is he dead? says the girl.

No, he's not dead.

Where did he come from?

The river.

He's all green.

He's alive, the boy says.

Why is he shaking?

He's cold.

What should we do?

They run off.

A little later they come for him. He hears a man's voice. He can feel their hands as they pull him sideways onto a plank and cover him with a blanket. It is a sled, he realizes, a toboggan. There are several people lifting him up, carrying him, talking over him. They carry him a long way. He keeps his eyes closed; he is too frightened to look.

He wakes in the near dark. If he isn't dead, then he has been saved. It is a stone hut. They've made a fire in the small hearth. The warmth is a gift. His hand is bandaged in gauze, and there's a splint on his leg. To accomplish this, it appears they've cut off his trousers and dressed him in loose flannel pajama pants and an old T-shirt. He is covered with wool blankets that smell of horses and hay and dung. The man sits on an old plastic lawn chair, watching the fire. His back is wide and strong. His hands are clamped as he waits for something, some messenger of judgment. His hair is long and silver. He stares into the flames. Rye too watches the flames. They share this time, the crackling fire, and Rye instinctively knows that he is a good man, determined to keep him alive. Finally the man stands, his shadow looming like a giant's on the wall of stones.

He gazes down at Rye with concern. Get some rest, he says. Then he leaves.

It is very dark, save for the firelight. Rye lies awake a long time in the quiet of this strange night, until he can no longer fight his closing lids.

Daylight. He opens his eyes. It is very quiet. Very still.

He has woken up inside a photograph. He fears he will never get out.

The pain is the brightest white. Even the slightest movement. His hand throbs and it comes to him that there is a hole in it. It's like a grenade, he thinks, knowing he should not move it, lest the whole place erupt in flames.

Water. The constant sound of it. The river is very close.

His skin is hot, and yet he's shivering. It is a fever, he knows. He can smell his own sweat, the soiled sheets.

He is going to die.

A woman comes. She heaps on more blankets. She works the thick wool socks over his feet. The hat is her husband's, she says, as she pulls it onto his head. Her breath smells of garlic. Her name, she tells him, is Lotus. But only a moment later he forgets. Her hair is long and dark. She wears a heavy coat and work boots with thick brown laces. As she leans and fusses, her hair sweeps down over her shoulder and he notices a tiny silver star pierced through her nose. With great care, she wipes his face with a warm cloth. We would've called for an ambulance, she tells him, but they wouldn't be able to find us. We're pretty deep in the woods out here and there aren't any roads.

Although he wants to, he can't begin to ask her where they are.

Do you have to pee?

He shakes his head.

Here, take these. You're in luck, I happen to be a registered nurse. And one of our residents is a retired doctor. He came in here to take a look at you, and he's the one who fixed up your leg. Other than the leg and a couple broken ribs that need to heal, you'll be okay. We've got a truck, but it's a good hike from here. We can figure it out, though, if you want to go—

I don't want to go anywhere, he muttered.

She helps him swallow some pills, an antibiotic and something for the pain, she tells him. I'll be back in a little bit. What happened to you? Can you remember?

I fell, he says with difficulty.

She nods and waits.

Off the—

The bridge?

Somebody—

She frowns, anticipating some injustice in his story.

Somebody pushed me.

Oh, my Lord, she says.

Somebody pushed me, he says again, and although he wants to, he is too weak to cry.

Should we call someone? The police?

He doesn't know how to answer this. He only looks at her.

She sits beside him on the edge of his mattress and takes his hand. You're safe, she says. You need to know that.

And he nods.

Rest, she says.

She stays there with him. For a while he studies her face, the creases and lines, the curve of her lips, a face that has been loved, he decides. She sings him a ballad of promises. And he finally shuts his eyes. No matter what it takes, she tells him, you are going to live. You are going to survive.

He wakes. He can feel the sunlight on his face, so bright under his closed lids. The sun streams in through a hole in the roof.

He can't feel his legs.

Later, he hears the children. The sound of their feet trampling the snow-covered ground. Their voices like birds.

The girl is maybe eight, the boy a few years younger. They stand there, looking at him with runny noses, dirty faces, their winter jackets zipped to their chins, their hats pulled down over their ears. A minute later they are gone.

Time.

It tells its own story in the light and darkness and all the colors in between.

He sleeps. Then he is awake. It is light, and then it is dark. And then it is light again.

He looks up and sees the clouds. The clouds move slowly, slowly, a whole herd of them. So much slower than he's ever noticed.

The woman is kneeling at his side. He sees the dark water of her hair. Her shoulder a pale, round stone.

The air smells of woodsmoke.

It rains. The raindrops fall across his face. They roll into his mouth. They roll down the side of his neck, into his ear. He can hear the rain on the river. He can hear it splattering on the steps that are made of stones.

* * *

A dog comes, a mutt of some kind. His fur is black and soft. He is squat, barrel-chested, his whiskers gray. He is smiling. He licks Rye's cheek, his tail wagging, wagging.

Plato! she calls into the hut. Leave him alone! He needs to rest! Come!

And he lumbers off to his mistress.

He tries to count the days but forgets. He lies there a long time without moving.

He's pissed himself.

He tries to remember his other life. Where is it? What did it look like?

Who is he?

He remembers a dark little room, the smell of chemicals. Paper in a tray of clear liquid. He is watching a picture come up, a face. A face appearing through the water, slowly becoming clear. It is a man's face. The face of someone he knows.

Simone

She can't seem to do anything. Can't work. Can't cook. Day after day, the dirty winter light hovers. Her life seems false, shambled with bad decisions. She trusts nothing. No one. Not even herself.

On New Year's Eve, she drinks a bottle of Veuve Clicquot, retrieved from the tomb of the cellar, sprinkled with the dust of a previous century. No matter, she pops the cork and pours the bubbling splendor into a crystal flute, somewhat pleased with herself for the moment, and watches the ball drop on TV, counting backward until the second hand on her watch maneuvers time like a magic wand. One year closer to death, she thinks morbidly.

A few days later, she hears Constance pulling into the driveway. Simone throws on one of Rye's T-shirts over her oldest pair of yoga pants. The shirt smells just like him, and as she descends the stairs, she fights a desire to run back up and crawl into bed, to stay there forever.

He's not here, she says when she opens the door.

Constance stares at her. Happy New Year to you too.

Sorry. It's been a weird time.

Do tell.

But Simone only looks at her helplessly.

You look horrible. What's happened to you?

I don't know where he is, she says, and begins to cry.

Coffee, Constance determines, and walks directly into the kitchen and fills up the kettle and sets it on the burner, then dumps a few scoops of Guatemalan into the French press. She inspects the refrigerator, scowling at the sight of it. What have you been eating?

Simone holds up her last tangerine. We can share this.

In the beginning, she had mixed feelings about her husband's assistant, a working-class girl from the Bronx whose parents scraped to send her to Riverdale, then on to Vassar, where she acquired the assured hip-speak of her affluent schoolmates. Constance—never Connie—wants to be a photographer, and Rye is one of her idols. It is a particularly intense adoration that sometimes annoys Simone, mainly because she follows her husband around like a stray pup. At first with Simone, she was overly polite, her flattery like costume jewelry, a bit too obvious. By now, though, she has proven herself to be entirely indispensable, and Simone considers her a friend.

Ah, caffeine, Constance says. Remedy for most ailments. She pours out the coffee into two cups. Now drink.

Thank you.

Simone offers her half of the tangerine and Constance takes a few sections and sits. She puts a bowl of pistachios between them. Breakfast is served, she says.

How was your break?

Good, until it wasn't. My parents—it's a very small apartment. Let's just say I'm glad to be back—sort of.

Simone concedes, I'm sorry about all this. It's really very strange.

She tells Constance everything she knows, including the stuff about Rye and Magda at the hotel. It's been nearly three weeks, she says. Maybe they've run off together.

No. That's not his MO. He would tell you.

What, then?

Maybe something happened to him.

Hard to believe, given his experience.

Have you tried tracking his phone?

How do I do that?

I'm guessing you don't have the find-your-family app?

She shakes her head. You know I'm technologically impaired.

Simone calls Verizon, but since her name isn't listed on the account, they won't tell her anything. You'll need a subpoena to see his texts, they advise, if it comes to that.

If it comes to what exactly, she wonders, all of a sudden feeling very worried. I think we should go to the police.

Constance nods. We're taking the Honda. You're in no condition to drive.

They hurry out to Constance's ratty old Civic.

This is surreal, Simone says.

Constance starts the engine and turns the heat on high. It reminds me of that quote by Cartier-Bresson, she says.

Which one?

About how photographers are always dealing with things that are continually vanishing.

Only in this case, *he's* the one who's vanished. Why is he doing this to me?

Constance shakes her head. Only Rye can tell you that.

The police station is in Chatham, a good twenty-minute drive, and there's nobody there save for one cop behind the desk. She tells him her husband hasn't come home for over two weeks. I think he's missing, she says. I think something's wrong.

He hands her a form to fill out, and she tries to answer all the questions. They ask for a photo. She searches her phone for the one she took of Rye sitting at the kitchen table in the old Windsor chair. Here, she says to the cop. Maybe you can print this.

She'd caught him reading the paper one Sunday, his eyes brightening with surprise and amusement, for she was rarely the one taking pictures. It was her favorite shot of him. The old Rye. The man she would always love.

She hands in the form, and the cop reads it over, checking to make sure everything's filled in. Then he looks at her curiously and asks her to tell him about the last time she saw him. For some reason she starts to cry. Because she can see that morning so vividly. The shy winter sunlight. His face as he climbed into the truck. How he'd waved to her out his window just before he turned, a gesture that, now, in retrospect, feels like a final goodbye.

Rye

Magda.

The taste of her, like the rain.

He is dreaming, walking in the city. He can hear footsteps, his own. He sees no color. The edges of the buildings are sharp, as though drawn with a very thin pencil. The shadows are deep. The sky is a perfect banner of gray.

The city is a carney. The people and the smells. The streets soaked with rain.

The buildings seem to be waiting. Vast apartments full of empty rooms, sloping camelback couches in raw silk, elaborate drapery, the secretary desk from before the Civil War, a half-written letter on the desk stopped in mid-sentence, an unfinished thought...and just beyond the window, the rain, a sky like hammered tin.

He is looking for someone.

The faces come at him, all the people he'd photographed, a whole lifetime's worth, a throng coming toward him. What do they want? *What do you want?*

He grabs the man in the long black coat and the man turns. He has no face.

You have a fever, she says, her hand on his forehead. She sets down her lantern and feeds him more pills. She holds the jar of cold water to his lips, and he drinks.

Sleep, she says.

He is better in the morning. His fever has broken.

She brings him breakfast, strawberry yogurt thick with berries that she feeds to him off a spoon, out of a small glass jar. She is gentle, precise, and while under any other circumstances he'd be embarrassed, with her he is not. She is procedural in her actions. A mother, he surmises. A wife. Her outsize wool sweater is gray as the sky.

Lotus, he remembers her name.

How are you? she says softly. Better?

Yes, a little.

She pulls the blanket under his chin. Warm enough?

He nods. He wants to ask her where he is. This hut, this place. But it is too much to put together. Too many words.

She starts to rise, and he catches her hand, and for a moment she is startled. Thank you, he says.

Her gaze softens. You're welcome. You're going to be okay.

She stokes the fire. The rain has stopped, she tells him. He can hear the rainwater plinking in a barrel.

Sleep, she tells him. You need to rest.

She stands there a minute, looking at him.

Rest now, she says. Then she leaves.

He tries to sit up, but he is too weak. He leans back on his elbows and looks around. The hut is small, the size of the king-size bed he shares with his wife. Simone, he remembers now. Simone is his wife.

He lies back down and shuts his eyes. Slowly he is healing. He is like a plant uncurling its leaves in the night, diligently repairing itself. His body is working very hard, and he is tired, with a sort of exhaustion you cannot imagine when you are well, like you are buried in sand. The dark drifts down, slow as paint. It covers the world.

Simone

A week of nothing; she can hardly bear the silence of her house. She can feel herself beginning to disappear. And then, on Sunday, a police cruiser pulls into her driveway. Two cops get out, a man and a woman. They stand there on her doormat. His name is Johnson; the woman is Sanchez. We found your husband's truck, Johnson tells her.

What? Where?

In a parking lot in Albany.

We were set to tow it, Sanchez explains, but when we ran the plates, your husband's name came up in our database of missing persons. Can we come in and sit down a minute?

Of course.

Simone leads them into the kitchen, and they sit at the table. Johnson studies her face, her already bereft expression, as if he'll find something there, some resistant truth.

Have you ever heard of Mohawk Island? It's a nature preserve.

She shrugs. Maybe. I'm not sure.

That's where he was parked, in the lot near the bridge. It's closed for winter, so the truck was immediately suspicious. Every year we get a few jumpers.

Simone just looks at them. Sorry, I'm not following you.

Off the bridge, Sanchez says. People who want to—

Johnson cuts her off. Your husband left the keys in the ignition.

He did?

And these items. He sets down Rye's wallet and his gold wedding band.

Simone sits there a moment, staring at Rye's things with disbelief. She reaches for the wallet. It is almost as if they have handed her an organ, her husband's beating heart. The wallet appears to be untouched, everything in place, his credit cards, two twenty-dollar bills neatly tucked into the fold. She sets it down and picks up the ring. It feels surprisingly heavy and cold in her palm. It is no ordinary ring. They'd had them made by a jeweler in the city.

We also found this note. Johnson presents a plastic evidence bag. Under the shiny plastic is a white scrap of paper. There are just the two words, written in pencil. *Forgive me.*

Is that his handwriting? Sanchez asks.

I guess it could be. His handwriting isn't—

She stops for a moment, her head pounding. We mostly text.

They sit there, looking at her. Then Sanchez asks, Was he at all depressed?

Not that I know of.

But now that she thinks of it, maybe he was. In truth, there were plenty of things troubling Rye in recent months. One night, after they'd had too much wine, he admitted to feeling disenchanted with his work. *Soul-crushing* was the word he used. The celebrities with their mansions and jets, the money, the lingering sycophants—he couldn't stand it. Things had gotten out of hand, he said, the disparity between rich and poor. For the past several years, he'd photographed an assortment of billionaires—movie stars, athletes, celebrities, industrialists, entrepreneurs, politicians—quite in contrast to his early days, when it was ordinary people who interested him, the ones so easily overlooked.

They take her to see the truck. Like a criminal, she rides in the back of the cruiser behind the metal grate. Distantly she wonders if they suspect her of something. Even in her heavy coat she is shaking to the core.

This weather, Sanchez says, and turns to look at her. They're saying a nor'easter is coming.

We got some time yet, Johnson says. Before it hits.

Nearly an hour later, they are driving through an industrial area near the river, past dreary row houses, curtains tugged over windows, pulled shades. No people anywhere—the street desolate, bleak, as if this part of the city has been erased. We've been hit pretty hard down here by opioids, Sanchez explains.

After a while, they come to a large, empty parking lot, a deserted fairground. Rye's old red truck is sitting there all by itself.

They get out and stand there a minute in the wind, gathering their bearings. Flurries of snow fill the air like the petals of cherry blossoms.

The truck seems to be waiting for them.

They walk over to it and Johnson opens the driver's-side door.

Keys were just sitting right there in the ignition, he says.

Odd, Simone says, almost convinced, now that she's here, that Rye is really gone. Still, she refuses to believe he'd jump off a bridge. It's not who he is. And she refuses to talk about him in the past tense. He always has equipment in here, she explains, valuable stuff. He always locks his door.

Why don't you climb in and have a look around, Sanchez says.

She does. She slides behind the wheel, the seat worn to his shape. She can smell him, his pine-smelling soap. Like an extension of his studio, the truck is his own little world. In truth, she's rarely ridden in it. When they go out together, they always take her Saab, and she does the driving. The truck is in its usual state, the floor littered with paper coffee cups, receipts, empty water bottles.

Where was the note?

Tucked right up here, under the visor.

And the ring?

Johnson points to the cup holder. Right in there.

Simone shakes her head. This is surreal. I'm not sure I believe it. It's almost too—

She doesn't want to cry here, not now, not in front of these strangers. She gets out and stands there a minute, trying to breathe. It's just very unlike him to do something like this, she says finally.

You have any idea what he was doing over here?

He may have been on assignment. She explains about Rye's work.

May have been? You don't know?

She wonders if it's some sort of a crime not to know your spouse's schedule. We kind of lead independent lives, she says.

But the cop only looks at her with troubled confusion.

We spend a lot of time apart.

I see—

He likes a lot of—

Ma'am?

Space.

Johnson nods, but she can feel him judging her, their messed-up marriage, their sprawling farm, their money. There's a bag back here, he says, and opens the back door, where Rye's canvas bag is nestled on the floor. Why don't you have a look.

He sets it on the seat and steps aside. Unzipping the black canvas, she thinks vaguely of a body bag. The dirty clothes inside are stiff and cold. She finds his camera, not his usual digital Nikon but an old film camera, and a couple canisters of film. There are Kind bars, a frozen bottle of water, half full. At the very bottom, there's a large manila envelope. She opens it carefully and discovers a collection of photographs, all of the same boy, not just any boy, but a version of her husband. Her heart beats a little faster. They have the same eyes.

Any idea who that is? Sanchez asks.

It's not easy to lie to this woman, this fierce, seasoned cop. But she isn't ready to talk about this, not with her. I have no idea, she says. It's probably something he was working on for his latest monograph. We have pictures of strangers all over the house.

They want to show her the bridge. They climb up the steps and over the rope. The wind is stronger up here. Simone grasps at her wildly blowing hair.

It's about four hundred acres, Johnson shouts, sweeping his arm over the river where the island sits. Most of that land's been donated to the state. There's an old hotel on it. Used to be a real showplace. It's been closed now almost fifty years. My grandparents were married there. The state's been trying to buy it, but the owner's in a nursing home someplace with dementia, with no heirs, and refuses to sell it. We got history around here with the river. You can find it all over these parts, just staring you in the face.

Maybe he fell, Simone says. Maybe he was trying to get a shot.

Could be. But that doesn't explain the stuff he left behind, Sanchez says. The note, the ring. The keys—

She looks out at the bleak sky, the icy water below. Could he survive it?

Ma'am?

She gestures with her chin, unable to say the words.

Let me put it to you this way, Mrs. Adler. Nobody has before.

When she gets home, she parks Rye's truck on the grass, just like he always did. The dogs run over expectantly, but when he doesn't step out, they whimper and whine with disappointment. It's only me, she says.

She grabs the bag off the back seat and brings it into the kitchen and sets it down on the table. She fishes out the envelope that contains the pictures of the boy and flips through them a second time. For the briefest moment, it's almost like he's theirs, the child they never had together. She'd always wanted to, but after Yana, Rye didn't want any more kids. At the time, she'd been all right with it, but now, with everything so crazy, she can't help rethinking her life and all the things she might've done differently.

Theo. She says his name aloud. Strange. He looks so much like his father. The eyes, the narrow chin, even the eyebrows. It's one of those school pictures. The shiny blue backdrop. He's maybe seven or so. Sitting there, smiling. She turns it over: *Theodore Ladd, Grade 2.*

Ladd, she whispers.

She opens her laptop and googles Magda Ladd. Sure enough, a website comes up: Celebrations Photography by Magda P. Ladd. Encouraged, she opens the site and finds Magda's picture, not the girl she remembers, but a woman twenty years older. No longer the wild beauty her husband had photographed, but a grown woman etched with her own fraught history.

She clicks on the contact page and a phone number appears. She forces herself to dial it and waits expectantly as it rings. She will tell her everything, she decides. She will confess that instead of giving her husband the letter, she buried it deep in the tomb of her closet. And like all things that are hidden, it has remained a symbol of distrust. A curse on their marriage. She will tell her that from the moment she first saw her, she envied her beauty, her exquisite power. And that she hated her for it. Yes, she will tell her that too. I never meant to hurt anyone, she imagines declaring. And she will admit how terribly sorry she is.

But it isn't Magda who answers. Instead, a recording informs her that the number is no longer in service.

In frustration, she walks into the field with the dogs. It is beginning to sleet, and she can hear her wind chimes jangling in the trees, an overture to the nearing storm. Back inside, she lights the woodstove and makes some tea, then thinks better of it and pours a glass of whiskey. She drinks it down like a cure, watching her reflection come clear in the darkening glass.

Sleep will not come. She lies there in bed, thinking about Rye. Wondering what might have been in his head to make him do such a thing. If in fact he has.

Julian

Julian had never been better.

Back in the city, ensconced in his usual routine, he felt lighter. Freer. Absolved.

It was over a month now, and nothing had happened. His greatest fear—waking in the night to police banging on his door—had not been realized.

That night, driving cautiously home on icy roads, he'd made the decision to turn his life around. What else could he do? That was how he'd described it to his mother when he called her the next morning. I'm a changed man, he'd told her. I've experienced a revelation.

The bad thing he'd done to Adler had inspired introspection more than guilt. What was the point of guilt? It didn't change anything. Even if he wanted to, he couldn't take it back.

Methodically he'd embarked on a crusade of change.

In the weeks that followed, he became a model citizen, courteous to his neighbors and coworkers, offering to help whenever it was needed, in some cases going out of his way to appease or comfort someone, like the old lady who lived above him with her little shrieking dog. His coworkers called him a workaholic, and he supposed it was true; he rarely left the office before ten. As a result, he'd garnered several new and important accounts.

If it weren't for his troublesome wife, things would be almost normal. Her lawyer had been sending nasty, irate letters.

He ignored them. He just couldn't—

In fact, things had been going so well that—

He had all but forgotten about Rye Adler.

It wasn't until he saw the headline in the *Times* that morning in late January that he could fully remember what had so compelled him to do what he'd done. Rye Adler, Renowned Photographer, Reported Missing, it read, along with an ominous picture of Adler's truck in the empty lot.

He sat down at his kitchen table and made himself read the article out loud, word for word. A note had been found in the truck; Julian hadn't been aware of one. They'd found his wedding band and wallet, and on the nearby bridge a footprint had been discovered in the snow that closely matched the underside pattern of Adler's sneakers, suggesting that he might have fallen or jumped. The article was so convincing, he almost believed it himself, that Rye's fall from the bridge had been deliberate, provoked by a deep and unbearable sadness.

It was becoming increasingly clear to Julian that there was a very good chance, an exceptional chance, in fact, that he'd gotten away with it.

Funny how life turned out. He'd always had a talent for operating under the radar. Somehow going unnoticed. Fading into the background. You could see an awful lot when nobody noticed you. He thought of his photographs, shoved into a box somewhere. The lovely sweeping open views he'd captured. That compelling horizon. It was so simple, really, two bands of color, separated by a perfect, infinite line.

It was strange not knowing where she was. Hurtful, really. He'd left several voice mails, none of them returned. He knew he wasn't supposed to call. She didn't want to talk to him. She'd made that perfectly clear. And the judge had warned him at his hearing, when he'd shown up to defend himself, that he had no business contacting her. More out of curiosity than anything else, he'd been tracking her phone and the strangest location kept coming up, in the Bronx. He'd been checking it obsessively, at least three times a day, and the location had not changed.

With their home in Westchester so obviously unbearable to her, he assumed she'd taken a rental, but when he flipped through his bank statements, he found no evidence of such an expense, and there were no charges on her credit cards.

Cleary, his spoiled immigrant wife had outsmarted him.

He didn't have a clue where she was.

A few days later, his Realtor called to say they'd gotten an offer on the house. It's full price, she declared. You might want to go out there and start cleaning up, the inspection's next Friday.

He broke down and rang his wife's lawyer in her Madison Avenue office. The assistant put him through right away. He explained about the house being under contract. I'm just letting you know, he told her. If she wants any of her things, she'll have to get them this week.

I'll tell you what your wife wants, Mr. Ladd. She wants those papers signed. You realize, it'll be a whole lot better for you if you do.

It sounded like a threat.

It may interest you to know that she's kidnapped our son. Last time I checked, that was a federal offense. I'm his father, he shouted. I have a right to know where he is!

She hasn't kidnapped anybody, the lawyer snapped. And your rights happen to be quite limited just now. Need I remind you that you have a restraining order issued against you? If I were you, Mr. Ladd, I'd get those papers back to me so you can both move on as quickly as possible.

With that, she hung up on him. Move on, he thought bitterly. The two most expensive words in the English language.

The next morning, he drove out to Westchester with empty boxes and cleaning supplies. The bare wood floors creaked as he walked around. For obvious reasons, he'd turned down the temperature, and the house was cold; it seemed relentlessly hostile to his presence. He wasn't going to miss this place, he was glad to be getting rid of it. He'd never really been comfortable on this street, and in all their years here, he couldn't remember ever feeling quite at home. It bothered him now to think that Theo probably hadn't either.

He grabbed a couple garbage bags and went up to their bedroom. He emptied the contents of her drawers, sweaters and sweatpants and nightgowns and underwear, fighting the impulse to pull the garments to his nose, to breathe in her scent one last time. Closing the last drawer, he heard something rattling around inside it. Annoyed by this minor disruption, he yanked it open and found the culprit, a small pink shell. He picked it up and examined it in his palm. It was shaped like a fan, the size of a nickel. He ran his fingertip across its scalloped edge.

It was a sign, he thought.

The following Saturday he drove out there. With the cold weather, there wasn't much traffic, and the small towns along the shore were fairly desolate. Montauk was just as he remembered it. More than twenty years had passed since that weekend, what Julian had always considered an invitation into Rye's exclusive little circle, but it hadn't amounted to much. For reasons that had never been explained, Rye had dropped Julian. That last day, when they'd moved out of their apartment, Rye merely muttered, I guess I'll see you around, before driving off in his mother's old station wagon. Julian had stood there a moment on the sidewalk, feeling like a spurned lover.

He turned off the old highway into a neighborhood of small cottages, angling down toward the beach, and retraced his memory to find the private, sand-covered lane that ran up to the house. With satisfaction, he drove slowly up the long hill. At the top, just as he had suspected, he saw her car sitting in the driveway.

He pulled over and parked in a cluster of seagrass. He felt a little sick. His mouth was very dry. He stumbled out, taking in the expansive horizon, the wind filling up his jacket, rippling the legs of his pants. This cliff, he thought, where nothing can touch you.

He looked out at the ocean, the red sun sinking into it.

It was the end, he knew. He had come to that point.

He walked up to the house, aware that Theo was standing at the upstairs window, gazing down at him.

Magda opened the door. She looked a little frightened. How did you—

He stood there, shaking his head. You've always underestimated me, Magda.

Why are you here?

There was so much he wanted to say, and yet, at that moment, he was unable to form even a single sentence.

He doesn't want to see you. He's not ready.

I know, he said. I understand.

You know you're not allowed to be here. You're breaking the—

Please, he said. Is that really necessary?

She sighed and shook her head, and he asked her if she'd seen the article about Adler.

It's horrible. Nobody seems to know what happened.

He's missing, apparently.

But his truck. Just sitting there in that lot. It's so eerie. Her voice trailed off. I don't know what to think, she said. You may as well know that I love him. I've loved him my whole life.

She started to cry, and it was in that moment that Julian understood he'd been a fool to think killing Adler would bring her back to him.

Well, he said. I brought you something. She waited as he took the envelope out of his pocket. I wanted to personally hand these to you. They're all signed. You're a free woman.

She stared down at the envelope in her hands. Thank you, Julian.

I need to say something to you.

Okay. She looked at him with interest, waiting, her long, thin arms crossed over her breasts like a shield.

I always thought I loved you more, he said. But now I'm wondering if I loved you at all.

She nodded that she understood. I know I did a terrible thing to you, Julian. I don't expect you to forgive me. I'm sorry. You need to know that.

I'm sorry too, Magda, he said finally. Then he took the shell out of his pocket. I thought you might want this. It was in your drawer.

He dropped the little shell into her palm. She seemed to recognize it and clasped her fingers around it. I thought I'd lost it, she said.

I think it belongs here. He looked at her a long moment. Good-bye, Magda.

With resolve, he turned and got into his car and pulled out of there.

He knew he'd never see her again.

Rye

He is better, stronger. Lying here for all this time, receiving the care of these good people, getting up only to use the outhouse out back, hobbling to it on a pair of crutches they have left for him, his feet pushed into a stranger's shoes. Wearing another man's clothes. Somehow, they give him strength. Again and again, he finds himself.

He thinks of Magda. That night when he'd held her, body and soul, in his undeserving hands. She is always in his head. He imagines her inside his mother's house. They called it the cottage—built in 1900 by a captain's widow—it has a widow's walk. There is a story people tell about the widow, how you can see her ghost up there on certain nights, waiting for her husband's return. With irony, he thinks of Magda now, staring out at the sea, waiting for him.

It was their safe house, his father used to say. The place you went to when you needed to disappear. You couldn't find it on any map. You couldn't see it from the road. The ocean embraced it. The cold bare floors and iron beds, the rooms smelling of the sea, the salt and the wind, the dampness. You understood the passage of time as the sun roamed the floors, the corners. You'd look out at an expanse of nothingness, thinking about your life, where you were inside it, what you wanted to do, your future, and your death—yes, you even thought about death. What it might be like once it came. Once it found you.

It's what the wild places do to us, he reasons. They remind us that we're vulnerable, expendable. And so briefly here.

In the afternoon, the children come. They have brought supplies.

The girl is Cleo. She kneels beside him and opens the jar of tea and waits as he struggles to sit up. He takes the jar with his good hand. The tea is green, tepid, and he can taste the honey they've added to obscure the bitterness. The children watch with fascination as he drinks down the entire jar. The girl's brother, Gus, holds the bread like a small, round shield. With dirty fingers, he tears off a piece and gives it to him. Thank you, Rye says. The bread is soft and fresh. He chews, swallows. It's good, he says.

Even this simple exchange exhausts him. For some reason, there are tears running down his cheeks.

He is a fascination to them, this man who fell from the sky. They entertain him with their games and plays. Handmade toys of felt, wood. They sing songs to him. Recite made-up poems. He is like Gulliver the giant, and they are his loyal attendants.

At night, alone in the hut, he lies awake. He is attuned to all sound. He hears the animals on their nightly rounds. There are coyotes in these woods. Foxes. The sway of the brush, like the rustle of a woman's skirt. A skunk loitering outside, she finally wobbles in. He lies there, unmoving, as she sniffs and investigates. Finally, disinterested, she wobbles out, and he can breathe again, relieved.

There is the constant music of the river. It laps and laps, like a dog drinking from a bowl. A dog that drinks, then waits, then drinks again. He watches the light. The colors. Colors that he once intensified in the darkroom. They are real to him now. The colors are bright. They are teaching him to see.

It's a social experiment, Lotus explains. What we're doing here. We're like a cult, but the only religion we practice is freedom. She has brought him coffee and a bowl of raspberries. The berries are small and sweet and dazzle his taste buds. The coffee is black and strong.

Freedom, she says. To be ourselves.

He watches her as she talks. She uses her hands. Her clothes are loose and soft, in the colors of the forest, brown and gray and mustard, and made by her own hand.

There's a field up yonder, she tells him. We've got a big garden up there in the summer, and our vegetables last us through the winter in our root cellar. There's a couple barns, some livestock. About a hundred and ten acres, all told. I can't remember the last time I went to a supermarket. It was a hunting camp back in the day, all these huts along the riverbank. I used to see them from the train, never knew what they were for.

I've heard the train, he says. I like the sound of it.

You haven't told me your name, she says.

He answers automatically, as if someone has just whispered it in his ear.

Her husband is Tracey Boyd. People call me Boyd, he says, tossing some more wood on the fire. It's a miracle you survived that fall. Do you remember it?

Rye shakes his head, but it isn't true. He sees glimmers. Flashes, as if from a dream. He remembers fighting with a man in black leather gloves. He remembers falling, the feeling of being utterly weightless, wholly intact as he turned through the air. Sometimes, when he concentrates very hard, the jagged outlines of the man's face come clear, but the image lasts only for a second. Somebody pushed me, he tells Boyd. Somebody threw me off.

Who would do that?

I'm trying to figure that out.

Boyd sits in the old lawn chair beside Rye's bed, a thin mattress they dragged in from somewhere, his face lit by the yellow light of a Coleman lantern. They are sharing a joint, the smoke earthy and fragrant. A man in his forties, Boyd projects the confidence he's earned through studied and determined progress. A student of life, as it were, Rye thinks, with an expressive, nineteenth-century air, his hair pulled back in a loose ponytail, his clothes strategically assembled for the late-winter cold: the canvas jacket over a down vest over a flannel shirt, his jeans held up with suspenders, a blue wool scarf around his neck. On his feet, well-worn hiking boots. His eyes are warm and brown, a man whose quiet, intelligent gaze induces trust.

Is there somebody we should notify? To let them know you're alive?

But Rye is unable to fathom it. No, he says.

Boyd looks at him curiously.

I need some time. I need to think.

It's your call. This is a real good place to do that.

Rye nods with appreciation. Truthfully, he doesn't feel ready to go home. He can't even imagine it. He is too broken now. But it's not just his physical predicament. A shift has occurred deep inside of him, a fear of the world beyond this quiet place, of the person out there who did this to him. The person out there who wanted him dead.

Over games of chess, he comes to know Boyd. Boyd tells him his life— his childhood in Buffalo, the son of two college professors, his BA from Cornell, a master's from Hopkins, the PhD from Rensselaer.

During my last year at RPI, I found this tract of land down in Albany, he says. It was all overgrown, full of garbage. People thought

I was crazy. I scraped together the money and bought it and put a fucking barn on it. This is a rough part of town, a lot of poverty. A barn was something to see. People started showing up, curious about what I was doing. It just kind of grew from there. We started a community garden. Chickens. Goats. I ended up raising a lot of grant money and opening a center for urban sustainability.

Rye watches the excitement light his eyes as he talks. He finds his confidence inspiring.

Then I met Lotus, he tells him. She came down to work with me. She's a nurse and an environmental activist—with a BA in philosophy. Smart as hell. We did a lot of educational programs with the schools, teaching kids where their food comes from. We were trying to show people how to get along without depending on supermarkets and places like Walmart. It was cool. We did a lot of good.

Then what?

We wanted to test ourselves. To see if this was really possible.

How long have you been out here?

It's going on two years. It's been a process. I think we're starting to get the hang of it. You learn to use your hands out here.

Boyd's are large and expressive. He holds them out so Rye can see the various marks and burns and scars. He's learned to hunt and fish, to build and to sew. Hunting and gathering, he says. It can fill up your day. So yeah, I've learned a lot out here; we all have. You get really tired. We don't compartmentalize. Everything shares equal importance. It's been a big change for me. I was one of those nerds staring into a computer screen all day, looking at statistics, living on pizza and good Kentucky bourbon. I used to have all kinds of health problems. Not anymore. What I've discovered is how well we can adapt as a species. The body changes. It gets more efficient when you use it right.

He tells Rye there are fifty-three people on the riverbank as part of this study of collaboration. We're an enterprise of ideas, he clarifies. You come out here, and, well, all that anxiety I used to feel kind of went away. Like was I making enough money? Did I have the right apartment, the right car, stove, clothes, what have you. The material world gets a whole lot quieter. You pretty quickly figure out that there's a lot out there that just doesn't matter, all of the distractions we think we need. It kind of changes how you see things, you know what I'm saying?

Yes, I think I do.

What about you?

I'm a photographer, Rye says. If I remember correctly, I'm pretty good at it.

I wouldn't doubt it, Boyd says.

Rye takes a moment to describe his professional history.

It sounds to me like we're sort of in the same business, Boyd says.

How so?

Figuring out what we're all doing here. The true essence of things, he says, making quote marks with his fingers. Humanity as a concept, a revolution.

Rye nods. Indeed.

Tracey Boyd smiles. As usual, I'm talking too much, he says. It's kind of an occupational hazard. Anyhow, when you're up to it, I'll give you the grand tour.

I'd like that, Rye says, and hands him back the joint. Soon, he says.

You're getting there.

After he leaves, Rye gives their conversation some more thought. Whereas Boyd and the people out here are all about making change— living off the land, sustaining the planet, pushing forward to something better—Rye's work is essentially about how things stay the same, moments that have passed, never to be again. With this idea, he perceives a conundrum that he will somehow have to resolve.

It comes to him that he is a little terrified, just being here. Without his camera to hide behind. For the first time, maybe, in his whole life, he feels exposed, vulnerable, and totally alive.

In the morning, the children come for him. They want to show him their house.

Slowly, on crutches, he maneuvers out into the cold fresh air. His senses are wild, ravenous. The green of the trees, the pale white sky. The smell of the earth, the air. He looks up into the trees, a little amazed by their fortitude, their branches constantly moving, the sound they make in the wind.

Like a small parade, Cleo holds one sleeve of his jacket, Gus the other. They show him the garden, the chicken house, the root cellar, one old goat. Bella, the horse. Up in a clearing, scattered among the distant trees, stand all variety of shelters, lean-tos of plywood and thick-plastic tiny A-frames, and mud huts with thatched roofs.

Welcome to the neighborhood, Boyd says, coming out of a small log house, opening his hands in the air like a ballet dancer.

This is really something, Rye says.

This is the future, Boyd says. As in right now.

Their house is small, adequate, comfortable. Built by loggers around the turn of the century, Boyd explains. The walls are decorated with the children's drawings.

I like the art, Rye says, and Cleo flushes with pride.

Please, take a seat, Lotus says, and he does, gratefully. The walk has made him tired.

The table is laid with crisp white cloth. They share a meal of bread and cheese, grapes, and several small salads, artichokes in olive oil, potato salad, thick wedges of purple beets, white beans. Sitting here with this family, he can only think of Simone and Yana, understanding, as if for the first time, the full reality of his situation, the fact that he is here and they are there, with so much space in between. He has fallen into a black hole, he thinks. He doubts his own strength to climb out.

After they eat, Boyd hands him a camera and a bag of film. I thought you could use this. It's nothing fancy, but—

It'll do fine, Rye says. Thank you. It's an older SLR. Elated, he holds it in his hands, a beloved relic.

It may help you make sense of things, Boyd says.

Rye nods. I appreciate it.

Take all the time you need, Lotus says.

Thanks for lunch.

They walk back along the river, just him and Boyd. The water is black and murky and freezing cold.

There, Boyd says, pointing up at the bridge. Thar she blows.

It's higher than he pictured. He stands there a minute, suddenly breathless, disabled by a sensation of vertigo, the vivid memory of falling through the air. He staggers a little and Boyd grabs hold of his shoulder. Hey, now.

That's a long way down.

It sure as fuck is. You all right?

I can't even look, Rye says.

Boyd studies him with concern.

My son almost died, Rye explains. We were at the hospital.

In his head, he is back in that parking lot. He can see Magda's taillights pulling out and can almost feel the cold wind on his back. He remembers thinking how quiet it was as he walked to his truck and climbed behind the wheel.

I was in my truck. Somebody banged on my window. Somebody—

He shuts his eyes in frustration. He isn't ready to see that face. Doesn't want to see it. I can't—

Rye cries. It's all right, Boyd says, and takes him in his arms, and they stand there, holding on to each other, two men in the middle of the forest, with no place else to go.

* * *

Later, alone in his bed in the dark, the face of his assailant comes clear, and a fresh terror consumes him. He pulls himself up, drenched in sweat. That such a thing could have happened to him...he can barely comprehend it. That Ladd's hatred was so great, he saw no other alternative than to throw him off that bridge. And even more unfathomable is the fact that he is still out there, living his life, a murderer disguised as an ordinary man.

At first light, he rises from the bed and puts on his clothes. He knows it is time to go, he must. But not just yet. Not before he photographs this place, this refuge, this haven. This figment of his imagination. He wants to show the world that this is possible. This place, these people, this simple, beautiful life. For he fears if he does not photograph it, he won't believe it exists. Once he leaves, it will be gone forever, like some strange, hallucinatory dream.

He loads the camera and sets out.

How to describe freedom in a photograph? What might it look like?

Maybe the old horse, Bella, with her skinny ribs, grazing in the long grass at moonrise.

Or the woman with a broken face, hauling a bin of summer vegetables from the root cellar, her large, callused hands.

Or maybe it is his solemn hut that has sheltered him all this time, its ancient black stones pulled from the river by the men of another century, stacked one upon another for all these years. Or the mattress on which he has slept the blackest sleep of childhood.

It isn't something you can own, he realizes. It is the thing inside you that makes you shine.

Later that night, under a sky vivid with stars, they have a great feast. Bread, baked in a large pan of water over the fire, a feat he never thought possible, but here it is, warm and delicious, served with homemade butter and honey. Yellow squash roasted over smoldering ash, its warm buttery pulp seasoned with pepper and salt. Sweet potatoes on skewers, half burned, smoking hot. Striped bass straight off the rod, sautéed in a cast-iron pan over the open fire.

After the meal, they build a bonfire out in the field. Standing there with all of these strangers, some of whom he feels closer to than life-long friends, he reckons with his own wild hunger, dislodged and freed from some deeper place, and watching the flames crackle and twist, he can think only of the word *rejoice*—for that is what they are doing. And for now it is enough.

Part Six

Raw

To photograph people is to violate them, by seeing them as they never see themselves, by having knowledge of them that they can never have; it turns people into objects that can be symbolically possessed. Just as a camera is a sublimation of the gun, to photograph someone is a subliminal murder—a soft murder, appropriate to a sad, frightened time.

—Susan Sontag, *On Photography*

Simone

They never find him.

Early in March, just after the stripers start running, his phone turns up in a fisherman's net. The same two cops, Johnson and Sanchez, appear at her door. They sit at her kitchen table and show it to her inside a plastic evidence bag. Written on the bag in Sharpie is her husband's name.

She asks if there could be some mistake, but they tell her no, the serial number checked out, there's no doubt.

He could have dropped it, she says.

Yes, Johnson says. That's true. But we also found this.

She waits while he retrieves another evidence bag from a black duffel.

At once she recognizes its contents, one of Rye's tennis shoes, the white Jack Purcells he's been wearing all his life.

She stares at it. Somehow this one thing convinces her more than all the others.

I'm sorry, he says gently. Stuff washes up with the thaw.

* * *

It takes her three more weeks to accept the fact that he's gone. Finally, the papers print his obituary, which makes his death a fact. It still feels strange and unreal, and part of her doesn't believe it, will never believe it. Nothing is what it was. Yana comes home, more mature somehow, sobered by the mystery of this life, the insistence of loss. They lounge around in their pajamas till noon, drinking strong black coffee. By four, they are drinking whiskey and smoking the pot Yana has been growing for years behind the barn. They are knitting long scarves with big wooden needles, using the wool from her farm share, soft and thick and a little damp, fragrant of a life in the open, of sheep content to roam the fields and nothing more. The scarves are blue and purple, yellow and green.

People call and write emails and texts. Letters arrive in the mail. An author proposes a biography. Simone meets with the rabbi. She decides to go ahead with the memorial. Even without his body. Even though they haven't found him. Even though he could still be out there. Somewhere. He could be out there somewhere, alive.

His name comes into her head even before he says it. Of course it's Julian Ladd. After the memorial, when they are all back at the house, he appears at her side like an apparition. She tries to conceal her surprise, not wanting to insult him. Nevertheless, there is something undeniably strange about him, something that puts her off. It's not anything you can see—not the Armani suit, or the shiny, expensive loafers, or his immaculate hands—but something about his eyes, a story sitting there, one he is keeping to himself. If memory serves, he and Rye were on awkward terms by the end of that year. Rye had told her he didn't trust Ladd, something about waking up in the middle of one night to find Julian standing over his bed in the dark. It had freaked him out, he told her. Maybe you were dreaming, she proposed, but he shook his head, he was adamant. That was no dream. They'd moved out of the apartment the next day and hadn't spoken since.

Somewhere in the middle of their conversation, her synapses begin to buzz, and she makes the connection about Magda, that Magda Ladd is Julian's wife. She's about to admit to him her revelation, when he abruptly begins to cry—to sob, actually—and launches into a soliloquy about his friendship with Rye, how that year had changed his life, and how he'd lost not just a friend but a brother. It makes her uncomfortable, how he's carrying on, and it occurs to her that there's something very wrong with him. That he is the very definition of a person unhinged.

He tells her he's missed his train, so she puts him up in Rye's studio. She doesn't want him staying in the house. It doesn't matter. She's up all night anyway, worrying because he's here. Worrying that perhaps he'll come into the house and do something, God only knows what. When he doesn't show up at breakfast, she and Constance go over to the studio to have a look. The bed is neatly made, and the place looks almost neater than before, as if all of its surfaces have been wiped clean. The only evidence of his occupancy is the heap of shredded paper on the counter in the darkroom, a photograph, she and Constance deduce, torn into a hundred pieces. With her agile fingers, Constance separates the shreds and moves them around like the pieces of a puzzle, reconstructing the image. The picture is old, worn at the corners, and all twelve of the Brodsky students are standing together on the marble steps of the building with their cameras hung around their necks, an unlikely army, elite, beaming with pride, ready to begin their fabulous lives.

A few weeks later, when the cherry blossoms are in bloom, an old pickup truck pulls up the driveway. Simone stands at the window, her hand on the glass. A man gets out, his long silver hair pulled back in a ponytail, his blue jeans held up by suspenders. He walks around to the passenger's side and opens the door, and another man gets out. This man is frail and has a walking stick nearly as tall as he is, and his hair, too, is long and gray. But he is someone she recognizes. In fact, she knows him very well.

Rye

After Boyd leaves, they hold each other for a long time, and Simone cries in his arms. I never believed you were gone, she says. Not even for a single minute.

They sit together in the kitchen and he tells her his story, including the night with Magda in the city, what it was like for him seeing her again, and how the past and the person he'd once been had rushed back to him like the warm oblivion of a drug.

I never wanted to hurt you, Simone. But I guess I did.

We've hurt each other, haven't we?

Yes, we have.

He looks at her face, something there in her eyes, a resolve he hasn't seen before.

I have something for you, she says, and hands him a small envelope. I should have given this to you a long time ago. It was an important letter, and I kept it from you. It was a terrible thing to do.

He knows what it is, of course, but he opens it anyway, unfolding the thick stationery. He can feel her watching him. The letter in question is very short and to the point, and he can hear Magda's voice as he reads the words. *No matter what,* it says at the end. *I will love you always.*

I was afraid I'd lose you, Simone says. I'm sorry, Rye. I'm really very sorry.

He nods.

It was stupid. And I regret it. She starts to weep. I was a young woman.

I know, Simone. But it's not entirely your fault. I was part of it. Part of why you felt you had to do that. And I'm sorry too.

Can you forgive me?

I'm not sure, he says.

They look at each other, their faces at once familiar and strange. He knows he can't stay. The house isn't his anymore. And he and Simone don't fit. They both know it. They've known it for a long time.

His old Porsche starts right up. He pulls out of the carriage house and takes a last look at the old house. He can see Simone standing at the window, watching. She raises her hand like a woman on a parade float, and he waves back, as if finalizing some obscure arrangement, then she tugs the curtain back into place and disappears.

The newspapers print the story about his discovery and his time in the hut in the wilderness. They all use the same photograph, the one that makes him look like Jesus, with his long hair and beard, the crazy look in his eye, one that's recognizable to anyone who's ever lived on the streets—the one that says *hungry.*

Magda

She's out on the beach when she hears his voice. She turns and watches as he slowly descends the stairs. As he nears, she sees the limp, the hard lines of his body, his blue eyes. Hey, he calls.

Hey, she says, and smiles.

They stand there for a moment, just looking at each other, and she can see in his face that he's been through something he can't fully explain.

It's about time you showed up.

He laughs and she does too, and then she cries. And he pulls her into his arms. And he holds her very tightly. And they stay like that a long time, holding each other under the bright sky.

This is my fault, she says. None of this would've happened to you.

It's all right. It doesn't matter.

You went through a lot.

We all did. How is he?

He's good. He went for a run. She looks off down the beach. There he is, see? Way down there. He's been running a lot. It's been really helpful.

That's good to hear.

It's been hard, you know. But we're getting there.

My God, you're beautiful.

She lets out a laugh. Am I?

Hey, I finally got that letter.

Okay, good. I'm glad. Took a while.

Yup. Sure did.

She must love you very much.

No, he says. That's not love. He touches her cheek. But this sure is.

It's like a bright heat inside her. She closes her eyes a moment, savoring it. And then he kisses her like it's the first time.

Hey, Adler, Theo calls, running up to them.

It is only now they break apart, and Rye and Theo hug.

I heard about what happened to you. You okay?

Way better than okay, Rye says. You look really good, Theo.

Theo accepts the compliment gratefully. It's been a gift to be here. Thank you for this.

You're welcome. I'm glad it worked out.

Theo smiles. I'll let you two lovebirds get reacquainted. I have another few miles to do.

See you inside, she tells him.

They watch him run off, each of them grappling with this new reality, the possibility of a life together as a family.

He looks great, Rye says.

I'm really proud of him. She sighs and laughs a little and shakes her head. It's been really good for him here, she says. Like he said, a gift. Thank you, Rye. Really. This place—

You don't have to thank me.

Yes, I do. You've helped us a lot. More than—

But now she's crying again.

Hey, now. It's okay, it's going to be all right.

She nods, wiping away her tears. I know. I know it is.

He takes her hands. I've been thinking about this moment for a long time. It kind of kept me going, you know? This feeling I have for you and Theo—

He shakes his head. There are no words to explain it.

You don't have to, she tells him. Because I already know.

Rye

He follows her into the house, nearly stumbling over her clogs. She takes his hand. Welcome home.

In the time she's been here, the house has come to life. It's no longer the empty old place. Now there is the smell of her cooking, the counters laden with oranges, avocados, dates the size of his thumbs, the table scattered with crumbs from breakfast, the leftover toast, the jar of jam. The open wings of half-read books.

Is it weird?

No. It's wonderful.

Are you hungry?

Very, he says, and takes her hand.

They hurry upstairs to his old bedroom and she closes the door. There are the tall windows, the pale blue sky, blocks of sunlight on the floor. There is the sound of the ocean. The cries of birds.

Even with Theo out on the beach they are very quiet, as if any sound might disrupt the ghost of his long-dead mother. The wood floors are cold under his bare, sandy feet. The bed, with its iron fists, waits. Slowly kissing, staggering like drunkards, they undress each other, and then she is naked, standing before him, her hands open at her sides, waiting to be filled.

Epilogue

Like everybody else, Julian was amazed that Adler had survived. He'd been flipping the channels one morning, getting ready for work, when he happened upon the report. Soon after, all the papers covered it, and most of the magazines, touting the renowned photographer as the most adventurous man of the year. *Vanity Fair* devoted several pages to Adler's story, beginning with a man knocking on his window in the hospital parking lot, a man he'd identified as a total stranger.

A total stranger? Hardly. Why had he said this? Maybe he'd been so traumatized, he didn't remember. Amnesia could happen to people when they experienced bad things. Something in the brain allowed them to forget. Julian certainly hoped it was the case. But what if it wasn't? What if Adler's statement had been deliberate? What if it had been meant entirely for him?

The article mentioned the couple who'd found him and nursed him back to health over a period of nearly four months and their strange little cult in the wilderness. All in all, Adler said, the experience had been life affirming; he'd been irrevocably transformed.

Truthfully, relieved as Julian was, it made him want to puke. Once again, it seemed, Adler had prevailed.

Over and over he reviewed that night in his mind. The drive in Adler's truck, the almost primal intimacy they shared, anticipating the unknown. How he'd forced Adler up on the bridge, his loyal prisoner, the satisfaction he'd felt during those precarious moments, how they'd fought in the shattering cold, the blood, the sounds they'd made, grunting and groaning like animals. How he'd had no choice but to finish it.

He'd disposed of the gloves, of course, which had traces of blood on the knuckles. He'd cut them to pieces with a pair of pinking shears and buried them in his mother's garden out in Jersey.

After the news broke, and for days afterward, a desperate panic set in. He lay in bed, feverish, his sheets soaked with sweat. His hair was long and shaggy, his skin oily, his eyes red and glassy. He felt unable to leave his apartment, his shades drawn. Only at night did he open them, staring out across the courtyard into the bright rooms of his neighbors. He didn't go to work and told them he was suffering from a prolonged medical condition. Often, he woke in the night, convinced there was someone in the apartment. He would turn on all of the lights and open the closets. He finally dug out his father's gold medallion, which he'd bought on a trip somewhere, with an evil eye on it, and wore the heavy chain around his neck to keep him safe.

When he finally had nothing left in his refrigerator, he walked the three blocks up to the market. He shopped quickly, impulsively, tossing random items into his cart—potatoes, sardines, a jar of pecans—and hurried home, avoiding the glaring faces on the street, convinced that they were watching him. Convinced that they all knew. As he shuffled past the news kiosk on the corner, he saw Adler's face on the cover of *Time*. He grabbed the magazine and tossed down his money, and the man behind the counter pawed the bills, staring at him with cold, knowing eyes.

The opening is at Henry Cline's new gallery. The critics describe Adler's photographs as transcendent. He doesn't plan on going in. Still, he buys a new suit for the occasion and a new pair of loafers. He pays a visit to the barber, enjoying the sensation of the man's fingers in his hair, the blade of his razor crossing his face.

It's a chilly night in October and he pulls on his old cashmere coat, the lining a little torn, and his stiff new shoes. They pinch his toes, and he regrets not getting a larger size. He rides the elevator down with the woman who lives next door to him. She nods but refuses to meet his eyes, and when the doors finally open, she flees.

Out in the cool air, he clutches the collar of his coat and hails a cab. The gallery is on 19th Street, between Tenth and Eleventh. There's a bar across the street. He orders a double whiskey and sits at a table by the window, watching the people going in and out through the wide double doors. With the drink inside him he feels more confident, and he heads out to the corner and crosses the street. It is a kind of theater, he thinks, glancing through the huge plate-glass windows at the bright space within, the white walls and high ceilings, the blond-wood floors. He can't avoid seeing the work, of course. Luminous, life-size photographs of the forest and its multifarious inhabitants, reminiscent of Adler's earlier work, but better somehow, more informed and truly, undoubtedly, brilliant.

A bitter taste fills his mouth. The taste of blood, he realizes; he has bitten his lip.

Aren't you going in? It's a man's voice. He turns to see a thin, bald stranger who has come outside to smoke.

No, Julian says. I'm not interested in photography.

Too bad, the man says. It's a great show, you should check it out. The guy's a fucking genius.

It's only then that he notices Adler, standing at the far end of the room surrounded by his acolytes. He sees Magda, the woman he called his wife for over twenty years, dressed all in black, beaming, you might say, with happiness, as she receives their guests, and Theo, the boy he raised from birth, standing beside her, wearing a blue work shirt and black jeans, just like Adler, seemingly content to be part of the celebration—to be alive, Julian imagines, here and now.

Feeling nothing, he stands there another moment before he notices Rye staring at him from across the room. Julian wonders if he actually sees him through the glass, or if he's looking at something, someone else. But his gaze persists, and Julian knows.

They stare at each other, transfixed.

They are like duelists, he thinks. Forever linked by this singular and final moment.

But it doesn't last.

Julian turns and walks away, instantly losing himself in a crowd of weekend tourists, a man in a long black coat against the gritty city night, indiscernible, anonymous, just one more stranger among many.

Acknowledgments

When I started this book, I knew I wanted to write about photography as an apt metaphor for our changing times, not only for its rapid technological ascent but for its reflection of who we are as a society. I began what I'd like to think of as a thorough investigation of the medium, reading countless books and magazines, interviewing photographers, and taking my own pictures. Some of the key books that helped to shape the characters in this novel are *The Ongoing Moment* by Geoff Dyer, a beautifully written investigation of several remarkable photographers and their work, as well as Dyer's *The Street Philosophy of Garry Winogrand;* Annie Leibovitz's *At Work,* a fascinating memoir about her extraordinary life and career; *The Nature of Photographs* by Stephen Shore, what he calls a primer, which helped me fundamentally understand how photographers see, and how one might understand what is happening inside the frame, as well as his collected photographs *Uncommon Places;* John Szarkowski's *Looking at Photographs* and *The Photographer's Eye;* Roland Barthes's *Camera Lucida; On Photography* by Susan Sontag; *Understanding a Photograph* and *Ways of Seeing* by John Berger; *Aperture Conversations* and *Aperture* magazine; *Master Photographers* by Roberto Koch; *Hold Still* by Sally Mann; *The Nine* and *The Ninety Nine* by Katy Grannan; *The Americans* by Robert Frank; *The Decisive Moment* by Henri Cartier-Bresson; *Half Past Autumn* by Gordon Parks; *Walker Evans: The Hungry Eye* by Gilles Mora; *Modern Color* by Fred Herzog; *Where I Find Myself,* by the extraordinary Joel Meyerowitz; *Revelations* by Diane Arbus; *2¼* by William Eggleston; *In the American West* and *Evidence* by Richard Avedon; *The Open Road* by David Campany; *Genesis* by Sebastião Salgado; *Road to Seeing* by Dan Winters; Lee Friedlander's *Street: The Human Clay; Saul Leiter, Early Black and White* by Max Kozloff; *The World of Atget* by Berenice Abbott; *Kodachrome* by Luigi Ghirri; *Miroslav Tichý,* edited by Roman Buxbaum; *Nationality Doubtful* by Josef Koudelka, edited by Matthew S. Witkovsky; *Edges* by Harry Gruyaert; *The Family Album of Lucybelle Crater* by Ralph Eugene Meatyard; and too many more to name. I also want to thank Magnum Photo's Learn with Magnum Workshops, Alec Soth: Photographic Storytelling and The Art of Street Photography, two excellent courses, as well as Dyanna Taylor's extraordinary documentary about her grandmother Dorothea Lange, *Grab a Hunk of Lightning,* which helped me to better understand what it feels like to be female in a male-dominated profession, and the sacrifices so many artists make for their work. I want to thank photographers everywhere, masters and amateurs alike, who continue to reaffirm what it means to be human in this complex and ever-changing world.

It has been a gift to work with Judy Clain, whose visionary insight and editorial precision helped me discover this novel's true and essential shape, for which I am entirely and wondrously grateful. Thanks also to everyone at Little, Brown, for their extraordinary expertise: Miya Kumangai, Jayne Yaffe Kemp, Laura Mamelok, Jeff Stiefel, and the incomparable copyeditor Pamela Marshall, whose remarkable detailed work greatly improved every page of this novel.

I want to thank my agent, Linda Chester, for always being the first person to lay eyes on my work and for her swift and critical feedback, which is worth gold to any writer and for which I am grateful beyond measure. Thanks also to the indispensable Gary Jaffe, Laurie Fox, Darlene Chan, and Michelle Conway of The Linda Chester Literary Agency, all devoted and outstanding professionals. Thanks also to Alice Deon, Robbert Ammerlaan, Elena Siebert, Michael Keusch, John Froats, Robert Zakin, Angelo Denoucous, Susan Turconi, Renee Pettit, Elizabeth Karl, Kevin O'Dea, Avie Hern, Patricia VanAlstyne, Guy Mastrion, and Donald J. Moore.

The book *Beyond Addiction: How Science and Kindness Help People Change,* by Jeffrey Foote, Carrie Wilkens, and Nicole Kosanke, with Stephanie Higgs, is a miraculous resource for anyone suffering from addiction and for their families.

Finally, I want to thank my husband, Scott Morris, who works harder than anyone I know and whose stories always inspire me to write better, to work harder, to keep going, and my parents, who, with their love and enthusiasm, keep the engine of our family running, every single day. And finally, and most important, this book is dedicated to my children, Hannah, Sophie, and Sam, who have taught me so much about life, and the changing rhythm of this world. I couldn't have written this book without them.

About the Author

Elizabeth Brundage is the author of four previous novels, *All Things Cease to Appear, A Stranger Like You, Somebody Else's Daughter,* and *The Doctor's Wife*. She is a graduate of the Iowa Writers' Workshop, where she received a James Michener Award, and has attended the American Film Institute in Los Angeles. A film based on *All Things Cease to Appear,* entitled *Things Heard and Seen,* is forthcoming from Netflix, starring Amanda Seyfried and James Norton. She lives with her family in Albany, New York.